TRAVEL

A PROJECT OUTRIGGER NOVEL

TRAVEL

A PROJECT OUTRIGGER NOVEL

KEVIN ROWLETT

atmosphere press

Published by Atmosphere Press

Cover design by Kevin Stone

Atmospherepress.com

CHAPTER 1

I woke up without opening my eyes.

I knew something was ... off. I had the feeling of familiarity, but I knew that there was something different about where I was. Inexplicably, I felt as if something had been *changed.*

I slowly opened my eyes and looked across the room.

My brother, Joseph, whom I hadn't shared a room with since I was a teenager, was sleeping on the twin bed that used to stand in the middle of our childhood bedroom, framed by the two windows that looked out into my childhood backyard.

The disorientation and sense of wrongness got worse. I stared across the room at my sleeping brother's back, not fully able to comprehend what I was seeing.

I felt the anxiety start to build and felt a jolt of adrenaline shoot through my system. I sat up in bed a little too fast and felt my head start to swim. I put my head in my hands and took a couple deep breaths, willing the dizziness away. When I looked up again, my brother was still there, snoring lightly.

What in the fuck was going on?

I looked at my hands, looking for anything to anchor me in the moment. The tattoo on my wrist was gone; there was nothing but blank skin. I looked at my left forearm, expecting to see the intricate, blue image of a lion, but that, too, was blank, and my smart watch was gone. I absently touched my forearm, my thoughts spinning. I pulled the sleeve up on my right bicep and was met with more blank skin. I didn't even look at the left side of my chest ... I knew that there was nothing there.

Somehow, even the permanent marks on my skin had vanished. No laser removal, no scarring; it was as if they had never been there in the first place.

I reached for my cell phone on the nightstand, intending to call someone—anyone—who could help me make sense of this. My fingers found the small, silver flip phone.

'*Holy shit,*' I thought, '*I haven't had one of these since I was in high school. What the fuck is it doing here?*'

I pushed one of the side buttons, hoping I remembered how to work the antique. The screen lit, and there was a small message icon on the blue cloud-patterned background. I flipped the phone open and saw the sender.

Sara C.

'*What?*'

I blinked.

'*No fucking way.*'

'*This is impossible,*' I thought. I opened the text and read the contents of the message. She was telling me she missed me and that she was looking forward to seeing me before symphonic band tomorrow. She'd also sent an old-school kissing face, the one that uses the colon and the asterisk.

'*What in the hell is going on?*' I thought, still staring at the device in my hand. I reread the message, this time comprehending what it was saying. A lifelong band kid, I had been in symphonic band in high school, both freshman and senior year.

I spotted my wallet laying on the nightstand and pulled it

toward me. Flipping open the soft, black leather, I found my driver's license.

'*Well, that rules out freshman year,*' I thought. '*Plus, I didn't date Sara until I was a senior. In a weird way, the license makes sense.*'

The picture on the license was familiar, although it was one I hadn't seen on a license in almost 15 years. My face was lean and rounded, without the sharper angles of adulthood, and my hair was medium length, parted just to the left of the middle.

The room gave a lurch, and I felt something dislodge behind my eyes—an unmooring sensation that seemed to cast my thoughts into an endless ocean of confusion.

I was back in high school.

Jesus fuck.

In a movie or some science fiction story, this is when all the memories would come crashing back into my mind of some failed time travel experiment. I'd either be the scientist who used himself as a guinea pig or be some starry-eyed volunteer who would follow the seemingly mad scientist to the ends of the earth. I would have gotten into whatever apparatus I had built and thrown whatever switch needed throwing. Something would happen, be it a bright light, loud noise, or searing pain. I'd black out. I'd wake up, just like I had.

None of that happened.

Yesterday, I was a 32-year-old teacher, living in my own house, talking to my girlfriend, and playing in the backyard with my dog. Why am I suddenly an 18-year-old again? *How* am I an 18-year-old again? Something must have happened last night as I slept to force my mind back to my younger body. The problem is that I didn't do anything to make this happen. In the science fiction story, the main character would know exactly what to do to fix the problem. They'd find the right person to help them who existed in both times. Sure, they'd have to convince them that this was really happening, but that might only take a few paragraphs—an impassioned plea and the revelation of information from the future.

This, on the other hand, was real—at least, I *thought* it was real—and there was no one to call to help me fix the experiment; it wasn't *Back to the Future,* and Doc Brown wasn't living in McHenry, Illinois.

I looked at the clock on my cell phone. 5:32, Friday, March 10. That meant I was supposed to go to school.

I actually let out a small laugh at that thought.

A laugh with a touch of hysteria.

'*How in the hell am I supposed to go to school when I don't remember anything about what I'm supposed to be doing?*' I thought. I had no reason, as a grown man, to remember my schedule from my senior year of high school.

'*Fuck that,*' I thought, shaking my head. '*I don't know how it happened, but I've got to figure out some way to get things back to normal. How to get back to my actual body and not have to live high school all over again.*'

How I was going to do that, though, was anyone's guess. I figured I'd better start by retracing my steps back to my house. I knew my house was still there in '06, but it would be nothing like when I lived there in 2020.

'*Well, at least it's somewhere to start,*' I thought. I got up, threw on some clothes, and grabbed my phone, wallet, and keys off the nightstand.

But then I stopped.

I probably shouldn't be trampling around the house, making a shit-ton of noise at 5:30 a.m. The last thing I needed was to explain to my family what was going on.

'*They'd think I was fucked out of my mind,*' I thought. '*Remember that time you took a nap and forgot what day it was? Mom asked if you were high. Just imagine what she'd think if you came with some* "I'm really supposed to be in the future" *story. You're apt to be committed.*'

I shook my head. I couldn't worry about that right now. Crazy or not, I had to figure out what was happening and find some way to fix it.

I found my boots downstairs and shoved my feet in. Then, I found my jacket and threw it on. I walked to the garage door, opened it, and looked inside. Sure enough, my 1995 Pontiac Grand Am was sitting in the far spot, backed in like I always did back then.

Or, now.

This time travel stuff is hell on linear thinking.

I shook my head and hit the button for the garage door, wincing at the squeaking noises it made.

After a moment of staring at the snow-covered ground, I got in my car and turned the engine over before carefully pulling out of the garage and around my dad's gigantic green conversion van. I drove down Turnberry Drive and out to Green Street, making a right. I drove for a few miles until I came to Illinois Route 120 and then made a left. I took 120 into Wonder Lake and turned down the road my future house sat on.

The house at the end of the street was in total disrepair. I stared at it in disbelief—I knew that the original owner didn't take care of it, but *Jesus*.

The yard was completely overgrown; the grass was about waist high and had been flowering before the snow had come. Now, it poked through the blanket of white, intermixed with the remnants of weeds and wildflower stalks. The house itself was beyond dirty. The siding was likely once white but had since turned a disgusting, dirty brown. Several of the panes in the bay windows were cracked, and one was missing entirely and covered in cardboard, duct tape, and newspaper. I wasn't even sure anyone lived in the place.

Pushing my disgust aside, I parked on the road in front of the seemingly derelict building. I got out and took a look around. Even in 2006, the neighborhood was quiet. I walked up the overgrown and snow-covered gravel driveway and made my way around the side of the house. The grass here was shorter, but the side of the house was drifted with snow.

I made my way to the backyard, still not sure exactly what my plan was.

Like the rest of the yard, the backyard was overgrown. Weeds had grown waist-high, and, like the front yard, there were snarls of pricker bushes poking through the snow. The tree that my neighbor had told me about was still standing, its long limbs coming dangerously close to the power lines that were strung across the easement between the properties.

I had a flash of memory: my kitty-corner neighbor, Reggie, telling me that, someday soon, the tree would be cut down because it was going to catch fire from the power lines. That day, apparently, hadn't happened yet.

'*This is all too fucking weird*,' I thought as I stood in the yard staring at the tree. I took a slow, deep breath, trying to center my thoughts. I turned toward the house, focusing my attention on something tangible—results and an objective I could focus on.

The back of the house was just as shabby as the front—dirt and stains marred the siding; gutters were full to overflowing with leaves and debris. The deck that would be there in 14 years was absent, and in its place was a simple concrete slab, forming the step up to a sliding glass door caked with dirt and muck.

It was jarring to see all the changes from what I was used to, and my knees started to feel weak. I sank to the slab, intending to take a moment to gather myself.

Something *had* to have happened yesterday to cause this to happen. The only kicker was that I had no idea what it could have been.

Yesterday had been as normal a day as possible in late June 2020. There was still a pandemic raging, so I didn't have much reason to leave my house. I had spent the majority of the day alone, working on plans for the shit show that was going to be the school year. The only real company I'd had all day was my dog, who I took out to play ball with in the afternoon. While he had run after the ball like his life depended on it, I'd smoked a cigar and enjoyed the afternoon sun.

Nothing stood out in my memory as out of the ordinary. I remembered scrolling through Google News on my phone and finding an article from PBS about some comet that was supposed to be passing the Earth in July.

Maybe the thing had been early.

The problem with that theory is that comets aren't magical—they're rocks trailing space junk that happen to fly past the Earth. If this were the fourteenth century, sure, I'd probably believe that some god somewhere was displeased and sent me back to right a wrong, or that I was some kind of messenger or hero.

Which was bullshit.

The fact that I was back in 2006, somehow inhabiting my 18-year-old body, was *not* bullshit.

Wallowing in the fact that it was happening wasn't helping me figure out why I was a teenager again or how to fix it. I took one more look around the backyard, scanning for anything that might be of use, but came up empty.

I trudged out of the backyard and down the driveway to the street.

I sat down in my car, turned the engine over, and began to drive out of the neighborhood.

I needed to be away from here and find somewhere to collect my thoughts.

CHAPTER 2

Two thousand miles away sat a nondescript office building. Officially, the room in the basement was called the Strategic Anomaly Observation Control.

Unofficially, it was referred to as the Overlook because that's exactly what everyone did to the people who worked there.

Project Outrigger had begun as something of a joke; it had been conceived by Major General Marcus Copland and Herman Samuel Baumann as a way to "ride alongside SETI—Search for ExtraTerrestrial Intelligence." SETI had come about as mankind looked to the stars and wondered, "Are we alone out there?" Project Outrigger sought to capitalize on the scientific possibilities afforded by SETI's team and funding.

In the original pitch, they had said the Project would supplement Berkeley's search, with Baumann as the lead researcher. As the project continued, it drew criticism from the mainstream of science—Project Outrigger became more and more esoteric as it continued. Eventually, SETI broke with Project Outrigger because their "views no longer coincided."

That was their polite way of saying Project Outrigger had

gone off the rails.

Rather than searching for extraterrestrial life as it had for the first years of its existence, Copland, Baumann, and Project Outrigger began to move away from searching space and began to search for anomalies in time and space on the planet Earth. Unfortunately for those involved, there largely were no anomalies on planet Earth. This did not stop the Project, though. Throughout the middle years of the project, Major General Copland acquired a number of investors—mostly billionaires with too much money and not enough going on to keep them occupied. Eventually, after the break with SETI, Project Outrigger went almost entirely underground.

In the thirty years between 1990 and 2020, Project Outrigger had detected a total of zero time-space anomalies. Even the few remaining billionaire investors were about ready to jump ship, as their cohorts had done years earlier.

Until late June.

CHAPTER 3

Javier del Carmen sat in the semi-dilapidated office, feet up on the console, reading a book. Truly, this was about the most boring job in the world. Fortunately for Javier, the billionaire investors kept paying his salary, even though the Project had gone thirty years without a positive result—or, really, any result at all. Although he was technically security, he had been assigned to sit in a chair and read a book for nine hours while "monitoring" the equipment, which was fine by him.

The Project paid well enough, at least.

Today, Javier had added headphones to his usual routine. As he looked up to give a cursory glance at the console in front of him, foot tapping in time to Johnny Cash's baritone voice, he noticed something new: a small, blinking, amber light near the bottom of the screen.

"Wait, what?" Javier said, dropping his feet to the floor and pulling his headphones off his ears. He noticed a soft, insistent beeping now that the headphones had been removed. "What does that mean?"

Vaguely, Javier was aware that there was a manual for this portion of his job, and he assumed that it would tell him what to do with this blinking amber light. Now, he just needed to *find* the damn thing. He rummaged around the filing cabinet to his left, pushing aside hanging files of memos and reports that all said the same thing in different ways. Coming up empty, he opened the drawers of his desk, hoping he still had the binder. He dug under empty coffee cups and snack wrappers, again coming up empty. Finally, shoved under a stack of magazines in his bottom-right drawer, he found the binder he was looking for: SAOC Agent-In-Charge Protocol.

He looked back at the screen, realizing for the first time that the blinking light actually said a small word.

-CONTACT-

Javier flipped the binder open, hands shaking slightly. He finally found the section labeled CONTACT and began to read. His eyes grew wide as he read the implications of the small, blinking word.

"Holy shit," Javier said, the binder slipping from his hands and landing with a soft thud at his feet. In a slight daze, he reached for the phone on the edge of his console, knocking that, too, to the ground. With a muttered curse, he picked the phone up and set it back on the console. It took him four tries to dial the correct extension—his hands had begun to shake.

"Yes?" The voice on the other end of the line said, sounding slightly annoyed. Javier, like most under-motivated employees, had a tendency to call his supervisor any time he needed a break, which was often.

"Jeffrey?" Javier said, his voice shaking.

"Who else would it be?" Dr. Jeffrey Phillips, Javier's direct superior, snapped. "What do you need?

"Something happened."

There was a pause at the other end of the line. Then, "The fuck does that mean, *something happened*?"

"The console lit up," Javier's voice was shaking more, and he seemed to have difficulty forming the words.

"What does the console say? Does it say detection or contact?"

"Contact."

The pause was longer this time, accompanied by some deep breaths.

"Jeffrey? What should I do? The binder just says to call you."

There was a sharp inhale on the other side of the phone; they had both been told that contact was a possibility, but no one had ever explained exactly what that would entail: "I have no idea."

CHAPTER 4

I drove out of the neighborhood and down IL Route 120 toward McDonald's. As I pulled into the parking lot, I instinctively reached down to the shifter knob for my mask. I was struck with yet another realization that I was no longer in the year 2020—the global COVID-19 pandemic wouldn't happen for another thirteen years. I have to say, I was excited by the prospect of being able to enter a restaurant and sit down for a coffee without fearing exposure or infection from the new coronavirus.

I parked the car on the far side of the lot, reaching down for the push button to turn off my vehicle, only to remember that I was driving a comparatively primitive Pontiac rather than my Ford.

'*Dammit*,' I thought, '*get it together. Stop forgetting* when *you are*.' I pulled the key from the ignition and got out of the car. I walked inside, ordered coffee and a sandwich, and sat down at a table. I went to pull out my smartphone and take notes but remembered that smartphones barely existed in this current year—technically, they existed, sure, but were most assuredly not accessible to the general population, let alone a teenager from a lower-middle-class family.

Shit.

Yet another thing I'd have to keep in mind until this nonsense was over ... whatever this nonsense turned out to be. I hoped to God it wasn't some kind of brain tumor or gas leak in my house. The last thing I wanted to deal with was waking up six months later in a hospital room hooked up to machines. Bizarrely, I almost hoped for some kind of time travel explanation; it was almost easier than hoping I had a mass growing in my head.

I left my coffee on the table and went to the counter. A sleepy-eyed, middle-aged woman stood there, effectively holding the counter up and waiting for the next customer.

What else did you expect at 6:12 a.m.?

"Excuse me, ma'am," I started. "Do you happen to have a piece of scrap paper and a pen I could have?"

She looked at me like I was an idiot, sighed, and nodded. She disappeared into what I assume was a back office or break room and returned with a printout of last week's schedule. She rummaged under the counter for a moment and surfaced with a pen. She handed them over and went back to sleeping while standing up. I thanked her and wandered back to my coffee.

Sitting at the table, I closed my eyes and tried to organize my thoughts.

What did I know?

I knew that, inexplicably, I was back in 2006. I knew that I was still myself and, therefore, inhabiting my younger body. I knew that, back in 2020, I didn't consciously do anything to cause this to happen.

I started taking notes, trying to find some pattern, some little detail, that would give me a clue to what happened and why.

I began by writing down what I knew for sure, which was a painfully short list:

- I hadn't left my house yesterday
- I hadn't done anything out of the ordinary
- I went to sleep at a reasonable time (around 11:15 p.m.)
- I woke up in 2006 (5:32 a.m.)

I stared at the list and wondered why I'd even decided to make it. There was no new information, no clue as to what happened, and certainly no help in fixing the situation. I leaned back in the chair and sipped my coffee. After a few minutes, my cell phone chirped. I pulled it out and saw the display: Mom. I'd known this was coming, so I took a deep breath and answered the call.

"Where are you?" my mother began immediately.

"I'm at McDonald's on 120. I'm safe, but I'm not going to school today. Something happened, and I need to figure it out."

"What are you talking about? Are you on drugs?"

I sighed. This was honestly about right for my mother circa 2006, considering this was the same woman who asked if I was high after I'd napped too hard and asked her what day it was.

"Well? Tell me what's going on!"

"Mom, trust me. Even if I told you what was happening, you wouldn't understand it. Hell, I barely understand it."

"I'm really worried about you. This isn't making sense. You need to come home right now before I call the police." She was getting more and more hysterical.

"Mom, please. I'm working on fixing this," I took a deep breath, "This isn't going to make any sense, but my consciousness has somehow been projected backward from 2020. You're not going to believe me, but I'm still your son, but I'm actually thirty-two. I woke up this morning here in 2006, but I still know everything about my life up until June of 2020. I'm working on finding out what the hell happened and how I can get myself back to my real body in my own time."

There was silence on the other end of the line. I knew my mother was staring ahead in disbelief, thinking that I had lost my damn mind or was high as a kite.

"You've just got to trust me. If you don't, I can't help that, but I'm going to do whatever I need to in order to fix this. If it works, and this is becoming history, you'll know I'm right when I get back to 2020. If it doesn't, and this is all wiped out, then it won't matter. Either way, I love you, but I'm going to hang up now."

"Don't you da—"

I cut the line and shut the phone down. I knew she was going to freak out, but what I'd told her was true—this was either going to become history and we'd talk about it in 2020, or it would be wiped out, and nothing would matter.

I sat for a moment, reflecting on the changes my mother had displayed over the years. Then, I packed up those thoughts and put them to the side. The primary focus remained the same: figure out what in the hell caused this time jump and do my best to reverse it.

I looked down at my wrist and realized that I no longer wore my watch. I pulled the piece of scrap paper closer and made a new list:

- Watch
- Backpack
- Notebook
- Pens
- Pocket knife
- Food (Clif bars, granola bars, etc.)

I packed up my new list and got up from the table I was sitting at. I went to the counter and ordered another coffee. I must have really looked like I needed it, because the woman behind the counter offered to give me a refill free of charge. I thanked her and left the McDonald's. I tried to remember if Wal-Mart had moved already.

'*Worst case,*' I thought, '*I drive a few extra minutes to pick up the stuff I need. Not the end of the world.*'

I got in my car and drove off toward Johnsburg.

CHAPTER 5

There was a flurry of activity inside the control room.

People who had never stepped foot inside the room were suddenly inhabiting it as if they'd always been there. Javier was unceremoniously pushed to the side by people who ranked much higher than him, never mind the fact that he technically had made the discovery.

Jeffrey, Javier's ever-pissy boss, muscled his way to the console, staring intently at the blinking amber -CONTACT-. He tapped a few keys, and a map popped up on the screen.

The map started out as a map of the United States. A blinking yellow box superimposed itself over Illinois. The map zoomed in automatically, and another blinking yellow box highlighted McHenry County. Jeffrey tapped a few more buttons, and the map zoomed in again. This time, a blinking yellow box highlighted the Wonderview neighborhood of Wonder Lake. The map refreshed a final time, and the blinking yellow box settled over a house at the end of a quiet street south of Wonderview Drive.

"We have the location of the temporal rift. It's in a United States city known as Wonder Lake."

"What's our game plan?"

That was Jeffrey's boss (thereby making him Javier's boss's boss), Lucas McDougall. McDougall was your average ladder-climber: he'd started in Javier's position, moved up through Jeffrey's, and finally kissed enough ass to be made Executive Director of Project Outrigger. He was the kind of person who loved talking about "gameplans" and "long-term projections" and "cost-to-result ratios." He had campaigned—unsuccessfully—to automate Javier's job, a fact that Javier never quite forgot.

Jeffrey stared straight ahead at the monitor, not answering McDougall's question. Javier thought Jeffrey looked constipated, but that was just him. After a moment, he took a deep breath before speaking.

"I think we need to get boots on the ground in Illinois. We need to secure the site and try to measure the output. We need to start loading the PC-804s and GN-192s, along with the TS-605Ts and YT-1300s. We may even need to bring along a T-65-AA-589."

Jeffrey rattled off the sensor numbers faster than Javier had ever heard him talk.

McDougall ran his thumb across his bottom lip.

"Do it," he said, "but make sure you don't cause a ruckus in town. Find out if it's a localized event or if it's something that's spreading. If it's localized, we can study it, and the implications. If it's expanding, we need to contain the spread so we don't have hundreds—or thousands—of people getting sucked away."

Everyone stilled for a moment, letting McDougall's words sink in. Javier stood quietly at the edge of the room, thinking of the implications of the temporal rift he had found. He was also thinking of the two options he'd read about in the binder. Right now, they seemed to be focusing on the first option: CONTAINMENT AND STUDY. What worried Javier was the other option.

ELIMINATION.

CHAPTER 6

I had just thrown my new backpack full of supplies in the passenger seat when it hit me.

My eyes seemed to widen, although my vision had decidedly tunneled. There was a high-pitched ringing in my ears, and the world before me seemed to shimmer. I felt my muscles seize up as I stared straight ahead into oblivion.

Then, my eyes snapped open.

I was staring up at a white ceiling. Vaguely, I was aware of a light affixed to the center of the room.

I heard a soft whimpering sound but was unable to turn my head to find the source.

The realization struck me: I was back in my own bed, in my own home, and my dog was the one making the whimpering sounds.

'*Now, why the hell can't I move?*' I thought. '*Is this some kind of sleep paralysis? Was all that other stuff just a dream?*'

I was trying to get my arms to move when I felt my eyes widen and my vision tunnel again. The high-pitched ringing was back, and the ceiling was starting to shimmer.

My eyes snapped open again. This time, I was staring at a

rounded, black shape. My face was resting on a rough, uneven surface I soon realized was the asphalt in the Wal-Mart parking lot.

I groaned and pushed myself up into a sitting position.

"Are you alright, son?"

An older man had walked up sometime during my blackout and was looking at me with a good amount of concern. I ran my hand through my hair, pushing it back from my sweaty forehead, and stood up.

"I'm alright. I have epilepsy, so sometimes I black out," I said, the lie coming easily. I'd rather not explain to a complete stranger that I'm actually from 2020, and I somehow glimpsed my bedroom at home in what I assumed to be the future. My own mother didn't believe me, so I'd fully expect this stranger to think I was some kind of lunatic. The last thing I needed was to get committed for talking about time travel, which was seeming—impossibly—more and more likely.

"Do you really think you should be driving? That seems dangerous," he said.

"I'm fine. Now, if you'll excuse me ..." I said, moving past the man and to my driver's side.

Unfortunately, the man persisted.

"Son, I really think you ought to get checked out. You could be hurt," he said, following me around to the driver's side.

"Look, sir," I said, letting irritation color my voice, "I told you I'm fine, so just leave it at that. I don't need your help, and I sure didn't ask for your opinion. Now, leave me alone so I can get on with my day."

The man gave me a disgusted look but shuffled off, muttering something about "damn kids these days" under his breath. I shook my head and got in my car. I turned the engine over and pulled out of the lot.

I worked my way back over to Wonder Lake, considering

my next steps. Judging from the abruptness of my flash-forward, the likelihood that I had somehow prompted my consciousness-travel seemed pretty low. Which really only left me with some kind of natural phenomena.

Either that or some fucked-up experiment that had gone awry.

I figured I'd need to take another look around my future house, although that would prove challenging.

I guess it's time to commit a misdemeanor.

CHAPTER 7

The helicopters touched down a little after 8 a.m., the sun already shining bright in the June sky.

As the equipment was being unloaded, McDougall, Jeffrey, and Javier disembarked and made their way to a large black van. Javier took the wheel, with Jeffrey seated beside him in the passenger seat. McDougall rode in the back like some kind of dignitary.

The little airport where they had touched down was called Galt Airport, and it sat a few miles outside the town of Woodstock. From there, it was about twelve minutes to the small town of Wonder Lake. The locals had been confused when the helo touched down—typically, Galt gets nothing more than the occasional puddle jumper. For the most part, the airport was known for flight school and the Young Eagles program, which took young kids up in planes and let them "fly." It was little more than a feel-good activity for kids and parents. To the man at the tower, the request to have two vans and a tractor-trailer was almost unheard of. He'd argued with McDougall on the phone for about fifteen minutes before he finally agreed to make the required calls.

When the two helicopters—one a passenger, the other

a cargo—appeared on radar, the man in the tower promptly shut his mouth. The cargo helicopter was weighed down with equipment—it took the better part of two hours to offload the cargo and load it into the tractor-trailer. When they were on their way, McDougall began to tell them what the plan was.

"What we know, as of now, is that a time-space anomaly appeared in the Wonderview neighborhood of Wonder Lake, Illinois. We are to proceed with caution but with the objective of measuring and studying this anomaly. This is the first time such an anomaly has been detected, and we do not know the full scope of its impact. Ultimately, we hope to control this anomaly and study it, although if it's viable, the repercussions could be enormous.

"I have files that detail what the Project coordinators knew about the scientists that defected." McDougall patted a leather-bound binder on his lap. "They didn't have specifics, but they suspected that one of their lead researchers purchased the home we are going to and set up a lab."

Jeffrey nodded, and Javier ran his hand over his stubble-covered chin, making a harsh rasping sound.

"What happens if someone is in this rift?" Jeffrey asked, turning back in his seat to look at McDougall.

McDougall sat quietly for a moment, staring out the right-hand window. Javier's eyes flicked to the rearview mirror and watched his boss's boss knit his brow.

"Sir?" Jeffrey prompted, looking over at Javier. Javier raised an eyebrow but otherwise drove on silently.

McDougall turned to face Jeffrey straight on.

"I don't know. We may have to put the poor soul out of their misery because I don't think anyone could survive something like that."

Both Javier and Jeffrey nodded solemnly. Jeffrey glanced at Javier, the unspoken question hanging in the air.

Javier reached down and felt for the 9mm he carried on his left hip. His hand found the butt of the gun.

He gripped the wheel tighter and pushed the accelerator.

CHAPTER 8

I'd been sitting in my car for the past 25 minutes, trying to figure out if there actually was anyone in the house. Nothing had moved or changed in the hours I'd been gone, so I wasn't completely convinced the house was occupied. Looking at the state of it, that made sense.

I sighed and opened the driver's side door. I went to the trunk and popped it open.

Inside, I'd stashed a pair of leather-palmed work gloves, my backpack of supplies, and a crowbar. I took the gloves and pulled them on, then threw my arms through the straps of the backpack. Last, I picked up the crowbar and considered its weight.

I set the crowbar back down in the trunk and took off my backpack. I rummaged around inside the pocket for a moment and came up with my knife. I clipped the knife to my belt and then picked the crowbar back up.

I closed the trunk and walked up the unplowed gravel driveway, moving around the left-hand side of the house as I had done earlier. Although I wasn't convinced anyone was here, I still moved with caution. A teenager in a letterman jacket sneaking around someone's property was bound to attract attention. As I tracked through the tall grass and snow, I kept my eyes and ears open for any signs of movement.

Birdsong floated through the brisk air, and a branch creaked from some remaining snow resting on it. I could faintly hear the sounds of traffic in the distance but no sounds of approaching vehicles.

From the house, though, there was nothing.

I continued around the back of the house and made my way to the sliding glass door leading to the main living area. Although the windows were horrifyingly dirty, I could see through them—after scraping off a layer of grime with my gloves. I pushed my disgust down and hefted the crowbar.

My first thought was to just smash the window, but then I realized what a bad idea that would be. I considered the door and shoved the crowbar into the small gap between the door and the frame.

Fortunately, both the door and frame were aluminum, so there wasn't any splintering or cracking. There wasn't any bending, either; the door slid open almost immediately.

I shook my head and dropped the crowbar into the snow drift next to the concrete step. I slid the door open the rest of the way and stepped in.

The first thing I noticed was the sheer amount of crap in the house.

There were stacks of boxes, nearly as tall as my 5' 9" frame, filled with all manner of junk; milk crates full of newspapers or bottles, some crumpled and broken, others nearly new; and piles of pizza boxes from all manner of local pizza joints.

The second thing I noticed was the smell.

It's that special kind of smell that everyone knows but can't put into words. It's the smell of a life gone to shit—stale cigarette smoke, old food, mold, and rot. Apathy hung in the air like a cloud, an almost tangible thing.

The whole place had the feeling of being forgotten. Wasted.

There was also the feeling of being watched.

I scanned the room, trying to take in the details. I moved slowly through the dining room and peered around the half-wall into the living room. There was a ratty, moth-eaten chair shoved to the side in front of a 1980s-era TV. Surprisingly, the thing still worked, although the channel was tuned to snow. I made my way to the front door and noticed that it was nailed shut with 2x4s attached haphazardly across it and into the drywall. There were doors on the front closet, and the one on the right was slightly cracked. I flipped open my pocket knife and reversed the grip, angling the four-inch blade down my forearm. I moved to the closet door slowly, turning my body into a profile. I eased my fingers into the crack of the door and rolled it open on its track.

Thankfully, the only thing in the closet was another stack of boxes; there was no room for anyone to be hiding and lying in wait, although I still couldn't shake the feeling that someone was watching my every move.

I moved through the living room to the hallway. My hand found the trio of switches on the wall and threw the first one, turning on the light to the hall—or, at least, it should have. The switch didn't seem to work. I tried the other two switches but got the same result. I glanced at the ceiling and was surprised to see that the light fixtures were bare; the bulbs and globes had been removed, and empty receptacles were visible.

What in the hell was up with this guy?

I moved down the dimly lit hallway, passing the door to the garage. I glanced at the deadbolt and saw that it was locked, so I pressed forward. I pressed my back against the wall and peeked around the corner leading to the bedrooms. The two doors on the left side of the hall were closed, and little light filtered through the crack at the bottom of the door; likely, the windows were closed, perhaps even nailed shut like the front door. The bathroom on the right was also closed. The closed doors made me uneasy, but I knew my objective was the master bedroom at the end of the hall—the last place I remembered being before waking up in the past.

The door to the master bedroom was cracked, unlike those to the two smaller bedrooms. I approached slowly, walking on the balls of my feet to try to minimize my footsteps. I used the toe of my left foot to inch the door open and looked inside. Surprisingly, this was the least cluttered room in the house. There were still stacks of boxes almost to the ceiling, but they were confined to one corner and the walk-in closet on the left side of the room. The windows were covered in newspaper, and there was a twin mattress lying on a box spring on the floor. The master bathroom door was open, and I carefully poked my head inside.

Nothing.

I turned around and was almost immediately grabbed by the front of my shirt and shoved into the doorjamb.

CHAPTER 9

A floorboard creaked again, the sound reverberating through the basement.

There was someone in the house.

The man stood in the basement, shrouded in darkness and surrounded by all manner of odds and ends, stacked to the joists above his head. The odds and ends were his treasures; he had long ago given up human interaction in favor of tinkering with the various pieces of equipment in his home.

That was different now, he knew; someone had invaded his space and was looking through his things upstairs. A pair of yellowing eyes narrowed in the semi-darkness of the basement. This would not stand.

The man crept, catlike, to the bottom of the stairs. Mentally, he ran through which board would make noise when he put his weight on it.

He didn't like his chances of making it up the stairs silently. He turned to the large window and egress point near the septic outflow pipe. He carefully slid the window open and made his way up the rusted ladder to the side yard.

He moved quickly to the back door and saw that it was

standing open. In the snow near the back door was a crowbar. He picked it up and made his way back into the house.

Down the hall, he heard the door to the master bedroom creak open.

That was where he would confront this stranger who dared intrude on his solitude. Quickly, he made his way down the hallway and to the bedroom door. Inside, he heard soft footsteps on the carpeting and the creak of a hinge as the bathroom door was moved.

He moved, whipping around the corner, fingers snagging the fabric of a shirt.

CHAPTER 10

I felt my back slam into the wall, a jolt of pain shooting up my spine.

"Who in the hell are you?" the man snarled, spittle catching in his long, matted beard, "What the hell are you doing in my house?"

I had been so caught off guard that I couldn't even form a thought; the only thing I could do was stare at the man gripping the front of my shirt.

"I just needed to look around," I said, throwing my hands up, "I don't want anything from you; I just needed to look around the house!"

"Like hell you did," he growled, his voice harsh and raspy. "You're here to steal my treasures!"

He let go of my shirt and hefted the crowbar I'd dropped in the backyard.

Shit.

I reacted, dropping my shoulder low and driving it into the man's chest. He grunted and was pushed back a step. I pressed in, grabbing for the crowbar; my knife had fallen from my hands when he shoved me into the door.

I got one hand on the crowbar, but he wrenched it away, growling again. He swung the crowbar, but it was awkward, and I saw it coming. I dropped low and felt the rush of air as it flew overhead.

"I really don't want any trouble!" I yelled, "I'll explain if you let me!"

The man tried to stop the momentum of the crowbar, but his wild swing was too forceful. The crowbar slammed into the drywall, burying the claw end about three inches into the wall. He tugged at it, but it was stuck.

I took the opportunity to scan the room, looking for something I could use to defend myself. Although I saw my knife on the floor, I really didn't want to have to use it. I saw an old, cracked baseball bat half-buried in a cardboard box. I reached for it and yanked it free.

The man had finally freed the crowbar from the wall and was turning to face me again. This time, when he drove in, I swung the baseball bat, aiming for the crowbar.

His second swing was just as wild as the first, and the baseball bat missed the solid steel of the crowbar, instead landing on the soft bones of his wrist.

The man howled in pain and dropped the crowbar, clutching his left wrist to his chest. I took a step back, putting some distance between the man and me, hoping the impromptu fight was over.

The man had other ideas.

He lunged for my knife.

"Shit, no!" I cried, instinctively cocking the bat back and swinging it at the man's arm. At the last moment, he lurched forward, putting the back of his head squarely into the path of the baseball bat.

With a sickening *thump*, the man slumped in front of the bathroom door.

I stared for a moment, letting the baseball bat slip from my hand. I knelt down and checked the man's throat.

Fortunately, there was a pulse, and it was steady; the man was unconscious, not dead.

'*Jesus Christ,*' I thought, '*I could have killed him.*'

I looked at the unconscious man for a moment longer, then made a choice. I looked around for something to tie his hands with—the last thing I wanted was to have to fight him again. I found an old length of rope in one of the boxes stacked against the wall and went to work tying the man's hands together.

That done, I grabbed my knife from the floor and wondered why in the hell I'd even thought to have it open. I looked around the bedroom again but felt no sense of familiarity; there was nothing here that jogged my memory or painted a clear picture of what had caused my shift backward in time.

I moved back toward the kitchen, completely unsure of what to do next. I glanced at my watch and saw that it was after noon. I decided I should go grab a bite to eat and reconsider my options. I went back down the hall and into the bedroom. I picked up the crowbar and the bat. I shoved the bat back into the box I'd found it in and made my way back through the kitchen and to the back door. I pulled the sliding glass door closed behind me and walked back out to the front of the house.

Back in my car, I slumped in the front seat.

I was exhausted; my brain was nearly overloaded from all the information I'd been processing since that morning.

Plus, I'd just defended myself from some raging asshole. Although, I guess I couldn't really fault him. I had broken into his home, after all.

I decided to drive to Woodstock and find somewhere to eat and think, preferably in that order.

I turned over the engine and drove back out toward Route 120.

CHAPTER 11

Javier hit the turn signal and moved into the turn lane at the intersection of Illinois Route 120 and East Wonder Lake Road. The ride hadn't taken long, but everyone in the vehicle was on edge: Jeffrey was constantly trying to crack his knuckles, and McDougall kept picking at a spot on his slacks. Javier himself kept drumming his fingers on the steering wheel and grinding his teeth.

McDougall reached down between his feet and opened the go-bag he had brought with him. He pulled out a binder, flipped it open, and began to read. Javier looked in the rearview mirror and noticed it was the same red binder that he had pulled out of his desk, the same red binder McDougall had read on the helicopter.

The van began to drift to the left as Javier looked in the rearview mirror. There was a blast of an air horn, and Javier tore his eyes away from the rearview and back to the road, just in time to see the 18-wheeler barreling toward them. He jerked the wheel to the right and brought the van back into the northbound lane.

"Jesus, where in hell did you get your license?" Jeffrey

asked, clutching the "oh shit" handle for dear life.

"It was just a mistake," Javier said, mentally telling his boss to go fuck himself.

In the back, McDougall was seemingly unbothered by their brush with disaster. He continued reading the binder, almost as if Javier and Jeffrey weren't even in the vehicle.

Javier glanced down at the GPS and made the turn toward their destination. He found the house at the far end of a quiet street, a well-maintained, pale yellow ranch set back at the end of a steep driveway. The lawn was well-kept; the driveway was clean and free of leaves and grass clippings. Javier pulled the van up the driveway and threw it in park. He turned and looked at Jeffrey, who in turn looked at McDougall.

McDougall snapped the binder closed and shoved it back into his go-bag. "Let's go."

The trio exited the van, and Javier stepped away, pulling the radio off his belt and calling the address to the driver of the cargo van. He clipped the radio back on his belt and walked back over to Jeffrey and McDougall. McDougall was halfway through a question to Jeffrey:

"... see what's inside. What information do we have on the suspected victim? What was his name again?" McDougall asked.

Jeffrey pulled out his iPad and tapped a command. "He's essentially a ghost; his social media presence doesn't extend much past the basics, and the only definitive information we can find about him is the public record of the real estate transaction and his employment record for the school. His name isn't even interesting. It's something ... generic." He tapped a key on his iPad, found the name, and gave it to McDougall.

"Not a very memorable name, that's for sure. That's all, though? How does someone have such a small online footprint?"

"From all outward appearances, he's just a teacher in a mid-sized town in Illinois who doesn't like social media very much."

McDougall frowned. "There must be more to him. Let's get inside and take a look around."

Javier opened the back of the van and pulled out his own go-bag. He opened it, pulled out a pair of black leather gloves, and pulled them on. He found a small, red leather case in the front pocket, flipped it open, and examined the set of lock-picks. He flipped the case closed and shoved it in his back pocket. He checked the 9mm on his hip, making sure the weapon was loaded and ready to go.

Javier led the way to the front door. He stopped and turned to Jeffrey.

"Does this guy live alone?"

Jeffrey furrowed his brow. He flipped open his pack and pulled out an iPad. He tapped a query and scrolled through the results.

"I don't know. We have to go on the assumption that he does, right, McDougall?"

McDougall grunted.

Javier turned to the door and rolled his eyes. He pulled the pick set from his back pocket and knelt down. He peered at the lock, selected a pair of picks, and set to work.

It took less than thirty seconds, and he was in.

He pulled the 9mm off his belt and pushed the door open.

The living room was tidy but lived in. Along the far wall, there was a large dog crate. Javier turned to Jeffrey and McDougall, motioning toward the kennel.

Javier moved quietly into the house, keeping the barrel of the pistol low and his finger off the trigger. He moved toward the kitchen, looking for any sign of life.

To his left, there was a darkened hallway. Javier moved toward it, making his way past a door that likely led to the garage, and to the corner where the hall turned toward the back of the house. He pushed himself up against the corner and peered around.

The hallway was lit only by a sliver of light filtering under the three doors. He rounded the corner and pushed open the first door.

Nothing important.

The second door led to an office. He made a mental note to have the support team break into and analyze the contents of the computer he saw sitting on the desk in the corner.

'*That must be the master bedroom,*' he thought, looking at the closed door at the end of the hall. He moved forward, footfalls light against the hardwood flooring.

He turned the handle and pushed the door inward.

As soon as the door was open, Javier was hit in the chest with something large and furry.

Something snarling.

Something with teeth.

CHAPTER 12

I ended up in Woodstock at a little restaurant on the square called Angelo's. Back in 2020, Angelo's went belly up and was remodeled into a brunch cafe, but in 2006, it was still kicking.

I asked for a table near the back, and the hostess was happy enough to oblige; the restaurant wasn't very busy, and the majority of the seats were unfilled.

She sat me at my table, handed me a menu, and wandered back to the counter near the front of the place and her magazine.

Fine by me. I didn't really think I had the mental capacity for conversation right now.

I'd brought my backpack in with me, and I reached down and got my notebook out. I didn't open it, though, because I saw the waiter coming and didn't need him to snoop on my notes about my fucked-up time travel experience.

I ended up ordering coffee and a Philly cheesesteak sandwich, which came with fries and soup. When he brought the soup, it was hot, with a good, creamy broth and plenty of chunks of chicken and wild rice. I loaded up with pepper and dug in.

I opened the notebook and turned to a fresh page. At the

top, I wrote the heading, NEXT STEPS. Below that, I paused, considering my options.

Under NEXT STEPS, I wrote:

- Investigate the house again—basement?
- Call family?
- Call Leigh?
- Talk to Mr. Dobkins (physics)

I figured my best bets were to try and talk to Mr. Dobkins at the high school and then investigate the house again, this time trying to get to the basement. With any luck, the guy who lived there would be incapacitated still, and I could take my time. I really should have investigated the house more while I was there, but given the fact that that guy had ambushed me, I had just wanted to get out of there.

I also figured I should probably get in touch with my mom; I had a strong feeling that she was going crazy, wondering what the hell was wrong with me. I wasn't looking forward to that conversation, though. I decided to let that particular dog lie, and I turned my attention to making notes for when I talked to Mr. Dobkins.

In 2020, I hadn't spoken to Harold Dobkins in years, but in 2006, I was still his student in AP Physics. Mr. Dobkins was the kind of man who, when faced with something ridiculous or borderline impossible, tended to respond with curiosity rather than outright denial. I figured, being a high school teacher, he'd just about seen and heard everything, most of it twice.

Hell, some of it probably three times.

I also figured, though, that he had never heard anything like this. I tried to piece together everything I could remember, looking at my earlier notes. I included my B&E excursion and my thoughts on what might have caused my jump through time.

My food came, and I snapped the notebook closed. I ate slowly, still mulling the whole situation over but not getting anywhere. I finally came to the conclusion that I needed a new perspective and decided to head to the high school to talk to Dobkins first. I checked my watch, and saw it was near the time school let out.

I grabbed my backpack, shoved my notebook inside, and turned to leave. I dropped too much money on the table; I didn't want to wait for the bill.

I stepped outside, took a deep breath, and moved toward my car.

In moments, I was off, making my way to Route 120 and into McHenry.

CHAPTER 13

I arrived at the school at about three o'clock. Knowing that I usually stayed late after my students had left, I felt confident that the teachers were still there.

There were only a few students in the school; the parking lot was almost completely empty of student vehicles. The only ones there were students attending one of the various clubs or serving detention.

Fortunately, that meant fewer people who might have known me.

Unfortunately, that meant I stuck out as one of the few students wandering the building.

Luckily, though, I still had the mentality of an adult, so I just looked like I belonged and walked purposefully into the building.

I walked up the main staircase to the "blue level" and made my way quickly past the band room. I turned my head away as I walked past, hoping to God that no one I knew was in there—if I was going to get busted for skipping school, it would probably be by one of the band kids. I was heavily involved in the band program back in 2006, and just about everyone in the program knew my face. Fortunately, I was clear.

I made my way down the hall and found Mr. Dobkins' room. The door was open, so I poked my head in. I found Mr. Dobkins at his desk along the far wall, grading papers.

"Mr. Dobkins?" I said, making my way into the classroom.

"Yes? Oh, hello. I believe we missed you in class today. Is everything alright?"

"Well, actually, no. It's really not. Do you have a few minutes?"

"Of course," Mr. Dobkins said, stacking his papers on his desk and turning toward me. I pulled the door closed and walked over to his desk.

"Mr. Dobkins, you're going to think I'm crazy, but I can promise you that what I'm about to tell you is the truth," I started, watching his face carefully. He raised his eyebrows, clearly expecting an excuse as to why I hadn't been in school today. "I'm not the person standing here in front of you, not really anyway. I'm still me, but I'm not a high school student anymore. In reality, my consciousness is from the year 2020, and I'm actually thirty-two years old. When I woke up this morning, I was here, in 2006, inhabiting my younger body. I ended up going to my future house in this time and tried to look around, but I had to incapacitate the owner. Ultimately, I found nothing, so I thought I'd come here and ask you about this whole experience, thinking maybe your physics knowledge could help me. This is damn near impossible to believe, but I promise this is the truth."

Dobkins sat in his chair, looking at me with an amused look on his face. He could clearly tell that I'd rehearsed the story, and he was trying to decide how to respond to it.

"That's quite the fanciful story," he said, leaning back in his chair. "It would certainly make for an interesting thought experiment."

"Okay," I said, realizing this was even too much for him to believe, "if we were to do a thought experiment on this, what do you think the most likely cause would be?"

"Well, if I had to guess, I would say some kind of wormhole. The only problem is that wormholes are largely thought to be theoretical. If they did exist, though, they would be one of the few things that could transport someone back in time. The biggest concern with this, though, is ... now, let me see here." He paused, getting up from his desk and walking over to his bookshelf. He selected a volume and returned to his desk. He flipped through a few pages and found a dog-eared page. "Ah yes, here we go. In order to move through time, that would require the discovery of negative energy and mass particles. Not only that, but it would require a wormhole large enough for a human to fit through. Aside from those two things, you'd also need to be traveling at roughly the speed of light."

"So, you can't think of anything on Earth that would cause something like this to happen?"

"Oh, heavens, no," he said with a chuckle, "this is all purely theoretical. That much energy contained in one location would be nearly impossible, not to mention the forces involved. I think the biggest limiting factor is the speed someone would need to travel at. We can observe the speed of light"—he pulled a small flashlight from his desk drawer and clicked it on and off in rapid succession— "we can measure the speed of light, but we cannot *travel* at the speed of light."

I heaved an internal sigh. I had a feeling this was going to happen. Hell, it was happening to me, and *I* barely believed it.

"Thanks, Mr. Dobkins," I said, grabbing my backpack from the floor where I'd dropped it, "I appreciate your time."

"Oh, no problem," he said, smiling, "it was fun to talk through that experiment."

I nodded and turned to leave.

"Oh, by the way, I expect to see you in class on Monday. Missing school isn't like you," he said, turning back to his work.

"Sure, Mr. Dobkins," I said and left the room.

I paused outside the classroom and leaned against a bank of lockers.

I was running out of ideas and getting progressively more annoyed with my lack of progress in discovering what the hell had happened.

I decided it was about time I let my family know I was okay. I pushed off the lockers and made my way back out of the building.

Minutes later, I was back in my car.

CHAPTER 14

I pulled up the contact for my parents' home phone number. Like a lot of things, in 2020, it no longer existed. In 2006, it was the surefire way to get someone to pick up.

I took a deep breath and punched the green phone button.

The phone rang.

Again.

A third time.

Midway through the fourth ring, my mother picked up.

"Where in the hell are you?" she all but yelled into the phone.

"Mom, I'm fine, and I'm safe. Look, I know you're probably worried—"

"You're goddamn right I am!" she shouted, causing me to pull the phone away from my ear. "You take off in the morning, skip school, and now you call me and tell me everything's fine? What, am I just supposed to believe that?"

"Honestly, yeah," I said, trying like hell not to get irritated; I'd forgotten just how in your face she was in 2006; 2020-Mom was a lot more chill. Still in-your-face at times, but definitely not the same person who existed in my memories of high school. I grit my teeth, took another deep breath, and continued: "There's something going on that I can't explain. I'll try if you want me to, but I can almost guarantee you'll think I'm lying or on drugs."

My mother fell silent. This was either the calm before the storm, or she was actually willing to listen. I was betting on the former.

What she said next surprised me, though: "Tell me what's going on."

Her voice was calm, and she almost resembled the woman I'd come to know in 2020.

I figured I'd better seize this moment.

"Okay," I started, shifting in my seat, looking for the right words, "it's the year 2006, right? Well, up until this morning, it wasn't. Not for me, anyway. I'm still your son, but the reality is, for me, it's the year 2020. This sounds like I'm making shit up, but I promise you I'm not. I'm not high; I'm not drunk; I just woke up this morning inhabiting my eighteen-year-old body. I took off this morning and went to the house I bought in the future. I wanted to look around and see if there was something—anything—that would give me a clue as to what happened and what I could do to fix it. I didn't find anything, though. I'm actually at East right now; I went to talk to Mr. Dobkins, my physics teacher, thinking he could give me some kind of answers. Just like you, though, he had a hard time believing what I was saying and thought it was some kind of thought experiment."

I fell silent, knowing full well it was a lot to take in. My mother was silent for a moment.

"This is unbelievable," she said softly.

"I know, Ma," I said, "but I'm telling you, it happened. It is happening."

"Something about the way you talk is different," she said; even over the phone, I could hear her frowning. "Your voice sounds similar, but the way you talk sounds ... different. More well-spoken. More mature."

I smiled at my windshield, "Because, mentally, I'm thirty-two. I'm not eighteen in my head."

"Maybe this makes me a sucker, but I think I believe you."

My heart leapt. Either this was some kind of trick, or she actually believed what I was telling her.

"Really?"

"I think so. Something in my gut tells me that you wouldn't make up something like this. You might do other stupid things and lie about them, but this sounds too unbelievable to not be true."

"I'm glad you believe me, Mom. I'm trying to figure this out, but I didn't want you to worry too much. I've got a couple more things I want to try, but if it doesn't work, I'll come home, and then we can talk about what to do next."

"Is what you're going to try safe?"

"Honestly, hell if I know."

"Would you tell me if it was dangerous?"

"Probably not."

"That scares me."

"I know. It kind of scares me, too."

"Will you call me later, after you've tried whatever it is you're going to try?" I could hear the worry in her voice.

"Yes," I said, "I promise."

"Okay, go do what you have to do."

"Okay. Thank you."

"Thank you? For what?"

"Believing me. None of this makes sense, but I'm glad you don't think I've gone crazy."

"You're my son. I know you lie about things sometimes, but I don't believe you'd make something like this up."

"You're right, Mom. I wouldn't."

My mother fell silent again. I knew she was still struggling to believe me, but it went a long way that she wasn't yelling or outright denying what I was saying.

"I'll call you later. I love you."
"I love you, too. Be careful."
"I will."
I cut the line.

CHAPTER 15

"Get this fucking thing off me!" Javier screamed, stumbling backward down the hallway.

Before Jeffrey or McDougall could react, the brown-and-white dog landed on the floor and began to bark.

Then, it began to whine.

The dog took off down the hallway toward the kitchen and scrambled toward the back door, barking repeatedly. It spun around in a circle and barked at the back door.

"What the hell was that about?" Jeffrey asked, looking down the hallway toward the kitchen.

McDougall looked at his watch and shook his head. "Haven't you ever owned a dog?"

Jeffrey shook his head.

"It's later in the day. The dog has to go to the bathroom." McDougall turned and walked to the back door, opened it, and let the dog out.

Javier picked himself up off the ground and brushed the dog hair off his clothes, grumbling about being "fine, by the way."

A few minutes later, McDougall walked back, a bemused

look on his face. From the kitchen, Javier and Jeffrey could hear the crunching sounds of the dog eating, the metal tag from the collar knocking against the metal bowl. McDougall chuckled and shook his head.

"Poor guy needed the bathroom and food. Now, let's see what's going on with his owner."

Javier moved toward the bedroom, his 9mm once more in his hand. He pushed the door all the way open and walked inside.

Inside, Javier found a figure lying in a bed along the north wall. On the bedside table, there was what looked like a .40 caliber handgun in a holster. Javier moved forward quickly and snatched the gun off the table, fully expecting the figure in the bed to jerk awake and reach for it.

The figure didn't move.

Javier cleared the gun, locked the slide back, and put it over on the dresser on the west wall.

Jeffrey moved into the room, pulling his iPad out of his satchel. He plugged an odd-looking device into the bottom of the iPad and tapped a few buttons. Javier holstered his weapon and stood near the window on the far side of the bed. McDougall stood in the doorway, arms crossed over his chest.

"What are the readings?"

Jeffrey tapped the iPad a few more times, studying the graph that appeared on the screen.

"I'm seeing a negative mass of -95.25 kilograms and an emission of both gravitons and tau neutrinos. They do not appear to be naturally occurring; they're being focused from a subterranean level. Something is focusing the gravitons and tau neutrinos to negate his mass and essentially open up a stable wormhole."

"A wormhole? You mean what we've been looking for all this time? We finally found one?"

Jeffrey ignored him.

"The weird thing is, though, that his body is still here. According to the research of H. S. Baumann, the body should travel through time, too, not just the consciousness."

Javier noticed McDougall stiffen at the name. Jeffrey didn't seem to notice. Javier made a mental note of the name for later on.

"Javier, when is the equipment getting here?" McDougall asked, rubbing his thumb across his bottom lip.

"Within the next half hour," Javier said, checking his watch.

"Good," McDougall said. "Jeffrey, continue to monitor the readings until the equipment crew gets here. Javier, come with me."

McDougall pulled out his phone and tapped a message. He turned and left the bedroom.

Javier looked at Jeffrey, who shrugged.

Javier nodded and moved toward the hall, following McDougall.

"Where are we going?" he called down the hallway. In response, he heard a door open.

"The basement."

CHAPTER 16

I was sitting outside the house, in the same place I'd been for the past thirty minutes.

I knew I was taking a risk sitting on the street outside the house, but I didn't care. As far as I knew, the neighbors were just as secretive in 2006 as they were in 2020.

I finally got out of my car and grabbed my backpack.

I made my way around the side of the house again, moving through the overgrown and snow-covered yard with more confidence than my previous excursion. I came to the back door and found that it was still unlocked.

I entered the house again and stood, taking in the silence. I was mildly surprised that the owner wasn't yelling his head off, trying to get one of the neighbor's attention.

I decided to leave the current owner alone and rummage around the house.

I started in the kitchen.

The countertops were old, cracked, pink Formica, and the cabinets were filled with a mix of seemingly random junk, spoiled food, and broken plates.

The sink was stacked with dirty and moldy plates, pots, and glasses.

The squalor made my skin crawl.

I left the kitchen and went down the hall, opening the garage door. Light filtered in through the dirty windows set high on the west wall. I flicked the switch in the hallway that should have turned the lights in the garage on, but nothing happened. I looked up at the ceiling and saw that there were no bulbs in the sockets.

I sighed and shook my head.

I pulled out my phone and went to turn on the flashlight—

—when I realized that my phone no longer had a flashlight.

I growled.

I squinted into the murky garage and saw there was no vehicle, just even more boxes stacked up. It looked as though no one had been in the garage for years—there was a fine layer of dust on just about every surface.

I closed the garage door and turned to the other two rooms. Neither of which held anything useful. More junk. More squalor.

I turned my attention to the only remaining room I hadn't searched: the basement.

I pulled the door open and threw the switch. Unlike every other light in this house, the basement lights fired up.

I made my way down.

CHAPTER 17

Javier led the way to the basement, 9mm drawn and angled downward. He threw the switch at the bottom of the stairs and scanned the room. A mismatch of exercise equipment was strewn about the basement: weights, a cable machine, a punching bag, and other assorted gear. There was a dog bed lying in the middle of the floor near the support pole connected to the I-beam. He looked to the left and saw the dark opening of the back half of the basement. He raised his weapon and moved slowly toward the maw.

He saw a bag target full of arrows and a light with a pull chain past it. He moved to the light and pulled the string. He turned and swept the remainder of the basement, checking the bathroom before holstering his weapon.

He moved back to the bottom of the stairs and called up to McDougall, "Clear."

McDougall made his way down the stairs, iPad in hand. He tapped a few commands into the machine and pulled up a map of the house. Javier stood near the bottom of the stairs, his hands clasping his belt in the standard-issue security-ready position.

"What's next?" he asked McDougall.

"We have to gain access to the lab," McDougall said.

Javier raised his eyebrows.

"The lab?" he asked, confused.

"Yes," McDougall said, "it's through the auxiliary sump pit in the back of the basement."

Javier turned and looked toward the back half of the basement. He pulled his weapon again and went to the south wall of the basement.

"The radon mitigation pit?" Javier asked, skeptical.

"There's no radon here," McDougall said. "It was put in to mask the entrance to the lab and deter anyone from looking in the pit. The former owner of this house was one of the researchers on the original Project Outrigger." McDougall fished the binder out of his bag again and held it up. "Remember, what you and Jeffrey work on is the descendent of the original. After he was terminated from the program, this man—the original owner—stole Baumann's research and disappeared. We became aware that he was continuing in the same vein in his own lab in the sublevels of this house."

Javier knit his brows. This was all news to him; as far as he had known, there was only one Project Outrigger. Evidently, there was a lot more going on than he was aware of.

"Hang on a minute," Javier said, "how the hell did they let this lab continue to exist with a normal family living here? Why wasn't this, I don't know, dismantled?"

For a moment, McDougall looked like he was going to just ignore Javier. He sighed and said, "The original Project ended in chaos. It seems to me that the existence of this secondary site was forgotten about. Besides, most of the records from that time were destroyed. There were a few that survived, but they were stashed away somewhere that was 'safe.' " He made air quotes around the word. "There were always rumors about a secondary lab, but it wasn't until I found those documents that I was confident it actually existed. When we got the address of the anomaly, I knew for sure."

McDougall went to the sump well in the back of the basement and knelt down. He pulled out a knife and flipped it open, plunging it into the seam between the plastic well cover and the cement floor. He pried the cover loose, detached the PVC pipe connected to the cover, and set the cover aside. In the well, there was a switch. The side of the switch box said "Radon Mitigation Fan Control." McDougall consulted his tablet, then pulled on the faceplate of the switch. Inside the switch box, there was a red push-button switch. McDougall pushed it, and a mechanical whir filled the basement. A fine spray of dust shot up from the sump well as the bottom cracked apart.

The sump well was actually a cleverly disguised hatch, which broke open like flower petals. Under the hatch, there was a ladder illuminated by caged incandescent bulbs. The ladder went down about 25 feet before coming to a stop at a dusty cement floor. McDougall propped himself against the top of the sump well and carefully lowered himself onto the ladder.

Javier followed.

McDougall stepped off the bottom of the ladder and looked around. Javier was down the ladder a moment later. He found a circuit breaker on the wall and threw the lever, illuminating a cavernous concrete laboratory. Over their heads, there were large, bundled wires, all connected to a massive junction box near the ladder; a single, thick cable ran up toward the top of the ladder and disappeared into the wall of the sump pit. The bundled wires crossed the ceiling to a large machine set under the north side of the sub-basement. Javier looked around, noticing that the only things in the sub-basement were the machine and a computer terminal. The terminal looked as though it were directly from 1997; the terminals were connected by a thick bundle of wires to a bank of monitors, all flickering with different readouts displayed. The CPUs were blocky, large cases with an array of keyboards attached. There was a bank of vacuum-column devices along the north wall with another thick bundle of wires connecting the CPUs and the tape memory.

"This stuff is ancient," Javier said, moving toward the CPU bank. He tapped a command into the terminal, and a red box flashed on the central monitor: ERROR—COMMAND NOT RECOGNIZED.

"Don't touch that," McDougall said, pushing Javier out of the way. He set the iPad on the edge of the terminal and brought up a PDF document. He found the heading he was looking for and tapped a string of commands. The central monitor flickered and displayed a plain-text readout, which was more a jumble of equations than a coherent image. Javier watched as McDougall tapped another string of commands into the terminal. He studied the readout for a moment and then leaned back in the chair he'd sat down in.

"Shit," he muttered, running his hands through his thinning hair. "This isn't good."

Javier remained quiet, knowing better than to ask questions—he knew that asking questions often went nowhere. McDougall rotated the chair to face Javier:

"I think I know what happened here."

CHAPTER 18

I made my way to the basement, wondering what in the hell I was looking for. I reached the bottom of the steps, found the light switch, and clicked it on. The yellow-hued incandescent bulbs caused the mountains of boxes and equipment to cast unsettling shadows.

I had just stepped off the bottom stair when my cell started to ring.

I jumped about a foot in the air before I realized what was happening. I looked around sheepishly, as people tend to do when they get scared out of their minds by something innocuous.

I dug the phone out of my pocket and stared down at the screen: Sara C.

Shit.

I thumbed the phone open and answered.

"Where are you? Why weren't you at school today?"

"I had things I needed to do," I said, still looking around the cluttered basement. "I don't really have time for this."

There was silence for a moment. Then: "What the hell do you mean, 'I don't have time for this'?" Her voice was rising and becoming angry.

I had a memory of dating her and how meek and compliant I used to be, how willing I was to believe just about anything any girl I was dating said. I remembered that she hated being talked back to and hated being defied even more.

I also remembered that, at some point, she was going to go to Jamaica with her ex and may or may not have cheated on me.

I remembered how I'd just blindly believed her and insisted that it didn't matter, even when she treated me like shit.

To hell with that.

"Look, I've got things I need to do. I don't have time to waste talking to you on the phone. There's some messed-up shit happening, and I've got to figure it out."

"What kind of messed-up shit?" To her credit, there was actually a tinge of concern in her voice.

"It isn't going to make any sense, so don't worry about it. Look, I know you're not used to hearing me talk like this, but you'll get over it. I've got stuff to do, and it's not like this is going to work out anyway."

"What the fuck does that mean?"

I sighed. I hadn't meant to reveal that little detail. I couldn't remember where in the relationship we were, but it sounded like she hadn't gone to Jamaica yet.

I sighed again, "Forget it. It's not something that really matters in the grand scheme of things."

"Excuse me? You can't just say something like that and then tell me to forge—"

I snapped the phone shut.

Ten seconds later, she called back. I silenced the infernal thing and let it go to voicemail. After it stopped ringing, I flipped it open and powered the device off.

I could do without the interruption.

I shoved the phone back into my pocket and started to search the basement.

CHAPTER 19

The main room of the basement was filled with boxes and equipment, much like the master bedroom upstairs. Most of the equipment was recognizable, now that I actually looked at it, but some of it was bizarre. There were heaps of old computer parts—parts that looked like they were modern back in 1983: Commodore floppy drives, tape backups, and CRT monitors stacked on top of one another. IBM tape mainframes covered in static-shielding poly sheeting surrounded the piles of parts, and large bundles of wires were hanging from the floor joists, spidering out from the south end of the basement and running to junction boxes near the main circuit breaker panel.

I stared in amazement. There was no trace of any of this stuff in my own time—whoever renovated the house must have essentially gutted everything and started from scratch.

A mental image of a contractor, an electrician, and a plumber popped into my head, the three individuals just staring in openmouthed horror at the code violations they were seeing. Comically, it also gave me the impression of some kind of bad joke: '*A contractor, electrician, and plumber walk into a clusterfuck of a basement ...*'

With a small chuckle, I shook the thoughts away.

I made my way through the boxes and to the magnetic-tape mainframes. There was a fine layer of dust on the static shielding, and it was evident the machines hadn't been powered on for some time.

I turned and began to pick through a couple of the boxes littering the floor. All I found were partially disassembled computer parts; nothing in any of the boxes was completely whole.

Next, I made my way to the junction boxes, which were locked in the on position by heavy-duty stainless steel padlocks. I pulled the main fuse panel open, and found that it consisted of one gigantic switch, also padlocked in the on position. There was a soft hum of electricity, making me wonder just how much juice this house was drawing.

I decided I really didn't want to find out, so I shut the fuse panel and gave the wires as wide a berth as I could.

Having looked through the main portion of the basement, I made my way past the furnace and into the darkened back half.

In this time, there was no third bathroom, nor was there the radon mitigation sump; rather, there was a standard sump well with a loose plastic cover.

I frowned.

The bundles of wires from the junction boxes went underground, passing through a hole that was bored into the concrete near the sump well.

"What the hell?" I muttered, absentmindedly moving toward the sump well.

I pulled the pull-chain of a light fixture as I moved toward the sump well. The yellow light washed over the back half of the basement, illuminating more boxes and tape mainframes. Another thick snarl of wires was secured to the floor joists and wrapped around the furnace back to the junction boxes.

Some of the wires joined the mix that was bored down into the concrete.

I wandered down the path between boxes toward the sump, registering on some level that it was the only clear path in the entire basement. I knelt down next to the well and considered the plastic cover. Unlike the cover I remembered, this one was just resting atop the hole—there was no seal, no check valve, no clear plastic viewport.

I pulled the cover to the side and peered into the sump.

"... the hell?"

CHAPTER 20

McDougall pulled the binder out of his go-bag and flipped to a section near the back. He set the binder on the console, near the iPad he'd propped against one of the monitors. Consulting the photocopies of handwritten notes in the binder, he tapped out another string of commands into the terminal. A second monitor lit up with plaintext, this time far more coherent than the first.

McDougall studied the readout and leaned back in his chair.

"Shit."

Javier waited, fidgeting slightly. He glanced toward the machine and then back to the readouts on the monitors in front of McDougall, wondering what the hell was going on.

"I need you to go get Jeffrey," McDougall said, sitting up and swiveling the chair to face Javier. "Is the monitoring equipment and support team here yet?"

"I'll check, and I'll send Jeffrey down." Javier walked past McDougall to the ladder. He saw the man pull out his phone again. Who the hell did he keep sending messages to? Curious, but not really any of his business.

Back in the basement, Javier pulled his smartphone out of his pocket and activated the GPS locator he had tagged the support team with. The map showed that the team was en route and would be there in minutes. Javier closed down the app and tapped another icon—one most people wouldn't have even noticed. A biometric password prompt appeared. Javier removed his glove and pressed his thumb to the fingerprint reader.

A messaging app appeared, and Javier selected a contact simply titled "Control." He tapped out a sentence, filling them in on his activities so far. He pushed send and watched as the message encrypted itself, becoming little more than an alphanumeric string. He tapped another button, and the messenger wiped all traces of the communication from the phone—a handy feature of the secure messaging app.

He shoved the phone back in his pocket, then glanced around to make sure he hadn't been observed. Fortunately, no one else was in the basement. He nodded and made his way upstairs.

CHAPTER 21

"McDougall needs you down in the sub-basement," Javier said, smiling internally as Jeffrey jumped about a foot.

"Don't sneak up on people like that," Jeffrey said, irritation coloring his voice.

"Fine," Javier said, "but McDougall told me to come get you and tell you to get to the sub-basement. He found something."

"What did he find?"

"Go look for yourself. It's through the sump well in the back of the basement."

"Sump well?"

"That's what I said, isn't it?"

"You know I'm still your boss, right?"

"Whatever. McDougall is waiting. Isn't he *your* boss?"

Jeffrey's left eye twitched. He flipped the cover of the iPad closed and shoved it into his satchel. "Keep an eye on him. If anything changes, let me know."

Javier grunted.

Jeffrey moved past him, and Javier heard his heavy footsteps descending to the basement.

Javier considered the man lying in the bed. His eyes were closed, and his breathing was rhythmic. All outward appearances suggested he was just in a deep sleep. It was bizarre to think that this man was the first person to travel through time.

Javier crossed his arms and leaned against the wall, still looking at the man. After a moment, he closed his eyes.

When he opened them, Javier started.

He reached for the gun on his hip but froze.

The man was sitting bolt-upright, eyes wide, mouth open.

A low, terrifying moan escaped his mouth, rising in a crescendo until it was a full-throated bellow—hoarse, harsh, and almost inhuman; the sound grated against itself, seeming to threaten to tear his voice box from his body.

As suddenly as it began, the noise stopped.

The man's head tipped back, and his torso followed, flopping back onto the mattress with an audible thump.

His eyes fluttered shut, and his mouth closed.

His breathing slowed and became regular again.

"What the hell?"

CHAPTER 22

I opened my eyes.

Once again, I was staring at something looming over me.

Something I couldn't identify.

That's when I remembered: I'd gone down the sump well into a sub-basement. Normally, a sub-basement in a house isn't a big deal; this one, though, was hidden down a sump well.

Which was bizarre, to say the least.

As I made my way down the ladder in the sump well, I came to an empty concrete room. The wires I had seen that bored through the basement floor continued into the darkened room on the far side.

Before I left the relative safety of the pool of light from the basement, I looked around. I found a junction box with a large switch on the side. The switch was down, so I figured it was some kind of power switch. I threw it, and fluorescent lights flickered to life around the sub-basement. In the back portion of the sub-basement, I saw a large, cylindrical machine. I moved forward, starting to look the machine over. I touched the machine in the sub-basement, just running my hand across its cold metal exterior, and blacked out again.

This time, when I woke up, I wasn't staring at the ceiling—I was staring straight ahead.

Staring straight ahead and moaning a noise I'd never known I was capable of making.

I swallowed, my throat raw.

'*Wait a minute,*' I thought, '*how does that work? Was I screaming here, too?*' Without anyone around me to tell me what happened, I had to assume that I wasn't just screaming in my adult body.

I shook my head. Like the rest of this experience, I figured it was something I wasn't going to readily understand. I turned my attention back to the machine.

I took a deep breath and placed my hand on the machine again.

Nothing.

Absolutely nothing happened.

'*Shit, that doesn't help. I guess I can't make contact whenever I want.*'

I shook my head and turned my attention to analyzing the machine itself.

The machine was a huge, nine-foot cylinder with four wide legs bolted to the ground. The end facing me looked vaguely like an airplane turbine but was spinning gently, rather than forcefully. The large bundles of wires that spidered across the ceiling seemed to split, with half of them going to the control panel and half of them going directly into the machine. Behind the machine stood more vacuum column devices, likely acting as a makeshift mainframe. More wires ran from the control panel to the mainframes.

There was a recessed, blinking control panel on the front of the machine, but the labels were just alphanumeric garbage—clearly, they meant something to whoever operated it, but, to me, it just looked like gibberish.

Below the control panel, there was a plastic-coated bundle

of wires running toward the east wall and out of sight behind the bulk of the machine.

I followed the wires, making my way around the machine, and found three smaller units: the first two had delicate antennae rising from a domed top, and the third looked like a late-90s satellite dish. The largest of the units had a small window set in the front of it, which was softly glowing blue in the dim light of the sub-basement.

I was aware of a soft hum, but I wasn't sure where it was coming from.

I decided to look in the viewport of the central unit, wondering just what I was going to find inside.

I made my way forward, stepping over the jumble of wires connecting the four pieces of the machine. I stepped up to the viewport and looked inside.

What I saw was anticlimactic.

Inside, there was nothing except a bare, blue lightbulb recessed in the bottom of the unit. The soft glow must have been for effect.

'*Figures*,' I thought. '*What kind of weird-ass experiments are happening here? Are any of them real, or is the guy who lives here just totally insane?*'

I made my way to the second unit with an antenna and looked into the viewport on that one.

I was greeted with the same thing, although this bulb was tinged purple.

I walked to the dish and looked at the control panel. There was nothing except for more alphanumeric gibberish and a few on/off toggles.

I left all three alone and made my way back to the main machine. As I made my way back around the front of it, I noticed that there was a red, seven-segment LCD display and a numeric keypad set next to the recessed control panel.

I decided punching random numbers into the keypad was probably a bad idea, so I left it alone and turned my attention to the control panel set against the west wall.

The main control panel was mostly dark; there were six CRT monitors set inside a metal frame, with four sets of gauges between the two rows. Two keyboards were attached to the desk portion of the control panel, and there was another numeric keypad on the right side. Attached to ports on the side were an array of disk drives, tape decks, and even an old wax cylinder recorder. The wires were all bound with black electrical tape and connected using wire nuts.

The whole setup looked janky as hell; it gave the impression that it could catch fire or spark at any moment.

'*It's a wonder this damn place didn't burn down,*' I thought. '*How in the hell did I not know this was here? Where did all this equipment come from?*'

I sat down in the ancient computer chair and considered the only active monitor.

In the top left-hand corner, there was a green symbol:

```
>:
```

'*What the fuck is this,* Lost?' I thought, scowling at the computer. '*This has to be some kind of fucking joke or dream.*'

I tapped out a command:

```
>: STATUS
and hit RETURN.
"ERROR: COMMAND NOT RECOGNIZED."
```

The mechanized voice erupted from the left side of the computer, the top module crackling to life.

"What the fuck?" I all but shouted. I glanced up and almost laughed as I read the words "Intellivoice Voice Synthesis Module" on the top unit. Whoever had kludged this computer terminal together had even attached pieces of video game systems from the early 80s.

I tried another command:

```
>: HELP
"ERROR: COMMAND NOT RECOGNIZED."
```

"Shit," I said, leaning back in the chair. I decided to try one more command:

```
>: DOSKEY
"RUNNING. COMMANDS DISPLAYED."
```

I leaned forward and peered at the central monitor. The list of commands began to appear:

```
DIR
CD_*
NETWORK.EXE
SYS A:/
TREE
*.EXE
[executable] /?
```

'*Alright*,' I thought, '*now we're getting somewhere.*'

Although my own computer knowledge was rudimentary, I remembered talking to my brother, Joseph, about his work with computers. I thought back to the days we had spent with the old Packard Bell computer in our bedroom, just a couple of kids messing around with a behind-the-times PC. I tapped in ">: DIR" and punched RETURN. A list of all the directories on the hard drive appeared on the screen under the list of commands. I scanned the directories and noticed something strange. One of the directories was listed as "HIDDEN." I narrowed my eyes and tapped the command, wondering if it would work. I hit RETURN.

The computer seemed to freeze, and then, moments later, a string of files and commands appeared on the screen:

```
LOG.TXT
GAME.EXE
GOTO
FORMAT
PING_MACHINE
TRAVEL.EXE
UNLOCK_A:/
```

I tried LOG.TXT, thinking I might get an idea of what this machine had been working on.

"ERROR: RESTRICTED ACCESS."

'*Shit*,' I thought. I stared at the screen. I had two executables as an option: GAME and TRAVEL.

I figured TRAVEL was too obvious, so I punched in "GAME.EXE."

The computer sounded about like it was taking off; the fans recessed in the terminal came to life and ramped up to full RPMs, forcing air into the control panel and trying to keep up with whatever heat my command generated.

The UI of the terminal flickered, and abruptly, the screen went black.

'*Shit*,' I thought again, '*I better not have broken the damn thing*.'

My first impulse was to start typing commands, but I made myself wait. The seconds stretched into minutes, and the screen remained black. I was starting to get worried, and as I was resting my fingers on the keyboard, the screen flickered to life. I yanked my hands backward, as if I had received an electrical shock. I looked around sheepishly, feeling embarrassed at my reaction.

'*Get your shit together; Jesus*,' I thought, shaking my head.

The UI of the computer had completely changed; where once there had been a blinking input icon, there was now a graphic interface. The rendered shapes started to shift and formed the image of the machine behind me. A text box appeared on the left side of the screen and filled with what appeared to be readouts of the machine. Most of the fields were labeled as "OFFLINE."

The only fields that indicated something different were the ones labeled "POWER MODE" and "BACKUP POWER," both of which were listed as "MINIMAL."

Under the power mode listing was a heading called "MEMORY." Evidently, this machine was able to access 15 different memory systems, all of which were two terabytes each.

I stared at the number. What could this thing need that much memory for?

I looked around for a mouse to try and explore the system.

As far as I could tell, there wasn't a pointing device attached to the system.

'Now, how in the hell am I supposed to navigate a graphic interface without a mouse?' I wondered.

I decided to try bringing up the command prompt, which I figured would give me at least a little control over the system. Unfortunately, the keyboard was not one I recognized—it was more reminiscent of a Commodore 64 or Apple III keyboard. I looked for the closest relative to CTRL + ALT + DEL and tried the combination.

Nothing.

"Shit," I muttered.

I looked at the control panel.

"Maybe ..." I trailed off, looking over at the second keyboard recessed in the console. I pushed the ancient chair I was sitting in across the floor and tapped a command into the second keyboard. A second CRT monitor flickered to life.

Slowly, the image of a command prompt appeared on the monitor. This time, there was no oddly-shaped text input; this command prompt looked nearly identical to the one in Windows 98:

```
C:\>
```

I tried "DIR" again, wondering if this would list the directories in this particular drive.

A listing of different directories began to scroll across the screen. I scanned the listing of directories, looking for something that stuck out. I didn't find anything that stuck out, so I tried the change directory command a couple times. Each time, the message "Error 633: Confidentiality protected reply" flashed on the monitor.

I leaned back in the chair and exhaled.

'*Shit*,' I thought, '*well, what are my options? I can continue to screw around with this, potentially breaking it, or I can get out of here and try something else. Messing with the machine doesn't seem like the best idea ... If I break this thing, I probably won't be able to figure out a way to get myself out of, well, whatever the hell this is. If I mess it up too badly, I could wind up killing myself.*'

I stood up, pushing the chair back from the console. I took one more look around the machines, finding nothing new.

With a shrug, I made my way back to the ladder and back up into the basement.

A few moments later, I was back in my car, heading out of Wonder Lake. The sun was starting to set, and I had to decide what my next move was going to be.

CHAPTER 23

Javier stood in front of the house, watching as the support team unloaded the sensitive, complicated equipment. Most of the equipment was to monitor the condition of the man at the center of this whole situation: electrocardiogram, sphygmomanometer, electroencephalogram, various intravenous bags in climate-controlled cases, and pumps and monitors for the bags. There were a few other machines, known only by their codenames, meant to monitor the device Javier and McDougall had found in the sub-basement.

Inside, the support team—consisting of various doctors and technicians—began hooking the machinery up to the man lying in the bed. A phlebotomist slid a needle into the man's arm and secured the peripheral venous catheter with a strip of medical tape. He connected the lines and started the drip of 0.9% NaCl; initial blood tests on the man came back with extreme dehydration and electrolyte imbalances, and the doctors monitoring him told the techs to start fluids immediately.

The neurologist employed by the Project had been studying the readouts of the EEG and had called for the portable CT scanner to be brought in. As she stared at the readouts, she called for an additional drip of D5W to be started, noting an increase in intracranial pressure.

Cables had been run from the bedroom to the kitchen, and several computers and monitors had been set up on the table, pushing everything from the table unceremoniously onto the floor. Techs sat at the monitors, waiting for the readouts from the monitoring equipment in the bedroom and basement.

In the basement, the specialized machines had been hard-wired into the existing circuit breaker panel. Various pieces of workout equipment had been all but thrown out of the way, allowing for the thick, bound cables to be attached to the breaker panel. The cables worked their way to the sump pit in the north end of the basement and down into the sub-basement. At the lip of the sump pit, several tables had been set up, allowing for monitoring equipment that was too large to fit in the sump pit to be set up.

Another set of cables ran up the stairs and snaked their way through the kitchen to the computers set up at the table in the dining room.

In the sub-basement, Jeffrey and McDougall were busy attaching cables and monitoring equipment to the IBM tape mainframes; they also began attaching smaller contact monitors to the pieces of the machine behind the interface console.

Jeffrey completed the connections and pulled out his iPad. He tapped a few commands and confirmed that the uplink to SAOC was operational. He turned to McDougall and nodded.

McDougall made his way back to the terminal and tapped in a command. A command prompt window popped up and confirmed that the interface between the modern and antique equipment had been initiated. After he made the connection, his cell phone chirped. He pulled it from his pocket and answered.

He motioned to Jeffrey, and Jeffrey made his way to the terminal. McDougall finished up his call and slipped the phone back in his pocket.

"Take over for now," McDougall said, getting up from the control chair.

"Where are you going?"

"I'm going to arrange our living situation while we're working on this issue."

McDougall made his way to the ladder and up into the basement. He walked back up the stairs, passing technicians and support staff. He made his way out the front door and out to the driveway. He found Javier standing out front, supervising the support staff.

"I'm heading to set up our hotels. Go open the garage, and get the rest of the equipment unloaded from the vehicles. After they're unloaded, make sure the big rig and other transport vehicles are removed."

"Alright," Javier said, scowling a little and turning away from McDougall.

McDougall moved past Javier and got in the van. Oddly, he sat behind the wheel for a moment, fiddling with his phone. He looked up, catching Javier's eye. He looked annoyed for a moment, but he also had a different look on his face. One that almost seemed like a kid caught with his hand in the cookie jar.

As soon as Javier saw it, it was gone, and the scowl returned. McDougall turned the engine over, put the van into gear, and left.

CHAPTER 24

Later that evening, after the monitoring equipment had been installed and the support team took over, McDougall, Jeffrey, and Javier met in McDougall's suite at the seedy Super 8, approximately 15 minutes from the site. The bed was littered with papers: reports from SAOC and handwritten assessments from the doctors and technicians at the site, as well as blueprints of the house and a rough sketch of the lab in the sub-basement. The small, round table in the corner of the room held a laptop, an iPad, and more notes, these written by McDougall himself.

McDougall sat in the wooden chair at the table, tapping away on the laptop. The screen showed an email chain at least twenty messages long, detailing the measures already in place to monitor the machine and the man unconscious in bed at the site.

Jeffrey sat in the upholstered chair in the corner near the window, rubbing his left temple. In his lap sat another iPad, open to an ever-shifting graph that showed the vital signs of the man at the site, along with the data readouts from the machine.

Javier leaned against the wall, looking at his boss and his boss's boss. They had been in this room for the better part of an hour, and no one had said much of anything. Javier was beginning to wonder if these two had any idea what the hell they were doing. He was about to voice his concerns when his phone buzzed in a distinctive pattern.

Excusing himself, Javier made his way to the parking lot on the west side of the building, looking out to Route 31. He pulled his phone out of his pocket, thumbing the fingerprint reader to unlock the encrypted messaging app. He was greeted by an encrypted alphanumeric string from a restricted sender. Tapping on the message, he was prompted by the phone to provide his fingerprint again. Thumbing the scanner, he was then asked for a retinal scan to fully decrypt the message. Although he knew his employers—his real employers—valued security, he was always annoyed by the number of steps it took to get to the damn message they sent him. Finally, when the algorithm was finished running, he opened the message. Inside, he found his next set of instructions. Javier felt his eyes widen when he read the words.

He had often done shady things within SAOC for his employers, but this latest message was beyond anything he'd been asked to do so far. If he wasn't careful, he would risk exposure, and he didn't need that kind of heat. He read the message again, knowing that he had little choice in the matter, especially with his end goal in mind. He tapped his reply and watched as the encrypted message was sent to his employer. He turned back toward the hotel and took a deep breath.

As he made his way inside, he started to form a plan in his head. His new assignment was going to take some planning and a lot of luck. He understood his employer's request, but he didn't like it. There was the possibility that things would get messy, and messy inevitably led to questions.

Questions Javier wasn't excited to face.

He let out the breath he hadn't realized he was holding and

made his way back to the room with McDougall and Jeffrey.

Back in the room, he found McDougall and Jeffrey both looking at the screen of the laptop.

"Did something happen?" he asked, moving to look at the screen.

"No," McDougall said, "Jeffrey is just pulling the latest readings up for me so I can keep an eye on the support team."

Jeffrey tapped a few more keys and leaned back in the chair.

"There," he said, "the readings should sync with your laptop and my iPad."

"Good," McDougall said, straightening and looking around the room. He glanced at his watch and then rubbed his eyes. "Why don't the two of you head to your rooms? We should be out of here and back to the site early tomorrow."

Javier and Jeffrey both nodded and moved toward the door. Javier was already filing away that he needed to get his hands on the laptop when his assignment was over—his employer also wanted the data from the subject back at the house.

He left McDougall's room and made his way down to the far side of the hallway where his own room was located. As the door clicked shut behind him, Javier allowed his shoulders to slump. Being a double agent was exhausting.

He turned on the lights and made his way into the bathroom, fully intending to take a shower before he slept. As he ran the water, he began to think again about how he was going to accomplish his current objective.

"An accident," he said aloud, nodding his head.

Yes, an accident would be the best way. Something that couldn't be predicted and was just an unfortunate circumstance.

Javier stared at himself in the mirror, watching as the steam slowly obscured his features. He made his choice and turned away from the now-blurred reflection.

When the time came, he would act.

And he wouldn't look back.

CHAPTER 25

I sat at the back of IHOP, staring into my coffee cup.

It had been an incredibly long night. Not wanting to go home and deal with the questions from my family, I made my way to Crystal Lake and wandered into the IHOP on Route 14. A sleepy-eyed waiter sat me near the back and brought a thermal carafe of coffee to the table. After he took my order, he moved away, standing at the register and looking bored.

That was fine with me—I didn't exactly have a lot to say to anyone right now.

I took the notebook out of my backpack and turned to a fresh page. I started to write down my experiences, documenting my moves and theories. Slowly, I filled one page and then another, noting the things I'd tried and the outcomes. Although I still didn't see a pattern, it felt good to get things down on paper and out of my head.

The waiter drifted over with my plate of steak and eggs. He dropped them off on the table, took the carafe, and refilled it with coffee. After making sure I didn't need anything else, he floated away and resumed his post at the register. I set my notebook aside and started on my meal.

When I was finished, I pulled the notebook back over to me and began to write again, recording as many details of the mysterious machine as I could. After I wrote down the description, I turned to a blank page and began to sketch the machine, trying to record the twisted mass of wires running from the panel to the machine, and from the machine to the smaller units behind it. I sketched the tape mainframes, all connected to one another, and the snarl of cables heading back to the console. I noted the voice module, floppy drives, and unknown components on the left-hand side, adding labels to the parts I knew.

After about half an hour of working on the sketch, I leaned back in the booth. I reached for the carafe and freshened my coffee, savoring the hot, bitter flavor. I closed my eyes and took a deep breath.

Glancing down at my watch, I was surprised to see it was nearly 2 a.m.

'*Well,*' I thought, '*fortunately, IHOP is a twenty-four-hour place.*' I yawned and stretched, feeling the vertebrae pop back into place.

Sometime during my sketching, the waiter must have drifted back and dropped the check on the table. I freshened my coffee one more time and sat back in the booth.

A little while later, I had drained my cup. Setting it back on the table, I pulled out my wallet and found some bills. I made my way to the register and paid the tab, thanking the waiter. He mumbled a response and went back to the magazine he'd been reading.

Back in my car, I sat staring ahead into the parking lot for a moment. I needed a place to stay, and with the temperature hovering somewhere around freezing, I didn't much feel like sleeping in my car. I pulled my wallet back out of my pocket and checked my resources.

I only had a few dollars in cash left, but I figured I had to have at least enough in my checking account for one night in a shitty hotel somewhere. I reached in my pocket for my phone, intending to check my balance when I realized I couldn't.

The past kept hitting me in unexpected ways.

I shook my head but powered the phone on anyway. After a moment, the startup routine was finished, and the home screen materialized.

The phone vibrated in my hand, and the message icon popped up at the top of the screen. I opened the flip and hit the menu button. I scrolled down to messages and saw that I had three messages in my inbox.

I opened the inbox and saw the first message on the list was my mom saying she hoped I was alright and that she was worried because she hadn't heard from me.

The second message was from Roy G., asking where the hell I was and why I wasn't answering my phone.

The last message was from Steph B., asking—like Roy—where I was and what was going on.

Roy and Steph, two of my best friends from high school, must have talked when I wasn't at school, and they must have decided to reach out to see if I was alright. I hit reply on both messages and—laboriously, because I was using T9—told them that I was fine and that I missed school because I had a doctor's appointment. After that was finished, I sent a text to my mom telling her that I was fine and that she shouldn't worry.

I shut the phone back down and tossed it on the passenger seat.

I tried to think of a place to stay in Crystal Lake, not being overly familiar with the hotels in the area. I decided to just drive and see if I could find a place.

I pulled out onto Route 14 and headed east toward Cary.

I ended up at the Holiday Inn on the outskirts of Crystal Lake.

I pulled into the parking lot at a little before 3 a.m. and grabbed my backpack from the passenger footwell. I made my way to the lobby and up to the counter.

The woman working the counter looked up as I entered the lobby. I smiled and asked her for a room.

"Sorry, kid," she said, "you've got to make reservations at least two days in advance."

"Really?" I asked, glancing around the lobby. "Business doesn't exactly appear to be booming."

She looked me over, pretty clearly taking a dislike to me.

"Like I said, kid, you need to make a reservation."

"Look," I said, "it's been a long, pretty fucked-up day. I just need a place to crash for the night, and I'm not exactly prepared to sleep in my car. It's, what, thirty-five degrees outside?" I scoffed. "I get that you have policies or whatever, but I saw the state of the parking lot. You've got to be at, what, one-third capacity, tops? I don't want to be an asshole, but just give me a damn room. I'll be out of your hair in the morning. Charge me the whole daily rate for all I care; I'll still check out tomorrow morning."

Her eyes narrowed, but she turned to her computer. She tapped a few keys and turned back to me, smirking.

"The only room I have available for tonight is the top-tier suite. It's $217 per night, with a $100 deposit. You still want it?"

'*Are you fucking serious?*' I thought, but said: "Fine, whatever, just book it and put it on the card." I tossed my debit card on the counter.

"Cash only."

"Are you fucking kidding me? Where's the goddamn ATM?"

She pointed to the far side of the lobby, still smirking.

'*Fucking Jesus*,' I thought, turning to the ATM. I shoved my card in the slot and punched in what I hoped was my PIN. Fortunately, I got it right, and I withdrew the $500 maximum. The machine displayed my remaining balance, and I was relieved to see that I still had a decent amount of funds left. I closed the window on the machine and returned to the desk, tossing $320 on the counter and scowling.

She made a show of counting the money, even going so far as to lift each of the twenties to the light to check for counterfeits.

I rolled my eyes and crossed my arms, waiting as patiently as I could for her little act to be over. Finally, she put the money in the register and handed me a beat-up Schlage key on an old-fashioned diamond-shaped key tag.

"Room 313, sweetie," she said, her voice dripping in manufactured sweetness.

"You've been most kind; thank you so much for your service," I said, matching her tone with my own sarcasm. I snatched the key from her hand and stalked out of the lobby toward the elevators.

I punched the call button and blew out a breath.

The elevator arrived, and I hit the button for the third floor, leaning against the wall. When the elevator arrived on the third floor, I got off and looked up and down the hall. The sign on the wall pointed me off to the right, and I made my way down to the end. My room was the last door on the left, so at least it would be quiet. I opened the door and walked into the room, tossing my backpack onto the luggage rack in the closet.

As I sat on the bed, a sudden wave of exhaustion swept over me. I groggily kicked off my boots and pushed myself onto the bed.

I was out before I even hit the pillows.

CHAPTER 26

I woke up without opening my eyes.

Something was different, but I didn't feel the same sense of disorientation that I had felt the last time I woke up.

As I opened my eyes, I saw the generic furnishings of a hotel room: the anonymous but stylish paintings on the walls, red curtains covering the windows, and the typical, generic white bedspread you find in hotels across the world. I sat up and put my head in my hands, wishing everything that happened in the previous 24 hours was just a terrible dream.

But it wasn't. I was still here, in the past, inhabiting the body of my younger self. As far as I could tell, my mental functions were still my own—unlike other science fiction, where I would slowly transform completely into my younger self, I seemed to be hanging on to my older personality.

I brought my head up and shook it, trying to clear the worry and negative thoughts away. It only partially worked.

I pushed myself out of the king-sized bed and rounded the corner to the bathroom. I stared at my reflection in the mirror, still taken aback at my appearance. There wasn't even the hint of a beard showing on my chin—no stubble, no five o'clock shadow. My face was still the thin, unrefined face of youth; there was no strong, square jaw, no wrinkles around the eyes or forehead from years of raising one eyebrow, and no gray hair poking through the dark brown.

I ran the tap and splashed some cold water on my face. I looked back at myself and took a deep breath. I looked down at my clothes and realized that I hadn't showered for at least a couple of days. I turned to the shower and began to run the water, turning it up as hot as it would go. I dropped my clothes on the floor and stepped into the shower.

The hot water ran down my shoulders, to my chest, which I was amused by (the shock was wearing off), seeing that I only had a handful of chest hair starting to poke through the skin. I turned away from the showerhead and let the hot water work on the knots in my shoulders.

'*Well, shit,*' I thought, somewhat amused, '*that's one thing that hasn't changed.*'

I stood under the hot water for a few more minutes, willing my tired muscles to unknot. Finally, I shut off the tap and grabbed a towel.

As I made my way back to the main room, toweling off my damp hair, I came to the realization that I needed to finally involve Leigh.

How was I going to do it, though?

What was I going to say? *Hello, it's me, your future boyfriend. No, you don't know me yet, but in about a decade and a half, we're going to be together. Well, since I've got you here, could you help me? I'm apparently the victim of some bizarre time travel episode, and I'm really a 32-year-old trapped in this 18-year-old body.*

'*Yeah,*' I thought, '*that's an awesome way for her to call the cops, and for me to end up face down on the ground in handcuffs. Hell, they'll probably give me a snazzy white coat that'll make me give myself a hug and put me in a lovely padded room to chill. Jesus. How am I going to get her to believe me without her thinking I'm some kind of batshit crazy stalker?*'

I finished drying myself off and pulled on the clothes I'd left in the bathroom. They weren't very fresh, but they'd have to do. I sat down on the chair in the corner of the room and pulled my boots toward me. I shoved my feet in and laced them up. I leaned back in the chair, looking up at the ceiling. I took a deep breath and held it for a few counts, finally releasing it in a rush.

I stood up and grabbed my backpack. I glanced at my watch, surprised to find it was a little later than I anticipated but still well before the check-out time the hotel required. I tossed the backpack over my shoulder and made my way back to the front desk. Fortunately, it was a different employee from when I checked in, and I was able to check out without incident. The new employee even refunded the deposit I was forced to put down earlier.

Thank God for small favors.

Back in my car, I turned the engine over and sat in the parking lot for a moment.

Sighing, I pulled out my cell phone and powered it on. This time, I didn't have a flood of messages; instead, I had a single voicemail. Wondering who it was, I punched the voicemail button, hoping I remembered the mailbox password I'd used.

Fortunately, I managed to get the password right on the second try, and I was greeted with a message from Ace Hardware, wondering where I was. My boss, Debbie, sounded very concerned—in the two years I'd worked there, I'd never missed a shift without calling.

Apparently, I had been scheduled to work last night. I deleted the message and snapped the phone shut. I decided not to call her back, still working on the assumption that everything would be erased when I figured out how to get back to my own timeline. If it wasn't erased, I guess I would deal with it when the time came.

I looked at the phone in my hand for a few minutes and

then made a decision. I tossed the phone in the cupholder and pulled the car into gear. I pulled out of the Holiday Inn lot and onto Route 14 and started to make my way to Harvard. I figured my best chance was to try and have Leigh meet me somewhere to talk in person, assuming she didn't automatically shut me down and think I was insane.

Which was a big if.

'*Fuck it*,' I thought. '*At this point, I'll take my chances. Hopefully, I can get her to talk to me and believe me. Or, at the very least, just hear me out.*'

CHAPTER 27

The drive to Harvard was every bit as boring in 2006 as it was in 2020. Shockingly, there was even less between Crystal Lake and Harvard than I remembered.

The road to Harvard hadn't been worked on in several years, and pieces of Route 14 hadn't been widened into a four-lane road yet. Either way, I passed through Woodstock and eventually came up on the intersection of Routes 14 and 23. I pulled through the intersection and through the downtown area, heading for the northeast part of town. If I was lucky, Leigh wouldn't be working today, and I would be able to get her on the phone.

I glanced at the clock in my car, hoping it wasn't too early to try calling her. The clock read 9:27 a.m.

'Fuck it,' I thought, *'it's worth a shot. I might as well give her a call and see if she'll meet me somewhere to talk.'*

I drove to the parking lot of a small diner at the north end of town called the Kozy Nook Restaurant. More commonly, though, the restaurant was simply known as Nick's. Leigh and I had been there many times, so I figured it was the best spot to try and meet her.

The parking lot was small, but I was able to find a parking spot on the south end of the building. I pulled out my phone and flipped it open. I took a deep breath and dialed the number.

"Hello?" Leigh's voice answered, sounding suspicious.

I sat for a moment, letting the relief wash over me. Her voice sounded almost identical to the one that I'd come to know so well. I actually felt tears well up in my eyes.

"Who is this?" she said, sounding more frustrated.

I shook my head and answered her: "Leigh, God, it's really good to hear your voice."

There was silence on the other end of the line. I realized how weird that must have sounded, so I pushed on.

"Look, this is going to be unbelievable, but I need you to try to believe me. Will you hear me out? I know you don't know me yet, but I need someone to listen to me."

"Who are you?" Her voice was still suspicious, but there was an edge of curiosity starting to creep in.

"You have no reason to trust me, but I need to talk to you. You don't know me yet, Leigh, but you will. You're the only person who can help me. Can we meet somewhere to talk? Nick's? It'll be easier to sit down and talk with you face-to-face. I promise, if you don't believe me after we talk, I'll disappear and won't bother you again."

There was silence on the other end of the line. I listened for the telltale click that signaled that she had hung up. As I was about to snap the phone closed, her voice came back on the other end of the line.

"This is crazy. I think you might be crazy, but you sound sincere," She paused, weighing her choices. I knew I had to wait, and I mentally crossed my fingers, "Fine, we'll meet at Nick's. Ten o'clock. Go and sit at the table in the back, and I'll come to you. If you look like a creep, I'm out."

"That's fair," I said, smiling into my windshield, "Ten o'clock it is. See you then."

CHAPTER 28

Javier turned off the water and grabbed the towel he'd thrown over the shower rod. He pressed the towel to his face, feeling the rough, cheap fabric against his freshly shaved jaw.

It had been a long, sleepless night. His latest assignment from his employer was weighing heavily on him, and he had stayed up most of the night trying to figure out how he was going to accomplish this seemingly impossible feat.

Although he'd decided on an accident, he had to figure out just what kind of accident would attract the least attention.

Of course, there was always the fallback of a car accident—faulty brake lines or crossed wiring; however, car accidents were usually investigated. Evidence of tampering would be found.

Game over.

He'd considered a fall down some stairs but couldn't quite figure out how he would naturally get McDougall to a place with enough stairs that he could shove him down to finish the job.

Then, there was the problem of possible witnesses. If

anyone saw him, it would be just like the car accident scenario: game over.

'*Think, goddammit,*' he said to himself, staring at his reflection. '*You're a trained operative. There has to be a way for you to do this clean.*'

But there wasn't.

If he couldn't do it clean, he'd have to do it messy. Messy was stressful, but there were ways to make messy work.

The only problem with doing it messy was Javier needed help.

He walked out to the bedroom of his hotel and found his phone. He thumbed the fingerprint reader and opened the encrypted messaging app. He typed up a message to his employer, requesting backup, and pressed send, watching as the message encrypted itself.

He knew his employer would question why he needed backup, but he figured it was better to deal with questions than a failed mission.

He wiped the messaging app and closed down the phone. He dropped the phone on the bed and started to get dressed.

A moment later, the phone buzzed.

Javier grabbed the phone off the bed and started to open the encrypted app but saw it was a text from McDougall. He looked the text over and then closed the phone back down. He finished getting dressed and clipped his 9mm to his belt.

He made his way down the hall and back to McDougall's room. He knocked and waited.

McDougall opened the door and motioned Javier inside. Jeffrey was already there, sitting in the same chair he'd occupied the night before. Both men wore the same rumpled clothes and had bleary-eyed looks on their faces.

"Let's grab our gear and get back to the site," McDougall said, looking from Javier to Jeffrey. "We've confirmed that the anomaly is coming from the machine. Now, we need to figure out just what the implications are. Is whatshisname actually being sent through time, or are we dealing with something else? We also need to figure out how to get this machine back to our lab intact. The bigger question becomes: can we replicate this result?" Both men nodded, although neither had the answers to the questions McDougall had just asked. Something in McDougall's voice made Javier think there was more going on behind the scenes, but he really couldn't be sure. In all likelihood, he was just thinking about how he was going to score a promotion and pay raise.

Since Javier had already brought his go-bag with him to the room, he stepped aside and let Jeffrey pass. He leaned against the doorjamb and crossed his arms. He watched quietly while McDougall gathered his laptop and documents and shoved them into his bag.

A few minutes later, McDougall, Jeffrey, and Javier were back in the van, heading back to the site.

CHAPTER 29

The activity had calmed down considerably at the site. Technicians were still monitoring both the subject and the output from the machine. Very little had changed overnight: the output from the machine toward the subject had been consistent. There had been no power fluctuations.

Importantly, there had been no episodes of the subject waking.

As they arrived, a white-coated technician opened the front door and ushered the three men into the dining room, which had been turned into an impromptu command center. Jeffrey made his way to the terminals set up on the table and plugged his iPad in, letting the new data sync. McDougall spoke quietly with one of the technicians, gesturing toward the hallway and the sleeping subject beyond. Javier made his way to the couch and sat down, looking over at the dog lying in the crate against the wall.

'*Poor guy,*' he thought. '*Hopefully, someone let him out. I'd hate to have to take care of both the owner and the dog if this thing goes sideways.*'

The dog looked up at Javier, eyes drooping in the characteristic boxer breed's sad eyes. Javier shook his head and looked back at the technicians in the kitchen.

Jeffrey unplugged his iPad and moved down the hallway.

Javier stood up and moved to the kitchen, looking around at the technicians.

"Javier, I need you to head back to the bedroom," McDougall said. "We want to keep someone familiar with both tech and security."

Javier nodded and walked down the hall to the bedroom. As he entered the room, he saw the subject, seemingly still asleep. The monitors hooked up to the subject beeped steadily, marking his slow, steady heartbeat. The IV bags had run down, and a technician was in the process of changing them as Javier cleared the chair sitting in the corner of the room.

He pulled his phone out and opened the notes app, starting to work through the steps he'd need to take to stage his "accident." The phone buzzed in his hands as he was organizing his thoughts.

He switched over to the encrypted messenger and looked at the reply from his employer. Smiling to himself, he wiped the messages and closed the app down. He brought up the notes app and continued taking notes for himself, written in a shorthand only he understood.

As the pieces began to line up, Javier realized his plan would be less messy than he originally thought.

Still messy but a little cleaner.

CHAPTER 30

In the sub-basement lab, McDougall and Jeffrey worked through the code on the computers. At first, they struggled to understand the complex language the UI had been written in. Nearly every menu and setting was written in some kind of code and was not easily decipherable. Fortunately, McDougall had discovered the key in the original operations manual for the Project, the manual written by Baumann himself.

Jeffrey had done some research on the former owner of the house. The records that McDougall had uncovered were lacking in information about who actually owned the secondary lab. There were conflicting reports of just how many of the original scientists had left the project. The only consistent name mentioned was "Bureat." Apparently, Bureat and Baumann had fallen out at some point, and Bureat had stolen the majority of Baumann's research. Although Bureat had made off with the research, the original operations manual had survived, detailing the programming of the prototype computers that operated the machine. The only problem with using the manual was that Bureat had made some modifications to the code, although—so far—the modifications were relatively minor.

As far as McDougall and Jeffrey could tell, the core programming of the machine and control console remained intact.

Although they could get to the core programming, there were still parts of the machine's functions that were not accessible to them.

Evidently, in addition to making things more user-friendly, Bureat locked down some of the readouts and functions. Fortunately, they didn't appear to be functions that were integral to the operation of the machine.

McDougall continued to sift through the menus of the machine, looking for anything that would tell them how and when the machine became operational. Evidently, both Bureat and Baumann had been dead for the last couple of decades, but for some reason, their death certificates were proving difficult to come by. Apparently, buried in the records, the existence of this secondary site had been rumored, but no one knew for sure just how far along in his research Bureat had made it.

As McDougall tapped away on the console, Jeffrey made his way to the main portion of the machine. On his iPad, he pulled up the schematics for the machine back at headquarters—the machine built by Baumann for the Project. Much of Baumann's design was shrouded in secrecy, and the schematics only gave minimal information about the workings of the machine. They labeled, albeit vaguely, the parts of the machine and listed an abbreviated description of their functions. According to the schematic, the main portion of the machine was the Travel Drive, which was responsible for creating the reaction that would send a subject through time-space. What that reaction was, however, was not given. The auxiliary structures connected to the Travel Drive were listed as Reaction Chamber A, Reaction Chamber B, and Output Antenna.

What exactly was in the reaction chambers was not listed.

Evidently, whatever reactions that took place in Chambers A and B were fed to the Travel Drive. Then—with the process complete—sent through the Output Antenna toward the subject.

Jeffrey closed the cover to his iPad. It was a simple enough process on the surface, although he was sure the inner workings of the machine and the reactions were far above his level of comprehension. He glanced over at his boss. Hell, they were probably far above *his* level of comprehension, too.

"Jeffrey," McDougall called, swiveling around in the ancient computer chair, "I think I've got something."

Jeffrey carefully made his way through the jumble of wires and joined his boss at the control panel. Displayed on the central monitor was a menu Jeffrey had not seen yet. The listing at the top called it the Access Log.

"You figured out how to see when this thing was activated?" Jeffrey said, his eyes flicking over the readouts. Times, dates, and durations lined up on the screen.

"Finally," McDougall said. "The log was hidden in one of the sub-menus. If I didn't have the key from the manual, I doubt I would have found it."

McDougall tapped the down arrow and scrolled through the list of dates. Most of them, Jeffrey saw, were from the late 80s and early 90s. The durations were relatively short—no more than thirty minutes at a stretch.

McDougall highlighted an entry—"SAT; 9-3-94; 12:32 a.m.; 0h, 12m, 47s—JBAUT"—and tapped return. The display changed and showed a waveform, rising neatly for the first few moments and then spiking. The spike was labeled as "Genesis." The waveform reached a plateau for the remaining time and then dropped severely. The final point was labeled as "Terminus." Under the waveform and labels, a chart diagramed the maximum power output, the reaction strength in both chambers, and the frequency of the output beam. Blinking below the chart was the word "SUCCESS."

"It looks like someone was running tests of this machine and logging the results," Jeffrey said.

"This is a different configuration than the machine back at headquarters," McDougall said, rubbing his chin.

"What do you mean?"

"The machine back at headquarters is supposed to *detect* time-space anomalies, not *create* them. The systems are similar, but this machine has been modified from the original schematics. The reaction chambers are supposed to create a feedback field that is output through the antenna, allowing for the detection of naturally or unnaturally occurring anomalies. Rather than looking for an anomaly, this version of the machine is creating one. I think the original intention was space-time travel, but Baumann couldn't figure it out, I guess."

"So," Jeffrey said, eyes wide, "Bureat stole the design for this machine and changed it to project time-space anomalies in, what, an effort to travel through time? He must have figured it out when Baumann couldn't."

"I don't know his intentions," McDougall snapped. "All I know is that this thing is what was projecting the anomaly that our machine at HQ detected."

"Shit," muttered Jeffrey, "the implications ..."

"Right," McDougall said. "It's good we got here first. Now, all we have to do is figure out how to control this thing."

"Can you imagine the funding we're going to get? The research opportunities are unlimited!" Jeffrey's voice had taken a manic edge. In his excitement, he missed the glint in McDougall's eye and the slight smirk that crossed his lips.

"Control yourself," McDougall growled, although he had been thinking much the same things. They didn't have time to get delusions of grandeur; they still needed to figure out how to operate the machine and how to get it back to the controlled environment of the lab. “First, we need to figure out how to work this thing. We need to decode the rest of the menus and gain access to the areas that Bureat encrypted. We also need to figure out how to get the witness out of the temporal anomaly and what to do with him once he’s out. We can’t exactly leave any witnesses floating around.”

“What does that mean?” Jeffrey asked sharply.

“It means we have to figure out what to do,” McDougall said. “We interview him. Find out what he knows, and figure out if we can use his experiences to further our research. After that ...” He trailed off, leaving the implication hanging in the air. He cleared his throat. “Right now, let’s focus on the operations of the machine and decoding the menus.”

Jeffrey nodded, although he was growing uncomfortable with just how far his boss was willing to go to keep control over this machine. Yes, it was important, but was it important enough to cross that line? If they did, there would be no going back. He shook his head, pushing those thoughts to the back of his mind. Right now, he needed to focus. He looked around for a moment, went to a dimly lit corner, and dragged an old, rusted folding chair over to the second keyboard on the control panel. McDougall pushed the computer chair to the side, and the two men began to work.

CHAPTER 31

Several hours later, McDougall and Jeffrey joined Javier and the other technicians in the kitchen of the house. They had worked on the code Bureat had used to encrypt the machine, but even after hours of work, parts of the code remained indecipherable. The parts they had been able to decode began to show the readouts from the machine's current operation. As far as anyone could tell, the machine was working properly; the power levels looked to be consistent with earlier tests marked as successful, the output beam was holding at what appeared to be the correct frequency, and the reactions in both chambers appeared nominal. The readouts from the modern equipment tasked with monitoring the machine appeared to confirm the machine's own internal readings.

One of the technicians, a scrawny young man who looked like he was barely out of high school, stood up and made his way to the coffee pot sitting on the counter next to the sink. He poured himself a fresh cup and turned to look back at McDougall and Jeffrey.

"As far as we can tell, our readings are the same as yours," he said, then took a sip from the mug. "We don't know for sure what the readings are supposed to be, of course, but they appear consistent with the previous tests you were able to export to our system from the one downstairs. We'll keep monitoring both our equipment and the primary control panel down in the basement lab."

McDougall nodded absently, still looking at the readouts on the monitor. Javier stood near the back of the group, arms folded over his chest. From behind him, a whimper came from the dog lying in the crate.

'*Fuck it*,' Javier thought, '*I'm going to let the poor guy out and feed him*.' He knelt down by the crate and opened the latch. The dog was on his feet in a moment, tail wagging in a helicopter-like motion. He barked once and ran to the back door.

"What the hell are you doing?" McDougall growled, looking up from the monitor.

"It's a dog. He can't just stay cooped up all day. Look, until I have to euthanize the subject in the room back there," Javier jerked his thumb toward the back of the house, "someone needs to take care of this animal. At the very least, let him out and feed him. That's what I'm doing."

McDougall rolled his eyes and flapped a dismissive hand in Javier's direction. Javier contented himself with mentally punching McDougall in the face and breaking his nose. Javier smiled to himself.

Imaginary or not, the image made him feel better.

He pulled the back door open and let the dog out to run around. He stepped out after him and stood on the back porch, watching the dog run laps around the yard. Javier felt himself smile—truly smile—for the first time in a long time. When the dog was finished with his business, he ran back to the deck and skidded to a halt at the back door. Javier opened the back door and let himself and the dog back in. The dog ran around the table and over to the bowls in the corner by the back door, loudly gulping down water. Javier looked in the dog food bag next to the door, found a measuring cup, and scooped up some of the kibble. He dumped it in the dog's bowl and gave him a quick scratch behind the ears.

"Will you stop fucking around with the mutt and get back to watching the subject?" McDougall grumbled, scowling at Javier. Javier ignored him.

"Alright, boy," he muttered to the dog, "let's get back in your crate."

The dog's ears flattened, and he looked up at Javier, whimpering slightly.

"I know, buddy," he said, patting the dog on the head. The dog turned and trotted toward the crate—

—before turning and running down the hall toward the bedroom. Javier started to go after him but decided to let the animal go by his owner. It might just be a matter of time before Javier had to neutralize them both.

Javier moved down the hall and around the corner to the master bedroom. The dog was standing on the far side, paws up on the bed, sniffing his owner's face. The animal's ears were pinned back, and his usually active tail was tucked. He let out a whine and nudged his owner with his nose.

Javier actually felt bad for the poor creature.

He left the dog in the bedroom and went back to the kitchen.

"Done playing dog whisperer?" McDougall said, glancing up from the monitor.

Javier glared at him but held his tongue. It wasn't worth getting into an argument with him. Instead, he asked: "What's the plan now?"

McDougall leaned back in the chair and rubbed his eyes. "We're going to keep monitoring this machine and keep trying to decode the menus. You're going to keep providing security, since this is a little above your pay grade. The support team will keep an eye on the subject and monitor his vitals.

"From what we can tell, the machine is working properly,"

he said, looking at Jeffrey. "The genesis was 12:27 a.m. yesterday. The machine has been running since then with steady power levels and output. There hasn't been a terminus yet, and, as far as anyone can tell, there isn't one programmed. Start picking through the log files and see if you can tell how the terminus was initiated in previous tests.

"I'm going to continue working on the menus. I've had some success, but there's a lot that is still encrypted. I want to have complete control over this thing before we try to transport it back to headquarters."

Javier felt his mouth drop open. "What do you mean, 'transport it back to headquarters'?" he asked.

"Just what I said," McDougall replied, "you don't really think we're just going to leave this thing here, do you?"

"What if we can't initiate the terminus?" Jeffrey asked.

McDougall swung around in the chair to look at him. "Then Javier neutralizes the subject, and we pull the plug. This research is too important to leave here operating indefinitely. We need to study it in our lab with our detection equipment. Weren't you talking about the implications before?

"Of course," he said, looking between Javier and Jeffrey, "we'll make every effort to extract the subject safely."

'*What a load of bullshit,*' Javier thought. '*He's going to pull the plug anyway just to get this thing out of here and back to the lab.*' He thought about the plans he'd been making on his phone. Suddenly, his plan seemed a lot easier to carry out.

"... back to work," McDougall was saying. "Javier, go provide security in the bedroom; Jeffrey, download and analyze the log files and see if you can find out how the terminus was initiated. I'm going back to the basement lab to work directly on the machine and try to finish decoding the menus so we can have full control."

Javier walked back down the hallway to the bedroom, once again taking a seat in the rocking chair in the corner. The dog had jumped all the way up on the bed and was curled up next to his owner, his head resting on his chest. The dog's eyes flicked over to Javier, and he let out a low whimper.

The dog readjusted his head, taking his eyes off Javier and focusing intently on his still-sleeping owner.

Javier pulled out his phone and began to finalize his plans.

CHAPTER 32

-36 hours earlier-

The estate was secluded, just like he liked it. Seated on 15 acres, the 9,000-square-foot mansion was perfect for a recluse who was, for all intents and purposes, dead.

Of course, the man himself was not dead. It had taken a lot of careful planning and a lot of money paid to the right people at the right time, but nearly all traces of him had been wiped out when he had been removed from the Project. Fortunately, the substantial fortune he had amassed in life was able to follow him into death through a myriad of shell corporations and holding companies, all with executives who knew nothing and could not be linked back to him, just like pawns in a game.

The $1.08-million-dollar estate had been purchased through a shell company shortly after his "retirement" and had undergone a number of changes during his occupation. An expansive basement laboratory, guarded by military-grade bullet- and blast-proof doors, steel reinforced concrete walls, and armed security personnel, had been outfitted for his continuing research.

Like the bankers, the guards knew nothing important. Their only thought was to be "shoot on sight."

The man himself emerged from the master bedroom, walking out onto the lavish balcony overlooking the pond. He ran his hands through his tousled, graying hair, smoothing it down on his head.

This was the man responsible for the original Project Outrigger—Herman Samuel Baumann.

Herman Samuel Baumann had been a genius from an early age. As with all geniuses, he had skipped several grades in school, graduating at the top of his class at the age of 15. He had gone on to MIT, studying advanced aerospace engineering, eventually graduating summa cum laude from both his bachelor's and master's programs. Ultimately, he had made his way to Stanford and obtained his Ph.D. in Aeronautics and Astronautics. When he had begun his work on Project Outrigger with Major General Marcus Copland, he seemed to carry the Project on his shoulders. Later, as the Project began to lose funding and investors, Baumann had turned to private millionaires and even a couple bored-but-well-connected billionaires. The money coming in from private donations had helped Baumann continue his research.

After a few years of work on his own, Baumann had been introduced to Jonathan Bureat.

Their meeting had gone splendidly. Finally, Baumann had found someone who could keep up with his research—someone who could challenge him to push his findings to their limits and, if all went well, unlock the secret to time travel, all under the guise of searching for alien life.

The two men had continued to work on the Project, even though the money eventually ran out. The lack of funding had begun to erode their relationship, and Bureat had finally had enough.

Secretly and behind his partner's back, he had begun to funnel Baumann's research into his own files. He had constructed a laboratory under a small house in Wonder Lake, a sleepy town far away from the primary laboratory, and had begun to feed the data from the Project to his newly completed, albeit hodgepodge, computer.

Unfortunately for Bureat, Baumann had come to find the leak in data. Baumann had been furious. He had cornered Bureat and began to hurl accusations at him. Bureat, for his part, had known he had been caught and had not tried to deny that he had been stealing the Project's research. Although Bureat had taken responsibility, Baumann's anger could not be sated. Baumann had attacked Bureat in their lab. In a fit of anger, he had nearly killed him; Baumann had grabbed a nearby piece of equipment and bludgeoned Bureat repeatedly until he was unconscious.

Standing over his bloodied and nearly dead partner, Baumann had known he would need to disappear. He had heard the last remaining investors talking—he had long ago bugged the conference room for his own protection—and he had known they were looking for any excuse to cut ties with their eccentric lead researcher. Apparently, even time travel was not worth putting up with his "peculiarities."

Baumann had ended up dragging Bureat to the entryway to the lab, pushing him roughly into a closet. He would eventually move him to where he could be found and rescued, but he needed him out of the way for the moment. He had returned to his office and pulled a file from a hidden drawer in his desk. Although the timeline had been moved up, Baumann had made plans for this situation long ago. He had begun making phone calls, working through his contacts to arrange his "retirement."

Within hours, his plans had been complete. His vast fortune had been strategically moved to offshore accounts, funneled through a myriad of shell and dummy corporations, until it was so convoluted that no investigation could trace the money back to one individual.

With his plans set, Baumann had initiated the final piece of his plan to disappear. First, he had gone to the closet where he had stashed Bureat, and he had dragged him to the clean room at the entrance to the lab. He had returned to his office, where, behind a bookcase, there was a hidden panic room. Although this room was meant to be used in the event of an emergency, Baumann had secretly converted it into a cold storage facility. There had been only one thing stored in this room: a corpse that had been surgically and dentally altered to be a near-perfect copy of Baumann himself.

Triggering a rapid thaw protocol—it wouldn't do to have his "body" be recovered frozen—Baumann had dragged the corpse to the Italian leather chair he typically sat in while working in his office.

'*It's a shame, really,*' he had thought, looking at the corpse resting in the chair. '*It really was a lovely chair.*' With a shrug, Baumann had pulled a pistol out of the small of his back and shot the corpse three times in the chest. Blood bags inside the chest cavity then ruptured, giving the corpse the lifelike appearance of ballistic trauma. With that task accomplished, he had triggered another protocol, this time from the doorway.

Above his head, the harsh fluorescent lights had winked out and were replaced with the dim red glow of emergency lighting. A loudspeaker had crackled to life, filling the lab with the soothing—but insistent—tones of one of the early female lab techs:

"Warning: Protocol Zeta-One has been initiated. All laboratory workers must exit immediately. I repeat, warning: Protocol Zeta-One has been initiated. All laboratory workers must exit immediately. The countdown timer has been set for five minutes. Please exit immediately."

Protocol Zeta-One had been designed to eliminate all lifeforms in the laboratory. Early in his career, Baumann had wanted a way to ensure that his research would not fall into the wrong hands. He had consistently backed his research up remotely, but he had wanted to be able to destroy the master copies. With the use of a high-impact thermobaric explosion, nearly everything in the lab would be cremated; the data and any living thing in the lab would be destroyed if he triggered the Protocol.

Assuming, of course, that the HITs did their job.

Baumann had known one of the security officers would make a hasty sweep of the lab, even with a timer running. He had known they would find the beaten Bureat and the "murdered" Baumann. With the timer winding down, they would not look too closely at the corpse; rather, they would leave it until the Protocol had been completed and take care of the barely living Bureat. Once they got back to the body, there would be barely anything left. Just enough to identify him.

Baumann had tucked the pistol back into the small of his back and made his way to his private, concealed emergency exit in the main laboratory.

Glancing back one last time, he had made his way through the emergency exit and toward his future.

That had been nearly thirty years ago. Since his "retirement," Baumann had continued his research. It had taken him years to reconstruct the machine he had built in the original Project labs, but he finally prevailed. He began running tests, but for all his knowledge, he continued to receive failing results.

Despite these failures, he continued to look for opportunities to continue the research he started on the initial Project. To do that, Baumann would need operatives to work inside the new Project. Slowly, he began to recruit officers into his Collective.

Baumann took a special interest in one of the technicians who doubled as a security officer. The man named Javier had served him loyally for several years (although he had never officially met the man) and helped him funnel information out of the new Project. Unfortunately, most of the information was moot—no time-space anomalies had been detected, and all the information being provided to the technicians was routine.

Other operatives in the Collective were placed at different locations in the Project. All of the operatives were low-level employees who could move about with little suspicion. By the time of the time-space anomaly detection, Baumann had five operatives reporting to him, although the remaining four continued their usual duties. He couldn't risk arousing suspicion of his involvement by pulling them all from their tasks. Javier would have to do—for now, at least.

On the morning the anomaly was detected, Baumann was sitting on his terrace enjoying his morning cup of coffee. Although he had not officially worked in an office for nearly thirty years, Baumann still woke early every day. His cook had gotten used to the timeframe and made sure to provide him with coffee and breakfast each morning.

As he was sitting on his terrace reading the paper, he had no idea what was in store for him.

About halfway through a story about local political woes, the satellite phone that was always with him chirped. Figuring it was just another meaningless status update, he casually folded the paper up and answered the phone.

What he heard would leave him speechless.

Not only had an anomaly been found, but it had been found barely five miles from his own home! Baumann asked his operative for more details, doing his best to work out what the next steps would be. He left his coffee and breakfast on the terrace and moved back inside, still listening to the voice on the other end of the line.

The higher-ups at the Project headquarters were tripping over themselves, just as Baumann had thought they would. They were, however, beginning to work out that they would need to go to the location of the anomaly and study it in person. Baumann would let them do that for the time being; his operative would be brought along to provide support and security. With his report finished, the operative asked what to do next. Baumann told him to stay accessible and in communication. After acknowledging this, the operative cut the line.

Baumann made his way through the mansion to the basement. He provided the necessary biometric data to enter his lab and made his way to the workstation. All the equipment in the lab was top-of-the-line, and the workstation came to life with little delay. He opened a terminal and worked his way into the out-of-date monitoring terminal located in the Project headquarters.

As usual, the security was a joke. He was in the system in less than five minutes. Smiling to himself, he brought up the monitoring data for the location of the anomaly. Turning to another monitor, he plugged the coordinates in and watched as the map centered and zoomed in on a location in Wonder Lake. It took a moment, but Baumann recognized the address.

Bureat!

'*Damn him!*' Baumann thought. '*That slimy asshole really did build a machine and get it working! The stupid motherfucker had better have used the same monitoring protocols ...*' Baumann began tapping commands into the terminal at the Project headquarters, opening up long unused menus. '*Ah, yes, good. Smart, but never that smart.*'

Baumann dug into the data.

CHAPTER 33

The minutes slowly crept toward ten o'clock in the morning. I sat in the booth near the back of Nick's, drinking coffee and trying not to fret.

Hell, I was trying not to look suspicious.

The brunch crowd was working their way through their meals, and the waitstaff was juggling refilling coffee, bringing food, and bussing tables vacated by other patrons.

A waiter floated over and dropped a menu on the table, asking if he could bring me anything. I told him that I was meeting someone here and that I'd wait until she arrived. He shrugged and refilled my coffee. I pulled the foil off a single-serve creamer and dumped it into the coffee, watching as the off-white, vanilla-flavored liquid mixed with the dark coffee. I stirred and took a sip.

I glanced down at my watch, noting that it had just clicked over to ten o'clock. I looked around the restaurant, scanning for Leigh. A moment later, I saw her walk through the archway connecting the counter area and the back I was sitting in.

Although I'm not normally overly emotional, I felt my heart jump to my throat. It was jarring to see someone I knew in this setting, even if she clearly didn't know me. I forced myself to take a deep breath and wait. She looked so much like the woman I remembered, but, just like myself, she had the unrefined look of a teenager: leaner, not as mature. Her eyes, though, were still the same ones I remembered. I noticed them right away, just as I had when I first met her, nearly twenty years from now.

She looked around the back area, clearly looking for someone around her own age. She saw me and moved toward the table.

"Hey," I said, forcing myself to stay sitting, fighting every urge to jump up and hold her.

"Hi," she said, pulling out the chair across from me and sitting down. "Well, you don't look insane."

I laughed.

The first real laugh I'd had in the last couple of days.

I couldn't help it. She had the same sense of humor in the future as she did now.

"Well, that's positive," I said, still smiling. "Thank you for coming."

"I told you I'd hear you out. I might not believe what you're telling me, but you sounded like you could really use someone to talk to."

I smiled, although it held a rueful edge. "Yeah, you're right about that. I haven't had anyone to talk to openly in days. It's all been cloak-and-dagger stuff so I didn't get myself committed."

"You mentioned something about a 'situation.' What exactly is going on with you? How do you know me?"

"Both of those questions are hard to explain," I said, running a hand across my chin. "I'll do my best, but frankly, I don't fully understand it myself."

Leigh sat quietly for a moment, thinking. "Look, if you're not going to tell me what's going on ..." She trailed off.

"No, it's not that!" I said, putting as much sincerity into

my voice as possible. "I just ..."

Sighing, I sat for a moment, looking down into my coffee. I tried to organize my thoughts into a coherent narrative.

I took a deep breath and started at the beginning.

CHAPTER 34

"So, I've been trying to figure out exactly how it happened and what I can do about it. I need to get back to my own time, back to my own body. This sounds completely insane, but I promise you I'm telling the truth."

Leigh sat, a mixture of emotions on her face. Shock. Sympathy. Fright. I hadn't left anything out, including my fight. I could tell that part bothered her, but I was hoping it wasn't a deal-breaker.

The waiter came back with our food, setting the plates down in front of us. He came back a moment later, dropped off Leigh's hot chocolate, and topped off my coffee.

I wanted to ask her what she was thinking, to ask her what was going on.

I made myself wait. I knew what I had just told her was a lot to take in.

"Okay," she said, drawing out the words, her skepticism clearly evident, "let's say, for the moment, that I believe you. What do you want me to do to help you?"

"Honestly, I don't know. I'm really not sure there's anything you can do ..." I trailed off for a moment, then said, "But

I wanted to reach out and, I don't know, talk it out."

She nodded.

I took a sip of coffee and gestured to our breakfasts. I pulled my fork out of the rolled-up napkin and began to work on my eggs.

We both sat in silence for a while, both of us working on our breakfast and digesting the insanity of the story I had told. The silence stretched between us, but it never quite crossed over into uncomfortable. It was comforting that the same amiable quality it had in the future existed here in this time, too.

After a few more moments, Leigh took a breath: "Okay, I'm not sure what I can do to help you, and this sounds completely made up, but you know things about me that, really, you shouldn't."

I opened my mouth to say something, but she raised a hand, cutting me off.

"I don't mean that you're some kind of stalker or anything. I think you might really be telling the truth with all of this, as crazy as it sounds. You definitely seem like this is something that's really bothering you. Maybe it makes me crazy, but I think I'm going to help you. At least, for now, anyway. But, honestly, the second something—anything—feels weird or creepy, I'm out. You can figure whatever this is out on your own."

I felt a mixture of relief and trepidation wash over me. Finally, I had someone on my side who seemed to believe my story, even if she wasn't fully committed to helping me figure the mystery out. I sat back in the booth and felt some of the tension I'd felt for the last couple days leave my body. It didn't change the fact that I still had no real idea how to get back to my own time, but it helped.

"Thank you."

"So, what are we going to do?"

I looked back down into my mostly depleted coffee cup.

"I don't know. I was at the house once, like I said. I found who I assume is the owner, and that machine in the sub-basement. I managed to catch another glimpse into my normal time, too, but the second time I touched the machine, nothing happened. I don't think I can control how I make contact with the future. There's got to be some way to control how the machine is working from here. It makes sense that the link between now and the future is the machine, right?"

Leigh nodded, "I'd say so. It seems to be the thing making all this happen, so it being the link between both versions of yourself makes sense. Did you try operating it when you were in the sub-basement?"

"Yeah," I said and nodded, "but the menus were coded, and I was afraid of fucking it up. The thing is built using old technology, and my computer skills aren't strong enough to operate it. I tried a few commands, and the information it gave me wasn't much help—it isn't like a normal computer with icons and a pointer. Did you ever play with the command line in Windows? It was more like DOS than XP—just lines of computer code and readouts. I was poking around and kind of panicked. A normal computer, I might be able to figure out how to fix it if I broke it. That thing? I doubt it."

"Okay," Leigh trailed off, looking out the cold-fogged window at what should have been a beautiful winter day. A shadow crossed her face. "Not wanting to mess it up makes sense. But what if we can't figure it out? Are you just going to live here in this time?"

"That's the million-dollar question. I guess it's a possibility I'd have to do that, but I'd really rather not live my teenage years again."

Leigh chuckled. I smiled.

"So, what do we do?"

"Well," I said, pausing just a moment as the waiter refilled my coffee, "I think the next step is to head back to the house and try to poke around the menus in that machine more. I was thinking about talking to my brother, too; he's the computer guy in the family and might have better luck with getting through the menus and into the thing's programming."

The question I still faced, though, was: *Would my brother believe me, and would he help me?*

"Will your brother help you?"

Ruefully, I smiled, "It's like you're reading my mind. I suppose the only thing I can do is ask him. If he says no, I'll have to try and figure it out myself."

I was pretty sure that my brother and I would be on good terms at this point in time. Like almost any siblings anywhere, we had our rough patches. I knew there was a pretty rough patch coming up, but I didn't think it had started yet. I figured he and I should still be alright.

"You alright?" Leigh asked, looking at me from across the table.

I shook my head, clearing my thoughts, "Yeah, I'm okay. I just got lost in my thoughts for a minute there.

"I'm going to call my brother when we're done here and see if I can get him to help me out. I'll give you the address, and you can head over to the house after I give you the go-ahead. Don't worry, I'll give you directions, too—I know you don't do well with road names." I smiled, expecting her to pick up on our joke.

"How do you know that?" she snapped, and then her voice softened. "Oh, right, the future. This is really messed up, you know that? It's like you have all this information about me, but I just met you for the first time today. It's really a mindfuck."

I nodded, knowing full well just how much of a mindfuck this whole thing was.

Our waiter came by again and dropped the check. I grabbed the check and my jacket. Leigh collected her things. I paid the tab, and we both left Nick's together.

Outside, I told her again that I'd call her when everything

was set. She nodded and turned toward her car. I made my way back to my own and got in, turning the engine over.

I picked up my cell phone and dialed.

CHAPTER 35

An hour and a half later, Leigh, Joseph, and I gathered at the house. It was a pretty hilarious circumstance: We were about to commit a misdemeanor—technically, I was about to commit the same one a third time—squeeze down into the sub-basement through the sump well, and mess around with a computer that none of us understood.

It had taken a little—okay, a lot—of convincing to get my brother to help me, but fortunately, he seemed interested in the opportunity to dig into a computer that might be the most complex thing he'd ever touched. The way I figured it, if anyone could figure out how to make the thing work, it was Joseph.

We made our way to the back of the house, but I told them to wait before we went in the back door.

"Okay, so, just a heads-up," I started, taking a step around them, putting myself between them and the sliding door, "the owner of this place is still here. I'm assuming he's still tied up in the bedroom where I left him, but I can't be sure of that."

"Wait a minute, what?" Leigh said, her eyes going wide.

"Yeah, what?" Joseph said, furrowing his brow.

"Leigh, I already told you I had to fight him," I said. "I just left out that I ..." My voice trailed off for a moment before I said, "I left him tied up in the master bedroom."

"Are you serious?"

"You tied him up and just left him?"

"What did you do?"

"Guys, I—" I started, but they cut me off.

"How did you do that?"

"Is he alive?"

"Guys—" I tried again but got cut off a second time.

"How hard did you hit him?"

"Is it safe to go in?"

"What if he got loose?

"Whoa, guys! Guys!" I exclaimed, holding my hands out in front of me to get them to relax and stop their rapid-fire questions. "First of all, he attacked me, so I really didn't have a choice. He came at me with a baseball bat. I managed to get it away from him, but he went for a knife. I ended up hitting him with the bat and knocking him out. I was really aiming for the knife, but he moved in front of the bat." I grimaced but continued, trying not to think too much about the fact that I'd clocked this guy with his own baseball bat. "Hopefully, he's still out cold, but I can't guarantee that. At the very least, he should still be tied up in the bedroom. I don't think he got loose, but I can't be sure of that. All I can do is tell you I tied him up the best I could."

It took another couple of minutes of convincing to get both of them to feel confident enough to enter the house. I told them I'd go in first and make sure everything was alright.

I stepped into the house and closed the sliding glass door behind me. I closed my eyes and stood quietly for a moment, listening to the sounds the house was making, listening for breathing, for the shuffle of feet, or for the rasp of clothing.

Creaks and ticks broke the silence. The sounds of a house settling and shifting. Common sounds that didn't give me the impression that my makeshift prisoner was loose.

I slowly made my way to the hallway, still keeping myself alert for the sounds of someone moving. I turned the corner and saw the bedroom door ajar. The rooms on either side of the hall were still closed, and dusty light still filtered out from underneath them.

I crept down the hall, wincing slightly at the creak my footfalls made. From the bedroom, I heard a faint shuffle.

I paused, listening again.

The shuffle came again, longer this time, followed by a grunt.

"Fucker," a voice drifted out of the bedroom.

I felt my lips press into a tight line. He was awake, but it sounded like he was still tied up and unable to get free.

'*Good,*' I thought, '*at least he isn't free and able to come chase us around the house. Maybe that'll give us a little time to work.*'

I made my way back to the sliding glass door and opened it carefully. I stepped out into the chilly March air and nodded.

"He's still tied up. He's up, and he's pissed, I think, but he isn't free. We should have a chance to get down to the subbasement and take a look at the machine that's down there."

Leigh and Joseph nodded.

We made our way into the house and toward the basement door.

"Good God," Leigh whispered, "who lives like this?"

I turned back and shrugged, gesturing toward the bedroom at the back of the house. I pressed a finger to my lips and inclined my head toward the basement door.

We made our way down the stairs, grimacing each time one of the steps creaked or groaned.

"Who the hell is in here? Hey! Come untie me, you little asshole! This is my house! You can't just tie me up and leave me back here!" The owner's voice drifted down through the floorboards, sounding muffled in the basement.

I felt myself wince. I knew it wasn't right to just leave him tied up—I'd have to at least give him some water and let him go to the bathroom at some point. Then again, I had shit to do and couldn't exactly have him running around while we were working on the computer. There might come a time when I would try to talk to him, but with the way his eyes looked when he attacked me, I wasn't sure he was lucid enough to answer any questions.

"Where is this machine?" Joseph asked, looking around the cluttered, dusty basement. "The only thing I see are tape mainframes. Those aren't going to help very much unless there's a computer to access them."

"It's in the sub-basement. I didn't even know it existed when I bought this place in 2020, but I managed to find it here in 2006. It's in the back through the sump well, over by the well pump. It's a tight fit, but the whole area under us right now is open—actually, the machine should be right below us."

We made our way to the southern side of the house. The well cover was still sitting ajar, and harsh fluorescent lighting was shining up through the hole in the floor.

"What the hell?" Leigh muttered, looking down at the hole in the basement floor. "How the hell did they build this?"

I moved past them and started working my way down the ladder, leaving the question floating in the air. Once we were all in the sub-basement, we made our way back to the machine. I moved toward it and took a deep breath. I laid my hand on the machine.

Nothing happened.

I let the breath out, along with a mumbled curse, and turned to face the other two.

"Well, that didn't work," I said.

"What didn't work?" Joseph asked.

"Last time he touched the machine, he was able to wake up for a few seconds in his other body. Right?" Leigh said, catching my train of thought.

I nodded. I hadn't had time to tell Joseph about that part.

"I was hoping I could get another glimpse of the future, maybe see something that would help. Hell, maybe get someone's attention, even if I wasn't able to move the other times it happened. Looks like that isn't part of the plan."

Joseph made a noise in his throat, a grunt somewhere between discontented and thoughtful. He gestured with his chin to the hodgepodge set up and said, "Is that the computer?"

I nodded, moving away from the machine to the control panel. In our phone call, I'd told him just how little luck I'd had with the machine and how navigating the menus was damn near impossible for me. Joseph pulled the ancient computer chair toward him, with it eliciting an ear-splitting screech as the immobile wheels dragged across the concrete. He winced but sat down and began to tap commands into the central keyboard. His light blue eyes absorbed the code, seemingly making sense of the gibberish on the screen.

Within moments, he had accessed a log file that seemed to show tests of the machine's mechanisms. The three of us peered at the screen, noting the start and end points of each test. There was a blinking icon at the bottom of the page that read "Current Simulation."

I gestured to the icon, and Joseph punched in another string of commands. A box appeared on the screen, flashing "Access Denied" and halting our progress.

"Damn," I muttered.

"Let me try something else," Joseph said, typing another command into the machine. The same menu as before appeared, but this time, he was able to get the information from the current test to display. "You'd think there'd be better security on something like this, but it's really just an MS-DOS operating system with custom menus. The whole thing runs like a really old Windows machine. I'm hoping … yeah, they left it in."

"They left what in?" I asked, starting to feel cautiously optimistic.

"The admin account. I can use it to work around the access denied sections. I just need to figure out the password …" He trailed off for a moment, tapping more keys. "Seriously?"

"Don't tell me," I said, crossing my arms, "they left it as something stupid like 'password' or 'administrator,' didn't they?"

"Yep," he said, nodding and looking over at me. "What kind of idiot programmed this thing?"

"Good question," I replied, flashing a wan smile.

"Clearly not someone who's good at their job," Leigh chimed in, "but it makes your job easier, right?"

Joseph nodded and then punched the execute key.

The top left monitor flickered to life, and the data from the current simulation appeared. A graph appeared, with its X-axis labeled as time and its Y-axis labeled as intensity. Under the graph, the terms "Genesis" and "Terminus" were displayed. A third category, "Duration," was steadily ticking upward. I found myself staring at the time listed next to Genesis.

12:27 a.m., two days ago.

'*So, this shit happened overnight? Is that why I have no memory of it? But, if that's the truth, how did this thing kick on at almost 12:30 in the morning? Something had to have turned it on. It can't have been a spontaneous event,*' I thought.

"It looks like this, I guess they call it a simulation, has been active for the last couple of days. Does that line up with what's been going on?" Joseph asked, looking away from the screen and catching my eye.

I nodded.

"So, something had to have triggered it," he said, turning back to the screen.

He tapped a few more commands. This time, the bottom left monitor turned on, and a series of dates was listed. The bottom one was flashing, just like it was on the other monitor. A few moments and a handful of commands later, he leaned back in the chair as Leigh and I looked at the screen.

"It doesn't look like it attached a start date to this test," Leigh said, reading over my brother's shoulder.

"Do the other simulations or tests or whatever have dates attached?" I asked. Joseph pulled up the menu again and selected a simulation at random.

"Yeah, they do," he said, working his way through a few simulations worth of data. "For some reason, this one doesn't have a date attached. Do you think that means it was started from the future, or does it just attach the data after the test is finished?"

Leigh and I shrugged, neither of us having the answer.

"Dammit," I muttered, turning away from the control panel. I thought there would be a way to see how the test was initiated. I figured that was my best bet to stop it and be done with this nightmare. "Alright, so it doesn't show when the simulation began. Fine. Doesn't matter. Does it show a way to end a simulation? Is there a command for that?"

Joseph brought up the menu and found an option listed as "Administrative Controls." He entered the command to open that menu but was prompted for a password and retinal scan.

"Shoot," he said, leaning back in the chair again, "it needs a password and retinal scan. I don't think I can do much about this. I might be able to brute-force the password, but that would take a long time and use hardware I don't have with me. The retinal scan ..." he trailed off, looking away.

'Unless I have the same eyes as whoever programmed this thing, I'm shit out of luck,' I thought.

"Shit," I said. I strung together a few more curses as I stomped over toward the machine.

"We just have to figure out the problem," Leigh said, still

looking over the graphs and text on the softly glowing monitors.

"And how are we going to do that?" I snapped. "We don't even know how this piece of shit works. We don't know who programmed it or who started this fucking 'simulation.' The only thing we really do know is that it somehow got turned on and dragged my ass back here to be stuffed in this body, and we have no idea how to fix it! I ..." I trailed off, took a breath, and continued: "I just want to go home. I just want to be me again. This isn't a simulation—it's my life!"

The frustration of the past couple of days seemed to bubble over. Anger started to well up, threatening to overtake me, but it was quickly overshadowed by despair. The hurt, the anger, and the sadness all fought for prominence in my mind. I felt my knees give, and I collapsed, my arm reaching for something to stop my fall.

The machine happened to be that something. Holding on, I propped myself up on rubber legs.

For what felt like the first time, sadness won out.

I felt the tears well up to the point of overspilling, running down my cheeks. I ran my hands through my hair, letting the tears flow, fat and wet, holding all the sadness and despair I'd been keeping at bay for the last two days. My brother and Leigh heard my sobs and turned to look at each other, not sure what to do. I sank to the floor, holding my face in my hands.

"Are you okay?" Leigh asked, kneeling down next to me. She put her hand on my shoulder. Although she was trying, there was no real comfort in the gesture.

Another slap in the face of how alone I was.

I couldn't answer. I just sat on the floor next to the machine that was ruining my life and wept.

CHAPTER 36

Baumann stood in the middle of his lab, papers strewn around him. His breath came in short, ragged bursts, and his face was blotchy and streaked with sweat.

"Dammit!" he shouted, his voice echoing off the cold, bland concrete walls. "God dammit! How did he figure it out?"

With another wave of his arm, he knocked a stack of folders to the ground, their contents flying out and mixing with the mishmash of papers already on the ground.

The data had taken Baumann the better part of the last two days to sift through.

What he had found had sent him into a barely controlled rage.

Bureat, somehow, must have figured out how to enhance his research, ultimately finding a way to do what Baumann had sought for so long. He had taken Baumann's base programming and adapted it, changing it in many small ways until the first successful test had been initiated.

All of it, with Baumann's own research.

Modified research, yes, but still *his*.

"He wasn't smart enough to figure this out on his own!"

Baumann roared, hurling a solid glass paperweight at the wall opposite his desk. "How did *he* do what I *couldn't*? It's not possible!"

As the fractured paperweight fell to the floor, glass shards reflecting the sterile fluorescent light like millions of stars, the smartphone that had been thrown into his chair chirped. Baumann whirled around, glaring at the device and barely keeping his destructive anger under control. He forced himself to take a deep breath, imposing his will on his anger, forcing it into a glass jar he could then set on the shelf in his mind. With any luck, the call would be one of his operatives giving him new information.

If it wasn't ...

Baumann stomped over to his chair and snatched the device. Opening the encrypted messaging app, he found himself staring at a query from his operative at the site.

He growled but answered the question. He dropped the phone back on the desk, taking perverse satisfaction in the loud *thunk* it made as the delicate device hit the unforgiving wooden surface.

Baumann sunk into his chair, leaning back and looking at the ceiling of the lab. The anger he felt was abating and leaving behind a remarkable and clinical clarity.

"How," he spoke aloud, asking the same question he had previously been yelling, "did he manage to modify my research to do what I couldn't?"

The speckled, pockmarked ceiling tiles had no answer.

He continued to stare up at the ceiling, mulling the question over in his head. It was true that Bureat was a genius. He wasn't, however, on Baumann's level. Baumann knew he was several steps ahead of Bureat. If that were true, then how could Bureat modify his research and create a wormhole stable enough to project a consciousness through time? More importantly, why was it some random person and not Bureat himself?

"Because he's dead," Baumann said aloud.

Unlike Baumann, Bureat had died several years earlier in a nursing home after a long battle with Alzheimer's. Even if Baumann could have spoken to Bureat, it was unlikely the conversation would have been helpful, let alone coherent.

'*What's next?*' Baumann thought, swiveling slightly in his chair. '*I've been in touch with my operative this whole time, and he's been feeding me information from Bureat's house. The kid that's in the wormhole is still alive, and presumably, his consciousness is still in whatever time he's projected to. That idiot McDougall is chomping at the bit to pull the plug, demolish the house, and extract and transport the machine back to SAOC. That can't happen. The experiment needs to run its course, and I need the data from it. I have to know what I did wrong and how that Bureat managed to create a stable, temporally sound wormhole. Not to mention, how he managed to focus it on consciousness ...*

'*That's the part that baffles me,*' Baumann thought, running his hands through his hair. He leaned forward in the chair and removed his glasses. He rubbed his eyes, suddenly exhausted.

Rage can be exhausting.

'*I remember that we managed to find out how to create a wormhole. We even came close to having it become stable. The problem is that we never figured out how to separate the consciousness and the physical body. We worked for years on that, trying with all manner of test subjects. I've lost count of the number of disgusting, useless vagrants we put through the process. Each time, their mind was ripped from their bodies, leaving them as little more than an empty shell, a husk of their former selves. What little information we could pull from them showed that we never succeeded in sending their mind through time; we merely threw them into a cloud of antimatter that destroyed brain tissue. It was always frustrating to fail, but being able to terminate the subject made it tolerable. A nice .45 slug to the back of the head before going into the incinerator. Worked like a dream.*

'*Bureat and I had talked a lot about how to fix the problems we were running across. It's impressive—but infuriating—that the little weasel played me. I never figured he was smart enough to figure this out for him-*

self. When did he figure it out? Was it before or after my so-called death? It had to have been before—when I retired, I made sure almost all the significant research was lost. Unless that little shit made backups and funneled information out of the lab.'

Baumann paused his thoughts, trying to recall Bureat's behavior in the weeks leading up to his "retirement." Bureat had always been eccentric—working with Baumann was enough to drive just about anyone over the edge.

'Come to think of it, he had been acting shifty in the weeks leading up to the destruction of the first lab. He was on edge. Bewildered. I figured it was just the stress of the job, but maybe it was the pressure of trying to funnel information from the lab to his makeshift one at home. It was easy enough for me to do, but I have operatives inside the SAOC who can get the information out for me. If he was working alone ...

'Now there's a thought. Was he working alone? Could he have found someone inside the Project to work with, smuggling information and materiel out of the lab? Who else could have been involved? Bureat didn't exactly have a lot of friends. Hell, he barely spoke to anyone in the Project besides me. Part of that was my doing; he was easy to manipulate. If he didn't have a partner, how else could he have done it?'

Baumann stood up and began to pace around his office, casually stepping on loose papers and nudging folders out of the way with his foot. The thought of another traitor inside the Project intrigued him. Was this possible, this other person continuing Bureat's research, even to this day?

'What if the machine was set on some kind of timer? No, that doesn't make sense. The logs my operative managed to send to me don't really have a rhyme or reason. That means someone is operating the machine. I don't believe it's anyone at the site—the idiot higher-ups at Command were surprised to get the readings; the stupid guy who bought the place couldn't know about it. I doubt the family that lived there before him knew, either.'

Baumann had uncovered everything he could about the previous owners of the house, eliminating the off-chance that someone other than Bureat created the machine. The current owner is nothing more than a teacher—of literature, of all things, as if anything was more important than science—and the people—what's his name? Baumann couldn't remember—the teacher bought the house from were just a couple with two small children and another on the way. No connections to anyone of importance. No government contracts. Nothing out of the ordinary.

The property records he'd found—ones that were currently scattered around his feet—indicated that the family had bought the property as a foreclosure after Bureat died. The house had sat vacant for about a decade, slowly decaying, even as Bureat was taken to the Alzheimer's care unit at Loyola, about forty miles away from the site.

Although Loyola didn't have a live-in care unit for Alzheimer's, a substantial "donation" had followed Bureat to the hospital.

The donation, of course, was money funneled out of the Project and used to keep Bureat quiet. It was exceptionally hard to get access to someone who was being kept in a long-term care facility.

Apparently, they made an exception and set him up in one of the rooms. Bureat lived the rest of his life while slowly descending into a fog in his own mind.

'*Good riddance*,' Baumann thought, '*I don't need the man; I just need to figure out how he created a stable wormhole that only works on consciousness. His research wouldn't be in the machine. Those log files only really track what the machine itself is doing. From what I heard from my operative, there hasn't been any significant movement in accessing the encrypted menus of the machine. That shouldn't matter, though; the majority of them will probably just be diversions. His real research is probably hidden away somewhere. I should have another operative do some research and find out if Bureat squirreled it away*.'

Baumann picked up his phone and began making calls. He was going to make sure something went right today.

CHAPTER 37

The team was back at the hotel. It had been a long, frustrating day with little progress. Although Jeffrey and McDougall had decoded parts of the log files, there was very little information in them. What little they could get out of the logs showed that the machine had been running what it labeled as "projection tests" and cataloging the results. All of the dates they could dig out were from various times in the past, which led them to believe that the machine was projecting whatshisname to some previous time. Unfortunately, the person who had initiated the tests remained unknown, much to their annoyance.

Javier sat on the bed in his room, his eyes slightly unfocused as he gazed at the wall. He was still put off by the way the man in the bed had woken up and made that horrifying noise.

It made him wonder just what kind of stress the subject was under and how long he could last like that. Javier kept trying not to think about it but always wound up imagining himself in that man's place.

What would it be like, he wondered, to inhabit a different version of himself? Could he change things? Would they change in the future? He had no idea how this alleged time travel worked, but he was pretty sure it didn't work like in the movies.

If this guy *was* changing things in the past, they sure as hell hadn't changed much in the future. At least, not that Javier had seen. Maybe the incident was isolated and wouldn't cause repercussions in the future. Or, maybe there were repercussions, and they were just that subtle; rather than getting the hurricane from the flap of a butterfly's wings, maybe they just got a light breeze. Hell, maybe the guy in the bed wasn't trying to change anything. For all Javier knew, he could have killed himself when he woke up in his past self. Maybe that awful noise was his death howl.

Javier shook his head slightly, blinking his eyes repeatedly to refocus them. No, he had a job to do, and he needed to make it as clean as possible. The Collective had finally made contact, and another operative was on the way to his location. He needed to finalize the plans and make sure everything was set. The next few hours were important, and everything needed to go as smoothly as possible.

As if on cue, his cell phone chirped. He stood slowly and made his way to the dresser on the far side of the bed. He picked up the phone and opened the encrypted app, looking at the contents of the message. What he found was not what he expected. His employer had contacted him, asking him to look into whether or not Bureat had a safe deposit box registered somewhere. He told Javier that the other set of plans was on hold and the second operative was not going to meet him.

The safe deposit operation takes precedence. Do not deviate from this, Operative #3. You are required to research the validity of the Bureat safe deposit box. You will contact me as soon as you have new information.

Javier took a deep breath and held it for a moment, letting the frustration he felt wash over him. He let the frustration bloom into anger for a moment and then cut it off. Anger would not be helpful in this situation. He pushed it all back down and considered his new options.

'*Fuck,*' he thought, '*the plans were already set. Why is this asshole changing everything now? Why can't I just take care of the other assignment and then look for the safe deposit box?*'

Still grumbling to himself, he tapped a response and tossed the phone on the bed. He returned to the foot of the bed and sat back down, still mulling over the events of the last few days.

He sighed and pushed himself off the bed. He made his way to his bag and found the pad of paper he kept there. He pulled out his laptop and then took both the pad and laptop over to the table. He sat down and powered up the laptop. He needed to make a list of all the places in McHenry and the surrounding towns that would rent out safe deposit boxes.

A few rooms down the hall, McDougall sat at his own laptop, working his way through another series of readings from the machine. As far as he could tell, the readings were all the same. The machine's output had remained steady since the genesis of the current experiment. The power input was routed through auxiliary power boxes and was not attached to the main house breaker. The power draw on the machine was colossal—the latest reading put power consumption at around 180 megawatts, which was just shy of the Large Hadron Collider in Switzerland. He was amazed that the machine had not attracted attention prior to this.

Of course, the machine only drew that much power when it was active. When it was passive, it drew barely enough power to light a standard 60-watt lightbulb—just enough to keep the core systems from degrading and the internal memory from being wiped.

McDougall shifted some papers around on the desk, looking for the dot matrix printout from the machine. He found it and took a look at the lapses between activations of the machine.

'That explains why it never drew attention,' he thought, looking at the readout right before the current iteration, *'it's been almost fifteen years since the last time the machine was activated to this extent. Monitoring systems weren't nearly as advanced back then, and given that it pulls power from about eight different substations, that much energy may have been able to slip past anyone monitoring.'*

He set the dot matrix printout to the side and returned his attention to his computer. He pulled up a diagram of the machine, studying the various parts. He had already done this several times and was starting to memorize the construction, but it never hurt to have a diagram. He pulled up a second window and began to work on mentally breaking the machine apart.

It was only a matter of time before they had to pull the plug and dismantle the machine to bring it back to the Project headquarters. The only problem with pulling the plug was whether the machine would come back online if the power was cut? Would the core systems remain intact? Could they wire in batteries to offset the power loss?

There was nothing in the schematics about a sudden loss of power, but since the machine was wired directly to the power grid, it stood to reason that power should not be abruptly cut off. The monitoring station in the sub-basement could conceivably lose power without irreparable harm, as it was wired into the house's primary circuit breaker.

McDougall shuffled through some more papers, finding a second dot matrix printout. This one showed the interruptions in the monitoring station's power input. McDougall confirmed that, over the last several years, power had been lost on several occasions. The fact that the machine was currently working—and working well—showed that power loss to the console was not a concern. McDougall flipped through the pages and found the one with the header for the machine itself. On this one, the data showed no power loss; rather, it showed that the power levels had been steady for nearly two decades. The only anomalous readings were from the times the machine activated. Those readings showed a colossal jump in power input, drawing enormous amounts of power from the power stations around Wonder Lake.

'*I'm still amazed that this thing hasn't drawn attention,*' McDougall thought. '*Yeah, there's been a lapse in activations, but it almost seems as though the machine's connections to the grid were purposefully taken off the radar. Those original Project guys must have had the power of gods. It's impressive that this site survived so long after Baumann's research was stolen and funneled out. The original machine was lost in a "laboratory sanitation" event where Baumann died. The question is, though: how do we operate and contain this thing?*' He leaned back in his chair and rubbed his eyes.

A few more doors down the hall, Jeffrey was hunched over his own computer. His iPad stood on a stand next to the screen and showed a slightly fluctuating graph of outputs from the machine. Before he had left the site, he had made sure the output readings were being relayed in real time to his iPad. The graph showed, more or less, what he expected from the machine. He tapped a few icons on the display, and another graph appeared, this time rolling steadily to the left. The ECG of the subject appeared steady, and the fluid drip they had started seemed to be helping.

Unlike McDougall, Jeffrey knew they had to keep this man alive and see what the full course of the experiment was.

Frankly, they needed to make sure it ended with the subject still alive—the machine was all but worthless if the subject died when the procedure was complete.

He pulled up a digital scan of the old dot matrix printouts on his laptop and scrolled through the pages until he found the one he was looking for. The list of previous tests held frustratingly little information about which—if any—subject was experimented on. Jeffrey figured there *had* to be a subject; running the machine without transporting someone or something just didn't make sense.

The pages displayed on his laptop screen were not especially helpful. He had made *some* progress deciphering the coded results the machine recorded. Digging through the monitoring station in the sub-basement of the house had provided a few more details on each experiment, even though it was most likely what the original programmer would have considered common knowledge.

The output gave the date, time, and duration of each experiment. The remaining data listed was primarily focused on the signal coming from the two reaction chambers and the frequency of the output beam that would presumably interact with the subject being transported. Earlier, he had pulled up the schematics and found that the output antenna was able to be angled and adjusted to aim it at the subject of the experiment. Someone had angled it to face the ceiling, which did not seem to be standard procedure. As far as he could tell, the antenna was meant to be angled parallel to the ground. Behind the output antenna, there were scuff marks on the floor which seemed to coincide with the "subject chair" that was listed on the schematics. McDougall had not been interested in this revelation, but Jeffrey found it intriguing.

McDougall, in their private conversations, had often wondered why the man in the bed upstairs had been involved at all. Jeffrey insisted that it was most likely an accident, that the man who lived in the house had no idea the machine was there and almost certainly did not experiment on himself. McDougall was skeptical:

"How do you explain the machine starting up and running the experiment, then?" he had demanded earlier that day.

Jeffrey did not have an explanation, and he told McDougall as much. The men settled into an angry silence, both staring at the readouts.

The only explanation Jeffrey could come up with was that the machine was under outside influence. In the snarls of wires, he was almost positive there was some kind of remote line that linked the machine to a console in another location. Hell, they were able to interface with the console, so why wouldn't someone else be able to?

The puzzle was maddening. He took a deep breath and held it for a moment, finally releasing it in a rush. He turned back to his laptop and continued digging.

CHAPTER 38

We ended up at a hole in the wall called Alex's Drive Inn. Despite the dive nature, it was far from being hidden away; it was right on one of the main roads through McHenry. The dingy but moderately sized building sat on Route 120 and was infamous for its owner, who was a crabby, bearded man who never quite made you feel like you were a "valued customer." It was kind of like Dick's Last Resort but without the back-handed charm or the Vegas tourism to boost it.

Walking in, we were greeted by line-management corrals and the owner behind the counter. We stood against the windows for a moment, looking at the ancient push-letter boards displaying the menu. Joseph and Leigh studied the yellowing letters, deciding what they were going to get. I wasn't hungry, but decided I should at least try to choke down some food. The owner did his best to look like he didn't care we were there, but you got the vague sense that he just wanted us to order our shit and get away from his counter.

We had left the house shortly after my breakdown. I had been able to pull myself together, but Joseph and Leigh had still seemed worried. I had told them that the stress of being forced here like this and not knowing what to do to fix it was messing with my head. In reality, I had been struggling not to just give up and resign myself to relive my teens, twenties, and on into my thirties. Joseph had been the one who suggested we leave the house and go somewhere to talk, away from the looming shadow of the machine. Leigh had been quick to agree. I had pulled myself off the floor and given the machine another look, silently cursing it. Without a word, I had turned to leave the sub-basement. Wallowing wasn't going to help.

We had made the drive back to McHenry, all piling into my red Pontiac. We had left Joseph's Corolla and Leigh's Taurus parked on the street south of the house. We had figured it would be a good idea to move the cars so we didn't draw attention, considering how run down the building was. Plus, the resident was pretty much a recluse, judging by the state of his house, so cars in front of the house or parked in the gravel driveway wouldn't have made sense to the neighbors.

I looked over at my brother and my future girlfriend, wondering if they were ready to order. I just wanted to sit down and relax for a few minutes. Both of them were still studying the menu, so I moved past them and walked to the counter. I ordered a gyro with fries and a drink, adding a cup of cheese to the fries. The owner took my order in his usual gruff manner, punching it into an old cash register. I pulled out my wallet and paid the man, making note of how much cash I still had to work with.

It wasn't much, but I hoped I would be out of this before my cash ran out.

I moved down the counter and grabbed my Coke from the other guy working back there. I walked to the dining room and sat in a booth near the pickup window, tossing my backpack against the half wall that the booth was built against. I felt the tension of the last few hours settle in my shoulders and neck, and I stretched them, trying to work out the knot that I knew was forming between my shoulder blades.

I took a sip of Coke, closed my eyes, and sighed.

We had gotten some useful information from the machine. Joseph had been able to recognize the programming language, even though it was an outdated version. After a few minutes of poking, he had been able to pull up the menu listing the current test. Most of it was made up of graphs that didn't really mean anything to us. It looked like technical readouts, focusing on power levels and beam frequencies. We had found out that the machine had been running—and drawing a colossal amount of power—since what had been labeled the "genesis" of the experiment.

I pulled the notebook out of my backpack and turned to the page where I'd started taking notes.

All of the other tests, or simulations or whatever, had dates, times, and durations attached to them. They all had output readings, too. There was, however, one entry before the current simulation that just looked like electronic gibberish. I decided to ignore it for the time being and focused on the current simulation.

The simulation that was running now didn't have a date attached; it just had the time it began, the steadily climbing duration, and the power levels of the output antenna and reaction chambers. I figured the reaction chambers had to be where the ability to travel through time came from. They were never defined in the notes on the machine, so what they contained was either meant to be common knowledge or was secret enough that whoever created the machine didn't want it getting out. Whatever was in them was being powered by the huge bundles of power cables fed through the basement floor.

For a brief moment, I'd considered rummaging around the garage, finding an ax or hedge clippers, and ferociously attacking the power lines to shut the damn thing down by force—until I realized just how stupid that would be. I didn't really feel like taking that much electricity across the heart.

Plus, for all I knew, losing power wouldn't just yank me back to the present; it could trap me here at best ... and completely destroy my consciousness at worst. I didn't really want to test any of those outcomes.

I flipped through the pages of my notebook, looking over the hastily scribbled text, wondering if anything in my notes would make a difference. Everything I'd written down was more about the machine rather than how to work it.

Leigh and Joseph had finished ordering and made their way to the table I'd staked out. Leigh slid into the opposite side of the booth, and Joseph grabbed a chair from one of the nearby tables. They both sat quietly, looking at me like I was a weird combination of a bomb about to go off and a fragile sculpture made of delicate crystal.

As much as I cared about them, I ignored their hesitant looks.

I flipped the notebook closed and brought my head down to rest on it. I took a deep breath and let it out. A bell rang, and I looked over at the pickup window. The guy who had dropped off my food was already moving back to the grill, leaving my meal standing on the cracked linoleum countertop.

Pretty typical of this joint.

I got up and grabbed my food. The smell of the gyro suddenly made me realize just how hungry I actually was. I brought my food back to the booth and slid in. I shoved my notebook back in my bag and waited a moment for the other two to get their food.

The bell rang again, and two more meals appeared on the counter. They both got up and grabbed their food. We dug in, eating in silence. No one seemed to know what to say.

I kept thinking back to the results and readings. We hadn't looked through every one of them, and we hadn't gone back too far, but I'd scribbled down a few of them, just for reference. Something seemed a little off about them. I couldn't put my finger on it, but there was something there.

I pushed the basket holding the partial gyro to the side and pulled the notebook back out. I flipped through the pages, looking for the one I had scribbled the results on. After a moment, I found the page and looked over the notes.

I wasn't really sure what I was looking for. I scanned over the familiar letters and numbers but still wondered at their arrangement. There was something about the last phrase that made me wonder.

It was always the same: JBAUT.

'*Jbaut,*' I wondered, rubbing my hand over my chin, '*is it a name? Some kind of code? I don't think there's any explanation in the menus of the machine; at least, not anything Joseph could find. Even when he pulled up the signature for the OS, all he found was the generic ADMIN label. It's almost like whoever wrote this doesn't want anyone to know who they are.*' I paused my thinking for a moment, letting that thought sink in. '*Why wouldn't they want anyone to know who they were? If I was someone who built a machine to travel through time, I'd try to show it off to anyone who would listen. Why is this person working so hard to keep things a secret?*'

I flipped through a few more pages of the notebook but didn't find any answers. I closed the notebook and pushed it back into my bag. I pulled my gyro back toward me and kept eating.

A few minutes later, all three of us were done with our meals. We sat at the table, still quiet. I broke the silence:

"When I was taking notes, there was something I noticed about the tests that were being run. I still can't put my finger on it, but I know there's something there. There's a series of characters that comes at the end of each test: JBAUT. What it stands for? I have no idea."

"I noticed that, too," Joseph said, "It doesn't seem like it would be part of the programming language. Nothing I know of would use a phrase like that."

"Even with how janky the machine is, you said the programming language is based on DOS, right? Just a simple command line?"

"I mean," Joseph started, "it is based on DOS, but there's elements of C++, Java, Perl, and even Python. To interface with the databases, there's script in SQL and standard HTML. The whole thing is kludged together behind an 'antique'"—he made air quotes around the word—"user interface. It isn't really antique, though; it's been programmed to look like it's still using software from the eighties. It's, like, a late-nineties, early two-thousands UI hiding behind a retro interface."

'*Now that's interesting*,' I thought. '*Why would they hide how modern the interface is? What's the point?*'

Leigh pulled the notebook across the table and began looking at the results I'd written down. She furrowed her brow, comparing the different lines of text.

"What if," she started but stopped herself, making a *hmm* noise. She pulled a pen out of her purse and began to write underneath each result. I craned my neck to look at what she was writing.

She began adding slashes to the numbers, breaking them apart into what looked like dates. It made sense, but it didn't point to any new information, as far as I could tell. She clicked her pen closed and returned it to her purse, unable to find any new information from the slashes she placed between the characters. The mystery of the all-caps JBAUT hung in the air around the table.

I flipped the notebook closed and shoved it back in my backpack.

"What do we do now?"

I was met with shaking heads and blank stares.

CHAPTER 39

The light hurt Joseph's eyes.

No, it did not just hurt.

It was excruciating.

He had never felt this kind of pain before. He had the occasional headache, but this was something completely different. He was nauseated, barely even able to sip at the glass of water Leona placed by the bed. He was barely able to lie there, damp towel over his eyes, without feeling as though a knife was slicing into his brain, cleaving out parts of it and grinding them to mush.

He normally would have logged in to work remotely, spending his days whittling away at the clunky, ineffective, drag-and-drop module his company used to create the back-end systems for insurance processing. Occasionally, if he was lucky, he would get to work on the front end, using more of his coding skills.

He might not have been upset about missing work, but he would have much rather have taken the day off for a more enjoyable purpose. His bosses were idiots, and they constantly tried to push their mistakes off on their subordinates. Joseph was only a few days away from throwing in the towel.

He groaned and rolled over, burying his face in his pillow. Even the act of thinking about his job increased the pain behind his eyes. He moved slowly, pulling the damp washcloth out from under his head and draping it across the back of his neck. He let his hand drop to the pillow next to him—even that small amount of movement left him exhausted. The simple act of rolling over made his head swim, and he felt a new wave of nausea wash over him. He willed it away—he got the distinct feeling that moving to the bathroom to be sick might actually kill him.

He groaned again, gently rubbing his right temple, which was the newest place he felt his head splitting open. The knife in his brain twisted more, gouging another piece of grey matter from its natural habitat. He could almost picture this piece of his brain being placed under the heavy, swinging meat tenderizer that must have been inside his skull, swung around by a pissed-off butcher who was only meant to inflict pain on his victims.

Leona cracked the bedroom door open, poking her head in to look at her fiancé groaning into his pillow.

"Joseph," she whispered, knowing the sound would be like a razorblade to his eardrums, "how are you feeling?"

Joseph didn't answer. He just repositioned himself on the bed and buried his face further into the pillows. It wasn't that he didn't want to answer—he just couldn't. Leona backed out of the room, closing the door softly behind her.

Somewhere in his pain-wracked mind, Joseph wondered why his older brother's name kept popping into his head. There were no other thoughts that went along with it, just the vague sensation that he was remembering something from long ago that had to do with his brother. Under other circumstances, he might try harder to figure out why his brother's name kept moving to the forefront of his mind.

Right now, he just wanted the pain to stop.

He heard the door open again and heard Leona move gently across the floor toward the bed. He felt her sit down and pull the washcloth off his neck. A moment later, he felt a comforting cool sensation across his neck; Leona had brought a fresh washcloth from the bathroom and replaced the drying, lukewarm rag that had been on his neck before.

He groaned a weak "thank you" before pulling another pillow over his head. The small amount of light spilling in through the crack in the door was enough to send another laser beam of pain through his brain.

Leona got up and moved carefully back to the door of the bedroom, stopping only for a moment to cast a worried glance back at Joseph. She had the distinct feeling that this was no ordinary migraine.

She wasn't sure how, but she knew something was wrong.

CHAPTER 40

'*There's something different about this migraine,*' Leigh thought.

She had suffered through many migraines in her life, but this one was a monster. She had managed to power through Sunday; her job had helped keep her mind off the splitting pain in her head. When the headache hadn't gone away the following day, she had resigned herself to pushing through another bad day. It wasn't common for her to have a two-dayer, but it wasn't unheard of either.

She was more worried about her boyfriend, though. Normally, they spoke on the phone at least a few times a day, although it was less when she was working. The last couple of days, though, she hadn't been able to get a hold of him.

'*I know he's a grown man,*' she thought, '*but something feels off. He doesn't usually go this long without getting in touch. I think I'm going to stop at his house after work today and make sure he's okay.*' She wasn't completely sure it would be necessary to head to his house, but she wanted to make sure everything was okay. Her gut told her to call off of work entirely, but she knew there was probably a perfectly logical reason she hadn't heard from him. Plus, she had used a fair amount of PTO already and probably shouldn't use the rest, especially when all she had was a vague gut feeling.

As she went about her day, she kept thinking about him—for some reason, his name kept popping into her thoughts. While it wasn't uncommon for her thoughts to drift during the day, these thoughts seemed different. They were more like memories than intrusive thoughts. The weirdest thing was that his brother's name kept appearing, too. It was almost as if she were remembering a time when the three of them were together ...

... but that hadn't happened. She'd never hung out with just the two of them; they had always gathered at his parents' house as a family. Even when they hosted a game night, Leona, Joseph's fiancée, had come along.

She kept trying to brush the feeling off but found it harder and harder to do so. She kept getting the feeling that something was different. Wrong. What it was, exactly, was harder to pin down, but she had a strong feeling it had to do with both Joseph and his brother.

During her lunch, she went to the tech lounge and pulled out her phone. She tried her boyfriend first, but the phone just rang until his voicemail picked up. She left another voicemail and hung up.

Tapping her fingers on the table, she tried to decide if it was worth reaching out to Joseph. Chances were he didn't know anything, but it might be worth a shot. She pulled up her messaging app and brought up his contact. She tapped a message to him and set her phone to the side, waiting for a reply.

The pain in her head made her nauseated, but she tried to choke down some food. She was only able to stomach a little of it, but she also drank some water, which helped ease the pain—but only by a notch. She picked up her phone and brought the messaging app back up, blinking her eyes several times to help them focus through the pain.

There was no reply from Joseph.

Probably not a big deal—he didn't usually answer in the family group message, either. He probably wasn't paying attention to his phone.

She decided to try Leona. Usually, Leona was much more attentive to the family group message—and messages in general. She tapped out a message to Leona:

Hey Leona, is Joseph around?

It took a brief moment, but Leona's picture popped up, indicating she was typing a response.

Leona: He is, but he's got a terrible migraine. I don't think he can talk right now. Why, what's up?

Leigh: That's weird. I have a bad migraine today, too. I just can't get a hold of his brother, and I was wondering if he heard from him lately.

Leona: I don't think so. He's been dealing with this migraine for the last day or so and hasn't really talked to anyone.

Leigh: Okay, thanks. Is Joseph okay, though? I had this bad feeling that something was going on with both him and his brother.

Leona: I mean, aside from the migraine, I think everything is okay.

Leigh: Okay. Sorry to bother you with all the questions. It's almost like I'm remembering things that haven't happened, and Joseph is part of it. If you talk to him

later, can you see if he, I don't know, has something like that going on? I know it's a weird thing to ask.

Leona: That is a little weird, but I'll ask him. I don't know when he'll be able to talk. He's pretty much buried his head in the pillows and has the lights off in the bedroom.

Leigh: Well, I hope he feels better. Migraines are the worst!

Leona: Thank you! Yeah, they really are!

Leigh: I'll talk to you later on. Have a good day!

Leona: You too!

Leigh closed the messaging app, more puzzled and frustrated than before. Leona didn't have the answers Leigh was looking for; even asking Joseph about his brother was a long shot. With his migraine, it was pretty much impossible. It sounded like his was really bad. It almost sounded like it was similar to hers.

Leigh decided she would get through the rest of the day as best she could and head over to her boyfriend's house after work. She had keys, so she would definitely be able to get in and see what was going on with him. She nodded, cementing her decision in her mind. She glanced up at the clock and, with a start, realized she was due back in the ER. She made her way out of the tech lounge and back toward the emergency room.

CHAPTER 41

'*This is fucking stupid*,' Javier thought, leaning back in the seat of the rental car. The van he had driven to the site from the airport had been appropriated by McDougall and Jeffrey, leaving Javier to figure out his own rental situation.

Fortunately, the Collective provided him with whatever funds he needed. It was nice to have a bottomless slush fund.

He had been driving around for the better part of the day, checking various banks in the area for the safe deposit box Bureat had stored his research in. Javier had been largely unsuccessful, mostly because every bank had the same response: "Sorry, sir, we're not able to give out that information." He had almost gotten into a fight with the last teller he had spoken to and had been escorted out of the bank by an overweight, red-faced security guard.

He was going to need to try another avenue. He pulled into the parking lot of the next bank on his list and reached into the back seat for his laptop. Maybe, if the security was weak enough, he could slip in through the firewall and find the safe deposit records. He powered the machine on and tapped the F12 key. A bootloader screen appeared, listing the typical

Windows partition. Javier tapped the down arrow and highlighted what appeared to be empty space. He tapped Enter and was prompted for a password. Pulling out his phone, he opened up the hidden administrator app and found the digital key he was looking for. He tapped the code, and the hidden partition booted. He closed his phone down and shoved it back in his pocket.

When the computer loaded, he pulled up the menu and selected a vicious-looking icon. The picture of a stylized, growling wolf glowed on the screen before opening to a web browser. The program aggressively found the Wi-Fi for the bank and connected. A status bar appeared in the browser, showing the progress of the brute-force cracker. As the program spammed passwords and passphrases to the Wi-Fi network, the status bar slowly reached the end. A moment later, a message appeared that acknowledged that the password had been accepted.

Javier pulled up a second program, this one with the icon similar to Moses crossing the Red Sea, but with a firewall rather than water. This program began its work, and Javier leaned back in his seat again. Getting through a bank's firewall could take some time. He closed his eyes, waiting for the soft *ding* that would tell him the program had finished its work.

He let his thoughts float up above his head and began to mentally organize them. As soon as he got through the bank firewall, he would need to determine whether or not there was a safe deposit box in Bureat's name. Realistically, there wouldn't be; Bureat couldn't be stupid enough to store his research under his own name, could he? Unfortunately, Bureat had no known aliases, which would make finding his research that much harder. If he had placed his research under an alias, Javier wasn't entirely sure how he would go about finding it.

'*If it comes to that,*' he thought, '*I'll probably have to research every name that's got a safe deposit box. That'll take for-fucking-ever.*' He let out an exasperated sigh.

The computer let out a soft *ding*, and a new window popped up on the screen. The background had the logo for the bank on it and had a series of icons on the left-hand side.

'*About time*,' Javier thought, sitting up straighter in his seat. He opened the bank's internal system, pausing for a moment to look over the various headings in the menu. He found the heading marked SAFE DEPOSIT REGISTRY and opened it. A box popped up, requesting a password. He moved his cursor to the list of programs on his own desktop and found the password cracker he had used in previous jobs. He opened the program, selected the appropriate window, and let the cracker do its work.

A few moments later, the program filled in the username and password and opened the registry. He pulled up the listing of customer names and started to sift through the results. He tried using the FIND function on the browser, but—because it was supposed to be "secure"—the action was blocked. He hung his head, grumbling a few choice words, and resigned himself to looking through the names manually.

From what his boss had told him, the safe deposit box would have been registered sometime between the destruction of the original lab and Bureat's death. That left about a twenty-year window for Javier to sort through. He was fortunately able to sort the safe deposit list by activation date and waited a moment while the list updated.

When the list was sorted by date, he found he was looking at safe deposit boxes that had been registered back in the 1930s—nearly ninety years ago.

Ancient history.

There was no way he would need to look through those for his assignment. Plus, most of the ones that had been registered that long ago were closed and reassigned. He needed to focus on boxes that were still in use today. Unfortunately, the list didn't have an open/closed filter, which was annoying.

He started to scroll down the list, slowing down as he

approached the 1980s. It was unlikely that Bureat would have registered the box in that decade, but he figured it was better to start earlier so he didn't miss anything.

He scrolled slowly through the names, glancing over them, even if he didn't read them completely. He skimmed through the list for the next few minutes, finally ending up in the early 2010s, about five years after Bureat's death.

No luck.

'*Dammit*,' he thought, backing out of the system. He clicked on another icon on his desktop, allowing the program to run and cover his tracks. '*Not registered at this bank. I guess I'll have to head back to all the other ones I've already visited and crack into their systems. This is going to take all day.*

'*What's in this fucking box, anyway? Files? It can't be money—my boss is loaded. It better be some Holy Grail of how this machine works, especially if I'm going to run all over creation finding this thing.*'

Javier looked at the clock in the center console of the late-model car he was driving, noting that it was already early afternoon. He cursed under his breath, annoyed that his employer would expect him to wander all over creation to track down an as-of-yet-unconfirmed safe deposit box.

But the man paid his bills, plus a hefty salary on top of it, so Javier couldn't complain too much. Plus, he didn't exactly feel like an ass-chewing for failing to exhaust all possibilities. When he was in charge, though ...

He closed the laptop and set it on the seat next to him.

If he was going to be driving all over the town, he might as well grab a bite to eat. Slush funds were good for more than just rental vehicles.

He put the car in gear and pulled out of the bank parking lot.

CHAPTER 42

Javier pulled into a roadside restaurant called Happy Jacks about ten minutes later. The GPS unit on his phone directed him to the building boasting hot air fries, deli-style sandwiches, and ice cream year-round. He parked the vehicle and pulled a facemask out of the bag he'd set on the front seat. As much as he hated wearing them, he didn't need to draw attention to himself; the more people who forgot he was around, the better.

He made his way inside, noting that the proprietor had a huge affinity for Coca-Cola products.

A *huge* affinity.

Every decoration in the restaurant was some kind of Coke memorabilia. An antique Coke machine sat against the wall near the counter where orders were taken. Signs hung on every wall bearing various incarnations of the Coke logo. There was even a Coke-branded shirt from the Olympics in a glass shadow box. Javier looked around in awe. He made his way past the ice cream counter near the entrance, still looking around at all the memorabilia. Just about every square inch of the wood-paneled walls was covered in signs, artwork, and

Coke bottles full of ancient soda.

'*Jesus*,' he thought, '*someone really has a passion for Coke products. To each their own, I guess, but Christ. I guess it is kind of cool to see all the vintage stuff, though*.' He smiled—a small one, but a smile all the same—under his mask and made his way to the counter. He looked up at the old push-letter menu, considering his options.

After a moment of looking, he moved forward and put his order in with the high-school-aged girl behind the counter. She rang him up, and he passed a bill to her. As she made change, he pulled out his phone and checked for any messages. He had updated his employer on his failure at the first bank, and he was interested to see if he had anything to say about it.

The phone didn't show any new messages. He clicked the lock button and shoved it back in his pocket. The girl held out his change, along with his receipt showing which number would get him his food. He thanked her and made his way to one of the tables that was available for indoor dining.

He sat near a window on the south side of the restaurant, pushing the bag holding his laptop into the booth next to him. As he waited for his food, he glanced out the window and saw a sign posted on the garage out back: "Jack doesn't discriminate! Enjoy a Pepsi!" He chuckled and turned his attention back to the mission he was on.

He had only cracked one bank's security so far. He needed to make a list of all the banks in the area, especially the ones that had been in operation for at least the last thirty years. Cracking the security and checking the safe deposit register of banks that had been built more recently wouldn't get him very far. He pulled the laptop out of the bag and powered it on.

A voice came over the loudspeaker: "Number 27!"

Javier pulled the receipt out of his pocket and checked the number. He was number 28, so he still had a few moments before they would call him to get his food. He booted the normal Windows partition of the laptop; the hidden partition was solely for the illicit—and highly illegal—software his employer had installed. He pulled up his web browser and ran a search for banks in the area.

Unfortunately, he was greeted with a lot of choices.

A few, though, he could cross off right away. Listed in the search results were several ATMs—completely useless for his current assignment. He began clicking through the websites of the remaining banks, looking for safe deposit boxes. He was able to cross a few more off the list, as they did not offer safe deposit boxes as a service.

"Number 28!"

Javier looked up from the computer screen and saw the girl behind the counter, pushing a tray of food in his direction. He closed the laptop and made his way to the counter, thanking the girl again when he took his food. He slid back into his booth, took his mask off, and started working on his food.

He was about halfway through his Italian beef, dripping wet, of course, when his phone rang. He dropped the beef, wiped his mouth with a napkin, and slid the answer button to the right.

"Report."

Javier hadn't looked at the caller ID, but the sharp, no-nonsense voice on the other end made it clear who was calling. His employer never wasted time with niceties.

"I haven't managed to find the safe deposit box yet," Javier said, grimacing at the report of his failure. "I cracked the first bank's system and looked through the records. If the target had a box at that bank, it has to be under an assumed name. I am going to exhaust all other possibilities at the other banks in the area before I consider the next steps."

He paused but continued before the voice on the other end could pick up the conversation: "Does the subject have any aliases you're aware of? It would make hunting down the box easier if I knew what name he might have put it under."

There was a beat of silence on the other end of the line. Javier waited, wondering just how pissed he had made his boss. He knew his boss didn't appreciate being asked questions—powerful men tended to ask questions, not answer them. Javier had worked for the Collective long enough to know to give the man on the other end of the phone a moment; inexperienced operatives would apologize and wonder if they could repair the "damage" they had caused by asking questions. Javier let the silence stretch, knowing the man on the other end of the phone would eventually speak.

"He has no known aliases," the voice said, clearly annoyed with having to answer the question. "I expect better news the next time you report in."

He cut the line.

Javier grimaced and put the phone back on the table. He knew he was pushing his luck. He could get away with treating Jeffrey and McDougall like that—they were both too stupid and weak to do anything about it. His boss, on the other hand, could make his life a living hell.

Hell, he could probably just have Javier disappear under mysterious circumstances. Javier would prefer that not happen. He didn't feel like ending up in a shallow hole in some Jersey backwater.

He picked his beef back up, mulling over his next moves. He knew he would have to finish his list of banks and crack the security remotely at each. Fortunately, his budding list only contained a few institutions. Safe deposit boxes weren't very common in this area. That made things both easier and harder for Javier. It left him with fewer choices, but he still had to find the right bank. Not to mention that he had to figure out how to get at the contents of the box after he found it.

Getting the contents was the part that worried Javier the most. Although he had broken into his fair share of businesses for his boss, he had never broken into and stolen anything from a bank. The security would be much tighter than the average business. Corporate espionage was one thing, but breaking into a bank vault was something else entirely. Undoubtedly, there would be tools at his disposal to make things easier, but he would still have to be the one infiltrating the bank. Infiltration came with risks. If Javier was caught, there was a good chance even his employer wouldn't be able to make everything go away. Javier didn't exactly want to sit in a jail cell while the Collective pulled the strings to get him out.

He finished his sandwich and pulled his laptop back toward him. He continued running searches of the banks in the area, pulling up each one's website to see if safe deposit boxes were offered. He ended up with five banks, in total, that offered safe deposit boxes as an option. Fortunately for him, they were all within a few miles' radius. He would probably be able to get to all of them before the day was done.

He saved his list of banks, along with their addresses, and closed the laptop again. He pulled his mask back on and went up to the counter, ordering another Italian beef, this time with a side of chili cheese fries. He asked for a refill of his Coke, paid his bill, and went back to his seat. He powered up his laptop once more and pulled a cable from his bag. He connected his phone, input the password, and imported his notes to the laptop's hidden partition. That done, he ran a program to wipe his phone's memory, deleting any trace of the notes he had been taking to finish his other assignment.

He opened a .TXT file on his laptop and imported the note, looking over the ideas he had already written down. The plan for the "accident" was still messy, but he thought he might have worked out a way to avoid suspicion. He would still need another operative, and that meant getting the Collective—and his boss—to sign off on it. He was confident they would ultimately give him the green light, but that plan was still on hold. He had to finish his first assignment before they'd bring the other one back to the front burner.

Still, it never hurt to be prepared. Not to mention, he enjoyed thinking through how he was going to complete his next mission. He set himself to work on his plans, waiting for the staff to call him with his next order. He organized his thoughts, laying out what he and the other operative would do, what their respective roles would be. The more he worked on it, the cleaner the "accident" got. There was one part he wasn't very excited about, but it would sell his story, helping him avoid most of the unpleasant questions he was anticipating. Sometimes, a little pain was involved in selling a story. As much as he hated parts of the training he had received from the Collective, it proved useful in a number of different situations.

Javier began to finalize his plans when the voice came over the loudspeaker again, calling him to the counter to collect his food. He closed his laptop and went back to the counter, thanking the girl one more time for his food. He went back to his table and started working through his sandwich and fries.

CHAPTER 43

McDougall set the phone down and flopped backward on the bed. It had been an incredibly long couple of days. Exciting, sure, but mostly exhausting for the middle-aged man.

It was especially exhausting when his subordinates were idiots.

Jeffrey had stayed at the site, still harping on about how to successfully terminate the experiment so they could work on dismantling the machine. If he had his way, he would pussyfoot around just pulling the plug until the last possible moment. McDougall, on the other hand, would happily cut the wires, terminate the experiment, and begin working on taking the machine apart so they could remove it from the sub-basement.

'*Actually,*' he thought, '*we could just excavate the backyard of the house. If the subject doesn't survive the test when we pull the plug, there won't be anyone to complain about us tearing up the yard and demolishing a wall to get this thing out. Hell, we could probably get it out all in one piece if we could do that.*'

McDougall's bosses were split, however. Some of the people on the board agreed with him: The team should pull the plug and be done with it. Others were in agreement with Jeffrey that they should let the experiment run its course. It made sense to an extent. They didn't know what would happen at the end of the experiment. The question of how the experiment concluded was valid, but it was exhausting from an administrative standpoint.

As much as he and Jeffrey disagreed, at least Jeffrey was present—Javier had largely disappeared. He knew it didn't really matter—Javier was just a glorified security guard who kind of knew how to run a computer. Honestly, McDougall could do without the smartass comments from the brooding security guard. He had already decided to terminate Javier's employment after this situation was resolved. The board might disagree, but he was going to ram his recommendation through this time. Last time, he almost had a majority. One too many board members voted to keep the security position, amending his proposal to add the monitor job so they wouldn't need to "eliminate the position."

What a load of crap.

McDougall was still sore about it, even though it had happened two years ago. Then again, McDougall was crabby about a lot of things right now.

Really, McDougall just wanted to get out of this shithole town. He was sick of staying in a two-star hotel next to a highway. Sure, it was quiet enough at night, but he still heard the idiots in the other rooms. For all he knew, hookers were using this dump to turn tricks. It made his own apartment seem like a palace. He was tired of having to put up with everyone's shit, tired of having to manage all the morons he had been assigned. It almost felt malicious, as if the board was intentionally punishing him.

Him, of all people!

Sure, he didn't work nearly as hard as he used to; when the Project started losing funding, he felt his motivation diminish. The pay cuts hadn't helped matters. Even though he had lost a lot of his motivation, he was still the best employee—hell, the best manager!—the Project had. There was no reason to saddle him with so many inferior subordinates.

As unfair as it was, McDougall would persist. He would put up with all the foolish questions, all the sarcastic responses, all the snide looks and under-the-breath comments. Greatness always comes with envy from lesser people. Sadly, McDougall was used to the envy of his subordinates. He would shoulder that weight, like he always did.

He picked up his phone and dialed Javier's number again. The phone rang, but he had no real hope the security man would answer. As it clicked over to voicemail, McDougall rolled his eyes and left another message, demanding Javier get in touch and return to the site the next morning. He hung up and dropped the phone back on the bed.

He needed some air. He needed some time to consider his options. He grabbed his phone and his room key and made his way out to the parking lot, glancing around for a sidewalk or path he could take that didn't involve walking on the side of a highway. Even though it wasn't fully dark yet, he still didn't feel like wandering the side of the road. He pulled out his phone and pulled up his map, noting that there was a park not far from the hotel.

Hopefully, it would be quiet. He was sure the fresh air would do him good.

He set out, walking for a few minutes down Route 31 toward Park Place. He turned left and walked down the dimly lit street, making his way past the McDonald's and to a gravel parking lot. There, he found some tennis courts, with a couple still playing under the lights. It was early evening, so he wasn't surprised to see a few people out and about. He made his way past the tennis courts, moving slowly across a gravel footpath that snaked its way through the park. The night air was much fresher than the filth he had been breathing in the hotel, and it helped clear his head immensely.

What he really needed to do was convince the board that they didn't need to see the experiment through to the conclusion.

'What those asshats don't see is that we'll be running our own experiments. We don't need to see how this one concludes because we'll be able to control the experiments and see them from start to finish. Why they think they need to see this one end is beyond me. I guess that's what you get when you deal with short-sighted morons. They really ought to let me be the director. I'd whip this Project back into shape.'

He continued his trek around the baseball fields, still thinking about how he was going to convince the board. He came to a junction and took a right, moving along the eastern edge of the field. The path he was on brought him toward a wooded path that climbed a hill. He made his way toward it, figuring the exercise would help clear his head, just like the fresh air did.

He failed to notice the dark figure lurking near the wooded area. The shadow was standing near the left side of the path, blending in with the early evening shadows the trees cast.

McDougall kept his eyes down, slightly unfocused as he wandered the path. The figure took note and moved slowly along the tree line, following the man up the hill. McDougall made it about halfway up the hill before he had to stop, bending over and putting his hands on his knees. He was breathing heavily and swearing under his breath about how the "fucking hill was too goddamn steep" for him to keep going. The dark, hooded figure shook its head. As McDougall turned, the figure melted backward, moving further into the shadows. The figure watched as McDougall passed by, making his way back toward the seedy hotel he was staying at.

McDougall followed the gravel path back the way he had come. The shadows were starting to grow longer, and he wasn't exactly excited by the thought of being out after dark. He knew next to nothing about this town, but he wasn't going to take any chances.

The dark shape he had passed stepped out of the wooded area and pulled its hood further over its head. It pulled out a phone, tapped a message, and closed the phone back down. It made its way up the hill, disappearing at the top.

CHAPTER 44

Jeffrey stood in the doorway, looking at the man who was stuck in the middle of the experiment. The IV drip was still running, and the soft beep of the heart rate monitor was audible in the background. The man's breathing was steady, and his face looked serene.

There was no outward sign that he was being torn between two worlds, as the PET, MRI, and CT scans all confirmed. His mind was under an unprecedented amount of stress. He was essentially powering two bodies with the same mind, although one body was essentially comatose.

His dog was lying on the bed, the creature's head resting on the man's chest. The animal's sad eyes looked at Jeffrey, almost begging for answers.

Jeffrey, for the first time in a long time, had none to give.

In the beginning, the bedroom at the back of the house had been abuzz with activity. Now, it had largely become a sanctuary: the shades had been drawn, and the overhead light remained off. The room was lit by the soft glow of the monitors and equipment attached to the man in the bed.

The technicians came and went, never remaining in the

room for more than a few moments. Even as they carried out their tasks, they spoke in hushed tones, as if they were afraid of waking the man up.

Word had spread about his "waking" incident. The horrible noise he made had scared some of the younger, more impressionable technicians. The older, more experienced ones were unnerved, too. Jeffrey hadn't witnessed the "waking," but it was fascinating for him. Did it mean there was the possibility of communication with a subject who is under the influence of the machine? How would he go about initiating that contact?

'*This is why those morons need to complete the experiment,*' he thought, shaking his head. '*Pulling the plug and letting the man either wake up or die isn't the answer. We need to know about all aspects of this thing, not just the convenient ones. There will be plenty of time to detain the subject, extract the machine, and get it back to the lab. We don't need to rush this like McDougall wants. He's just anxious to climb the ladder; he doesn't actually care about the science.*'

Jeffrey was getting more and more frustrated with his boss' constant complaining about letting the experiment run. Yes, he wanted the experiment to end so they were able to move the machine out of the sub-basement, but he didn't want to do it at the expense of valuable information. He had no idea what would happen during the course of the experiment. For all he knew, there could be invaluable insight into the workings of the machine—and even time travel itself!

If they pulled the plug now, there was no way to ensure that they could replicate the experiment. Just because there was a working prototype didn't mean they could reproduce the results. It happened in labs all over the world: one group would have a huge breakthrough, and the next group was unable to satisfy the requirements to repeat it. Without knowing all the steps, all the variables, they would never be able to repeat the process.

Time travel would be lost to them.

Jeffrey caught movement out of the corner of his eye. He snapped his vision into focus and stared at the man in the bed. The movement hadn't come from him, though; the dog was adjusting himself to push in closer to his master.

Jeffrey let out a breath he hadn't realized he was holding. This whole thing was giving him anxiety.

He turned to leave the room but stopped when he heard the dog whimper. He looked back at the bed, and the creature was looking at him with his sad, brown eyes. Moving before he realized he was doing it, Jeffrey walked across the room, dodging the tangle of wires strung from the various machines to the man in the bed. He knelt down, putting him at eye level with the dog, and petted the poor creature.

"It's alright, boy," he said softly. "We're trying to figure out what's going on with your master."

The dog looked at him, whimpering slightly again. He looked away from Jeffrey and back to his owner. Jeffrey glanced at the man, noting that he still looked serene, as if he were just sleeping peacefully.

"What is it, boy?"

The dog woofed lightly, nudging his owner with his nose.

Jeffrey didn't believe in such things, but it almost seemed as if the dog was trying to tell him something. The thought of that was laughable; the dog is a barely sentient creature. There was no way it was trying to intelligently communicate with him. Sure, dogs had thoughts, but they were nowhere near coherent enough to think they could be communicated to a human. Even warnings from service dogs were just training masked as thought. Jeffrey was just about to stand up and leave when he heard a sigh come from the man.

The sigh sounded like a word: "help."

Jeffrey shot to his feet, staring at the man. There was no outward sign that he had done more than breathe, but Jeffrey was sure he had heard him say the word "help." The dog whimpered again, pushing his nose into the side of the man's face.

Jeffrey bent to put his ear next to the man's mouth, wondering if he had actually heard what he thought he heard. Suddenly, the man shot upright, baring his teeth. Jeffrey was stunned, completely unable to move. The man reared back and sank his teeth into Jeffrey's neck. The man's teeth gnashed and tore a piece of flesh from Jeffrey's neck, even as Jefferey pulled back. Bewildered, he watched as the man began to chew the flesh, blood oozing from his mouth. Jeffrey's hand shot to his neck as he tried to staunch the bleeding from the vicious, gaping wound. For a moment, he thought he could stop the bleeding; then he saw the spurt of blood from his destroyed jugular splash across the window next to the bed. The dog howled and jumped at Jeffrey, his big paws pushing him fully to the ground. As he began losing consciousness, he became aware the dog was beginning to tear at his stomach and that the man was pulling himself off the bed to follow him to the floor. Within moments, Jeffrey had blacked out; the last thing he felt was the two sets of teeth tearing at his flesh.

Jeffrey yanked his head back from in front of the man with an audible "What the fuck!" With wild eyes, he stared at the man who, as he had been for two days, remained unconscious in the bed. Shaken, Jeffrey collapsed to the floor, leaning against the wall for support, terrified of the vision he had just had.

'*That's impossible,*' Jeffrey thought. '*He's under the influence of the machine downstairs; he's not some kind of zombie. What the hell is the matter with you? How could you hallucinate an attack like that? The stress must be getting to you. Pull yourself together!*'

He leaned over again, placing his ear next to the man's mouth. He stood silently for a moment, listening. The only sounds he heard were the steady beeps of the machines the man was attached to.

He could feel the gentle brush of air against his face from the man's breathing, but he wasn't able to make out any words.

Knitting his brow, he started to straighten up but heard the dog whimper again.

Jeffrey hesitated for a moment and then spoke: "Can you hear me?"

The steady beep of the heart rate monitor quickened. Causing Jeffrey to jump. He glanced over at the machine, noting that the heart rate was a few numbers higher than it had been a moment ago. He bent back down, placing his mouth near the man's ear.

"You can, can't you?"

The man sighed, but Jeffrey caught a faint word: "Yes."

"Holy shit ..."

CHAPTER 45

"What is it, boy?"

Those were the last words I remembered hearing before my vision whited out, Leigh, Joseph, and the booth at Alex's fading to white. It was like I was trapped in a snowstorm—I couldn't see anything, but I could hear a voice reverberating deep in my head. I had no idea what was going on, but I knew it wasn't a voice I'd heard before. It was an odd sensation: the voice sounded both very close and very far away, muffled but resonant. I tried to shake my head or blink my eyes to clear my vision, but I found myself unable to move.

'*Now, what the hell is going on?*' I wondered, '*All these side effects and other random shit that keep happening because of this goddamn machine are getting old.*'

I heard a whimper, one that sounded an awful lot like Mazer.

"Mazer? Is that you, boy?" I said aloud, completely unsure if my voice would reach my poor, neglected dog. As if in response, I felt a wet nudge against my cheek, almost as if he had pushed his nose up against me. "Mazer! I need help! Come on, buddy, I don't know what you can do, but I need help!"

"Can you hear me?"

The voice was back, and it seemed to be addressing me this time, not Mazer. It was more directed, more present.

No way.

I felt my pulse pick up and began to hope—albeit somewhat hesitantly—that someone from the future was trying to make contact. Who that person was, I didn't know. At this point, though, I didn't care. If I could make contact with someone on the outside, maybe I could finally get out of this hell.

"Yes!" I called into the white void. "Help! I don't know what the hell is going on, but I'm trapped here!"

"You can, can't you?"

The voice seemed like it couldn't hear me. '*Fuck,*' I thought, '*if they can't hear me, what the hell am I supposed to do? Is this guy just guessing I can hear him, or does he have some way of telling that I can? This is so goddamn frustrating!*'

"YES!" I shouted, straining my voice and wincing at the crack it made. Then again, as long as this guy heard me and was able to help, I'd be happy to sound like a twelve-year-old.

"Holy shit ..."

'*You're damn right, holy shit,*' I thought, still trying to work out a way to get this man to fully understand me. It seemed like he was only able to pick up a word or two at a time. '*Maybe a full-fledged conversation is out the window, but maybe I can at least make some kind of contact.*'

I took a deep breath: "HELP!"

I waited, but the voice didn't return. I couldn't hear Mazer's whimper or feel his wet nose on my cheek anymore.

Shit.

"HELP!" I shouted again, pushing my voice as loud as it could go.

Next thing I knew, my vision was back, and both Leigh and Joseph were staring at me. I looked back and forth between the two of them and then pitched forward into a coughing fit; the last shout had strained my vocal cords past what they could handle, and I got the familiar tickle in the back of my throat.

My coughing fit subsided, and I reached forward for my drink. A moment later, although my throat still hurt, the tickle was gone. I looked back up at Leigh and Joseph and then around the restaurant. Several people were watching me with strange looks on their faces. The owner was looking through the pick-up window with a mixture of annoyance and concern on his face.

"You alright, kid?" he asked, glancing at the other two teenagers with me. "Did you say you needed help?"

I tried to keep the shock that I had actually spoken aloud off my face but failed.

"No, I'm okay," I said, pushing my hair out of my face, "I'm prone to seizures, and they can sometimes make me say weird things."

The lie came easier this time, and the man behind the pick-up window shrugged and made his way back to the register. The customer at the counter threw a wide-eyed glance toward our booth but seemed to shrug it off and then ordered her food.

I looked back at Leigh and Joseph. They both wore wary looks, partially concerned, partially scared.

"What happened?" I asked in a low voice.

"You looked like you had a seizure, but I don't think that's what it was," Leigh said. "You zoned out and then started muttering things under your breath. I couldn't make out what you said"—she glanced at Joseph, who shrugged and shook his head—"but the last thing we heard was you basically yelled the word 'help.' It seems like that's what snapped you out of it."

"I think," I started to say, looking down at the table, "I think I could hear someone's voice from the future. I don't know how, but I just remember hearing this voice, but it was like a voice inside a snowstorm. My vision went white, and the voice seemed to kind of be coming from everywhere all at once. It started off faint, directionless, but then it got more ...

direct? I guess that's the closest I can describe it. I felt my dog's nose pushing against my cheek, too. It was so real. It had to be something from the future; otherwise, I don't know what else it could be."

"How is that possible?" Joseph asked, his brows knitting in concern and confusion.

I shrugged, pressing my lips into a thin line.

I didn't have any answers for him.

The real question became: what the hell was I supposed to do next? I kept wracking my brain, and I couldn't come up with a plan. It was almost like being in the past was affecting my ability to think like an adult.

'*Am I going to be stuck here, reverted back to being a teenager both mentally and physically? Jesus. I can't let that happen. Come on, think. What are your next steps?*'

I found my mind turning to the science fiction books, movies, and shows I'd watched over the years. Even if it was fictional, maybe it would give me some kind of Hail Mary avenue to try.

I remembered one of the later seasons of the show *Lost*, where Desmond was trapped in a time-travel loop. According to another character, he had to find his constant—someone who existed and knew him in both times.

'*Well, that's out the fucking window,*' I thought, looking at the two people in front of me. '*Both of them know me in both times, and I haven't snapped out of it yet. So much for finding a constant to anchor me.*'

The machine had to be the key. There had to be some way to operate it from this time and shut it down. All experiments had to end, so there had to be some way to shut it down from inside. I mean, if the subject of time travel got stuck and was reliant on someone in their original time, it wouldn't be very effective. Hell, it would essentially be a trap.

"The machine has to be the key to all this," I muttered, still looking down at the chipped surface of the Formica table.

"We're missing something."

Joseph and Leigh nodded, although their eyes appeared to hold some doubts about what I was saying. It was comforting to know that they weren't giving up, even with how hopeless the situation appeared to be.

After a few more minutes, we tossed our garbage and made our way back to the car. I tossed my keys to Joseph and got in the back seat, laying across the bench and putting my arm over my eyes. The time shifts, blackouts—and now white-outs, I guess—and general stress of existing in two times at once was wearing me out. I heard Joseph and Leigh get in and the engine turning over. After that, the darkness of sleep descended on me.

CHAPTER 46

First Midwest Bank sat quietly, bathed only in the light of the streetlights from North Illinois Route 31. The moderately sized, two-story building sat on the corner of Route 31 and Pearl Street, surrounded by asphalt parking lots and well-kept lawns. The main entrance faced Route 31 and was lit by decorative sconces framing the front door, giving it a faux Victorian look. The interior of the bank was dark, save only for the light of a security panel of fluorescents.

The crowd control stanchions stood empty; the lines for the tellers had exited the building long ago. On the wall, an analog clock slowly ticked away the seconds, marking time for no one but itself. The face of the clock read 2:03 a.m., although the face was hard to make out in the dim light of the lobby.

The office doors stood locked, many lit only by the faint, pale yellow glow of the computer monitor's power light, indicating it was in sleep mode until its owner returned the following morning. File cabinets with locking bars stood stoically next to the sleeping computers, almost like they were guardians of forbidden information.

The second floor of the bank held conference rooms and offices for the higher-ups employed there. These, too, were locked and dark. The secrets held in the administrative offices would remain just that: secrets.

The basement was the target.

The basement where the safe deposit boxes were stored.

It had taken hours of research and a number of illegal activities—not to mention a handful of bribes to the right people—but Javier had finally found the safe deposit box his employer had assumed existed.

He was marginally surprised that the safe deposit box wasn't located in the same town as the house, but anyone worth anything knew to separate the lock and the key when it came to hiding information.

Surveillance cameras stood like unblinking eyes on the walls, unmoving and stoically keeping watch over the safe deposit boxes and other parts of the bank. A wave of static crossed the recording, causing the image to flicker slightly, although not enough to cause alarm.

Javier looked up from the soft glow of his laptop and gazed through the passenger side window at the bank. He was parked across the street, sitting in one of the end spaces of the apartment complex that had been constructed a year and a half earlier.

Most of the windows in the complex were dark; there were a few night owls who were burning the midnight oil, but they weren't paying attention to the nondescript black sedan parked in the parking lot.

Javier glanced down at the clock on the dash. 2:18 a.m.

Almost time.

He had done some more digging on the employee register at the bank, looking to see who was employed as the night watchman. More specifically, he had been interested in the hours the night watchman was on duty. According to the employee handbook he had found in one of the servers, the watchman was on duty during the graveyard shift—his time-card showed he typically punched in around 10 p.m. and was off duty when the bank opened at 9 a.m.

Javier had decided that 3 a.m. was the time to make his move on the bank. By that time, the guard should be settled in his office and have his mind on other things. Assuming nothing happened to put him on alert, Javier should be able to make his way into the bank, incapacitate the guard, and find the safe deposit box he was looking for. With the guard out of commission, he should be able to wipe the security feeds and get out before anyone knew he was there.

'*If I have some good luck for once,*' he thought, snorting through his nose. '*This whole operation has been one fuck up after another, so why should I expect this to go smoothly?*'

He looked back at the clock. 2:23.

He still had more time to wait, so he shut his laptop and leaned his seat back. He closed his eyes and began to work through the next part of his plan, mentally tracing the route from his entry point to the guard's office.

From the schematics of the building he had been able to obtain, it looked like the bank was equipped with cameras and door and window sensors. Surprisingly, there was no mention of motion sensors within the bank.

Although he found this odd, it wasn't unheard of. Banks had all manner of different security systems. Perhaps, because of the guard they employed for the graveyard shift, the managers of the bank didn't find it necessary to make use of motion sensors.

Whatever the reason, it made Javier's job just a little easier.

Planning done, Javier switched his thoughts to his next objective. One that was significantly more satisfying to plan. As soon as he got the green light from his employer, he and the second Collective operative would put the plan into action.

If all went well—with both plans, really—he might be able to get out of this town soon and, finally, back to his low-key existence inside the control room at the Project headquarters.

Or, maybe his boss would reassign him to somewhere that wasn't a windowless control room scanning for time-space anomalies that may or may not happen. Maybe somewhere warm. Somewhere with a view. Maybe somewhere away from incompetent middle managers who thought they were more important than everyone else around them.

A guy could dream, anyway.

CHAPTER 47

The security guard was named Bill. A simple name for a simple man, he always said. He sat, as usual, with his wiry, vaguely catlike body coiled behind his desk in one of the back rooms of the bank, partially watching the security feed but mostly watching reruns of *Pretty Little Liars*. He was mid-way through season six and was engrossed in the plot, watching intently as Alison invited the girls to dinner.

Just as she was laying out her argument that Aria was in on the murder of Charlotte, he noticed the surveillance feed flicker. He absently reached a hand out and slapped the side of the monitor. Although the monitor was an up-to-date LCD, hitting it still seemed to do the trick, just like it would have for an old CRT. He turned his attention back to the cell phone propped up against the desktop tower.

Before he let himself get fully enthralled in his show again, Bill glanced at the clock high up on the guardroom wall. 3:06 a.m. He was still in for a long night. The morning crew wouldn't show up until at least 8:45 a.m., so he had at least a few hours to kill.

Fortunately, nothing ever really happened in McHenry.

Now, if he were a guard at a bank in Chicago, or Detroit, that would be another story. Hell, here in McHenry, he didn't even carry a gun.

Bill was scheduled to do rounds at 3:15 a.m., but he decided he would do them early tonight. The sooner he got his obligations out of the way, the sooner he could find out who was really terrorizing the girls. They'd already figured out the whole "who is A?" mystery, but the hits just kept on coming for the girls of Rosewood, PA. That was the real mystery he wanted to solve.

Bill paused the video on his phone and left his radio on its charger. Why in the hell they wanted him to carry one was beyond him: He was the only person even at the bank right now, so carrying a radio was useless. He pushed himself out of the chair and stretched his arms over his head, hearing the vertebrae in his back pop back into place.

Leaving his phone propped up against the computer, he grabbed his nightstick and flashlight from their customary place on the end of the L-shaped desk. He slipped the nightstick into its steel ring on his belt and clicked the flashlight on. The weak beam reminded him that he really needed new batteries.

He shrugged. He could replace the batteries later. This would do for tonight. He opened the door to the guard room and stepped out into the lobby of the bank.

CHAPTER 48

Javier moved a little earlier than he probably should have. The boredom of sitting in the car outside an apartment complex was killing him, so he decided that 3:05 a.m. was as good a time as any. It would take him a moment to gather his gear from the trunk of his car anyway.

He made his way to the trunk of the car and popped it open. Inside, there was a Pelican 1660 equipment case. He popped the clips on the front and side and opened the box. In the box, he had stored a number of different items for various different purposes.

Tonight, stealth was the name of the game, so he pulled out an Under Armour balaclava and a pair of Spyder gloves.

After donning those, he grabbed a duffel bag and unzipped it. From the crate, he took two IMT Vacuum Suction Cups and a Red Devil industrial-grade glass cutter. He put both items into the bag and turned back to the crate. He pulled a heavy-duty 36v Hilti drill with a side handle out of the crate and checked to make sure the massive battery was holding a charge. It was, with the lights on the battery showing a full charge. He put the drill in the bag and then found a set of

Milwaukee carbide drill bits, sliding them into the bag next to the drill.

He found a modified firearm case and popped it open, checking the battery level on the military-grade cracking device. Although Javier was more than capable of hacking a computer, he found it easier to let this little piece of tech do the hard work for him. He closed the case and put it into the duffel bag.

He pulled another case out of the trunk and clicked the latches open. Inside, he found a remote signal monitor specifically tuned to commonly used silent alarm frequencies. He powered the machine on, checking its status. Finding it nominal, he put the machine back in the case and put it in the duffel next to the cracking device.

He found the final firearm case in the trunk and popped it open. Inside, there was a black .380 Walther PPK with a threaded barrel. The silencer, although highly illegal, was in a cutaway next to the pistol. He removed the weapon and locked the slide back. After taking a moment to screw the silencer on and insert the six-round magazine, he thumbed the slide release and heard the comforting *snap* as the weapon chambered the round. He took a moment to pop the magazine back out and insert the "plus-one" round.

Although he didn't anticipate too much trouble, nor did he really feel like killing anyone tonight, seven rounds were better than six.

He slid the silenced pistol into the vertical shoulder holster and snapped the catch closed. He didn't bother filling the empty magazine holsters—there was no way he was going to need 19 rounds for this mission.

The last thing he grabbed was the 20-gauge shotgun loaded with beanbag rounds. Even if he was prepared to kill the security guard, he would really rather not leave a body around; the PPK was more to make himself feel better than for actual use tonight.

He pumped the shotgun and ducked his head into the shoulder strap. He pushed the gun behind his back and grabbed the duffel bag.

Time to go to work.

CHAPTER 49

Javier made his way across the street, grimacing at the shadows he was throwing from the street lights. Fortunately, at 3:09 a.m., there were very few people out. Those that *were* out were in no real condition to notice anything—they were too busy white-knuckling it, trying to keep their car in the correct lane so they didn't get what would probably be yet another DUI.

His target was the drive-up servicing center. After he scouted the bank earlier that day, he found that the only real points of ingress were the tall, plate-glass windows in the drive-up center. The rest of the windows were small, built into white-painted wooden frames.

Much too small for a grown man to fit through.

Well, fit through comfortably, anyway.

He originally thought of cutting one of the panels and opening the window, but with the window sensors, that would never work. From his research, he found that the only way the alarm would go off from the drive-up was through a concussive hit to the window; each of the plate glass windows was equipped with a break sensor, but not a contact sensor.

As he made his way to the drive-up lane, he pulled out the Walther. He took aim at the overhead lights and squeezed the trigger. The muffled *pzzt!* of the weapon sounded full volume in the early morning silence, but no one seemed to take notice. Even the shattering plastic of the light casing failed to draw attention. The lights winked out, and Javier became no more than a darker shadow under the overhang of the drive-up.

He took a moment to pick up the shell casings and slip them into a side pocket of the duffel. Although he had worn gloves when he loaded them, he didn't want to take the chance that some latent DNA would be found on the casings and tie him to the break-in.

He moved to the center window and set the duffel bag down. He pulled the frequency monitor out of its case and pressed the suction cupped back to the window he was about to cut. He punched the "scan" button on the monitor and waited a moment until the display turned green. When it did, he turned his attention back to the duffel bag.

He withdrew the suction cups and glass cutter. He pressed the first cup to the window, pumping the button on top with his thumb. When it finally stopped pumping, he repeated the process with the other cup.

Once both cups were secure, he traced the glass cutter around them, creating a minute break in the glass. He scored the soon-to-be opening again, working his way through the glass so it would come loose without shattering. He scored it a third time, just for good measure, and then put the glass cutter back in his pocket. He grabbed the handholds of the suction cups and jerked the glass backward.

The glass audibly cracked but did not shatter. Javier froze for a moment, staring intently at the frequency monitor, looking for any sign that a silent alarm was being sounded. When the light stayed green, he released his breath and pulled the chunk of glass all the way free.

He initially thought about just dropping it on the pavement, but he figured the shattering sound might still set off the alarm. He glanced around and found a flowerbed not too far away from the windows. He hefted the glass and made his way to the flowerbed, setting the glass down. As he let go of the handles, the glass settled gently into the dirt.

He looked at the glass, surprised that it hadn't shattered, when he got an idea. He would try to replace the glass to mask his escape. Maybe it would work, maybe it wouldn't. At the very least, maybe it would confuse the cops who would inevitably investigate the break-in.

Leaving the glass in the flowerbed, he made his way back to his point of ingress. He popped the portable notification unit out of the side of the sensor and put it in his pocket. He grabbed the duffel bag and shoved it through the hole he cut in the window, sliding it across the counter so it wouldn't fall to the floor as he pulled himself through. Taking note of the sharp edges—leaving blood evidence was a great way to get busted—he hauled himself through the window and into the lobby of the bank.

CHAPTER 50

Crack!

Bill didn't know what it was, but something was wrong.

He was making his way to the stairwell to check on the upstairs offices, but he turned toward the front desk instead. The area behind the counter was dark and still. He made his way deliberately across the lobby, his hand resting on his nightstick, directing the weak beam of the flashlight over the desk.

As he reached the desk, he squinted his eyes against the darkness; the overhead security light was at the far end of the lobby above the doors, and its light didn't reach behind the desk. His flashlight was doing little to pierce the darkness, so he made his way to the locked door at the far end of the teller windows.

He pulled the keyring off his belt and selected the appropriate key. He slid the key into the lock and opened the door. Making his way behind the teller counter, he drew his nightstick, just in case something was actually going to happen.

'*Chances are nothing happens, but, hey, it makes sense to be prepared,*' he thought. '*Besides, who would be breaking into the bank from this side? If anything, someone would just break open the front door.'*

Bill swept the flashlight along the wall, looking for anything out of the ordinary. He moved the light back to the teller counter, shining it underneath each of the stations.

Everything came up empty.

He made his way to the archway that marked the difference between the teller area and the drive-up, shining the light across the plate glass windows.

Until the light stopped.

There was a giant hole in one of the plate glass windows that wasn't there earlier in the night. A hole that looked like it was deliberately cut. Next to the hole, there was the dark rectangular shape of something stuck against the glass.

As Bill swept the light across the drive-up counter, he also saw a black duffel bag sitting in front of one of the microphones used for communicating with the drive-up lanes.

'*Fuck*,' he thought as he drew his nightstick, '*someone actually broke in. This doesn't look like a smash-and-grab; it looks like a pro. Shit. That's not what I need tonight!*'

"Who's there?" he called into the darkness, sweeping his flashlight around the drive-up area. "Come out with your hands up!"

Bill moved forward, slowly making his way to the drive-up teller counter. He nudged the duffel bag with his nightstick but pulled it back quickly. For all he knew, it could be a bomb. The thought of a bomb made him decide to call the police. He reached into his pocket for his cell phone—

—only to remember that it was back in the security office.

'*Dammit*,' he mentally yelled at himself. He turned and started toward the main teller line when he heard the soft sound of footsteps on the carpet. He whipped around and came face-to-face with a masked figure.

CHAPTER 51

Javier eased the door open, thankful for the well-oiled hinges. He moved forward slowly and carefully, shifting his weight smoothly between his feet, staying as quiet as possible.

Even with his footsteps light, the guard still heard him.

"Shit!" the guard yelled, swinging at Javier with the nightstick clutched in his hand. Javier took the blow on his forearm and shoved the guard back. His finger found the trigger of the shotgun, and he squeezed back, applying the four and a half pounds of pressure to discharge the weapon.

The shotgun barked and discharged the beanbag at 1,580 feet per second, the two-ounce projectile hitting the guard square in the stomach, all but lifting him off his feet and throwing him to the ground. The guard's breath left in a rush, and he was left gasping and writhing on the ground. Javier moved forward and stood over the guard, looking down at the man as he rolled back and forth, clutching his stomach.

Javier gripped the barrel of the shotgun and brought the handle down, striking the guard across the left temple, knocking him out. He knelt down and checked the man's pulse. It was elevated but steady. He pulled the gaiter facemask off the guard—why the man was wearing it when he was supposedly alone in the building was beyond him, but Covid paranoia was pretty common among people now—and tossed it to the ground next to him. The guard would be fine, but he was going to wake up sore, out of breath, and with a killer headache.

He made his way back to the counter and grabbed the duffel bag. He swung the shotgun around his back and threw the strap of the duffel bag over his shoulder. As he crossed the teller lanes, he knelt by the guard, pulling the ring of keys off his belt. He shoved the keyring in one of his thigh pockets and stood back up, moving toward the door to the main lobby.

His first stop was the safe deposit room in the basement of the bank. The schematics showed a locked door just to the right of the guard's office. Fortunately, both doors were labeled, at least according to the schematics. Javier made his way across the lobby, still on alert. There was only supposed to be one guard working, but for all he knew, things had changed.

He decided to check the guardroom first, ensuring that there was only one guard on duty. As he approached the door, he set the duffel bag on the floor next to the entrance to the safe deposit room and drew the Walther. He found the key-ring in his pocket and flipped through the keys. They were all the same, save for the multicolored key caps on each one.

Fortunately, there were only five keys to try. Number three did the job for the guard room. He pushed the door open slowly and slid inside.

The guardroom was small, the majority of it taken up by the large, L-shaped desk that held the computer. There was a single chair tucked under the lip of the desk in front of the monitors, obviously where the guard sat while he was monitoring the security feeds. Propped against the desktop tower was a cell phone; its screen still showed the image of a group of girls gathered around a dinner table. Javier picked the phone up and swiped his finger across the bottom of the screen, bringing up the navigation bar. He closed out of

Netflix and brought up the phone's menu. After a few quick taps, he brought up the administrator menu and searched for any hidden partitions or encrypted drives.

He found nothing.

'*It must be the guard's personal phone*,' he thought, closing down the admin menu and dropping the phone on the desk. He turned his attention to the computer. He nudged the mouse to wake the three screens, squinting at the bright, harsh green light from the night vision security feeds. He glanced at the feeds, looking for anyone else prowling around the bank in the dark, but only saw the unconscious image of the guard he had laid out.

He nodded and turned to leave the room.

The cell phone on the desk buzzed, causing Javier to jump.

He shook his head and holstered the gun. He picked up the phone and woke the screen.

A text from someone named Hannah sat on the lock screen:

Hey, are you going to be able to make it to dinner this weekend? My parents are excited to finally meet you!

Javier rolled his eyes and pushed the lock button. He dropped the phone on the desk a second time and left the guardroom, leaving the door open behind him.

He picked his duffel up again and pulled the keyring back out of his pocket. This time, the second key did the trick, and he opened the door to the basement stairwell. He made his way down to the safe deposit room.

The safe deposit room was smaller than he expected. The schematics of the building made it look like it took up the entire basement level, leaving little room for anything else. In reality, it was about 75 feet long, with different-sized safe deposit boxes lining the walls. Against one wall, there was a computer. Its screen glowed with the soft light of a screensaver; the bank's logo was slowly bouncing around, similar to the old DVD player screensavers.

Javier ignored the computer. He already knew which box he needed to get into: Box #325, registered to J. M. Bueareaux. The radically altered spelling of the man's last name had given Javier a little trouble tracking the box down, but he was finally able to confirm that it had been purchased in the correct time frame and that it held an indefinite, prepaid lease. Average citizens didn't lease safe deposit boxes for indefinite periods, and banks didn't tend to grant indefinite leases unless there was a lot of money involved. Or a lot of power.

Or both.

Javier walked quietly through the safe deposit room, glancing from side to side at the numbers on each box. About a third of the way down on the left-hand side, he found the box he was looking for.

As he knelt in front of the box, he noticed something strange. The keyholes—one for the bank manager, one for the patron—had been filled with some kind of gray sealant. It was evident that whoever the owner of the box was had no plans of letting themselves or anyone else into it.

Seeing the gunked-up keyholes only made Javier more sure he had the right box. Bureat was dead, and he must have intended for his research to die with him, even if he couldn't bring himself to destroy his notes and observations.

All the better for Javier.

He pulled the duffel closer and opened the zipper. He withdrew the 36-volt monster he would use to drill through the locks. He pulled out the carbide drill bits, found a quarter-inch bit, and loaded it into the chuck. He hefted the drill and pressed the bit against the first lock. The titanium-carbide bit ate through the stainless steel lock in a matter of moments. With the first pilot hole complete, Javier began work on the second lock.

After finishing the second pilot hole, he pulled the 1/4" bit out and replaced it with a 7/16". He lifted the drill again and shredded the remainder of both locks.

The whole process had taken less than 15 minutes, but Javier was in the box. He pried the door open and pulled the inner box out of the casing. He shuffled some things in the duffel around and slid the 24" × 12" × 6" box into the bag. He shoved the drill back in on top of the box and zipped the duffel up.

He hefted the duffel onto his shoulder and made his way back up the stairs. At the top, he set the bag down and unzipped it again. He found the modified firearm case with the military-grade cracker inside and popped it open. Leaving the case in the duffel, he went back into the guardroom and sat in the chair in front of the computer. The computer was still logged in and showed the same image as before. The guard was still unconscious in the lobby, and nothing else was moving.

'*Shit*,' Javier thought, '*I probably shouldn't leave the guard just knocked out in the lobby. I'll have to bring him back here and lock him in the guardroom.*' He left the cracker on the desk and went back to the lobby. The guard hadn't moved, but Javier still approached with caution. If it were him, he would play dead until his attacker got close. Then, he would finish the job.

The guard, however, did not spring to life and attack. His breathing was still labored from the bean bag round, and the lump on the side of his head was about the size of a golf ball. Javier knelt down and checked the guard's eyes. His pupils were dilated and unequal—a sure sign of a concussion. Javier nodded grimly and hauled the man into a sitting position. He draped one of the man's arms across his shoulders and straightened his legs, pulling the surprisingly light man into a fireman's carry.

He carried the man back to the guardroom and let him come to rest on the long end of the L-shaped table. Then, he sat back down at the computer and plugged the device he had brought into a USB port.

The computer screen flashed, and a command prompt window opened. Several dozen lines of code flashed in the terminal as the machine forced its way through the firewall and encryption on the hard drives. Several moments later—although it felt like a lifetime to Javier—the screen flickered again, and the command window disappeared.

The display on the device showed a green checkmark, indicating that the drives had been wiped and the backups had been corrupted on the server. Javier pulled the USB and watched as the monitors on the computer began to glitch, and finally as the dreaded Blue Screen of Death appeared on the central monitor.

Javier left the computer and went back out to the hallway. He found the key to the guard room, locked it, and broke the key off in the lock. He tossed the keys into the planter of the nearest decorative bush and then picked up the duffel bag.

He quickly crossed the lobby and went through the door leading behind the teller lanes. The hole he had cut in the plate glass window stood open; it hadn't been bothered in the roughly half-hour Javier had been in the bank.

He dug the transponder out of his pocket and glanced at the miniature screen. No silent alarms had been sent out. The primary alarm hadn't tripped, either. Javier put the transponder back in his pocket and jumped up on the counter for the drive-through. He pushed the duffel bag through the hole and then slid through himself. He made his way back over to the flowerbed and picked up the cut piece of glass by the vacuum handles. He hauled the glass back to the hole he had cut and, as carefully as he could, hefted the piece back up to the ledge. He fit the glass back into the slot and carefully let go of the handles. The piece seemed to stay, but Javier wasn't confident. He reached into the side compartment of the duffel bag and found a roll of Duck tape.

'After all, if you can't Duck it, fuck it,' he thought, sardonically misquoting the Duck brand's motto. He tore off a couple of pieces and pressed them against the seams in the glass. It looked like shit, but he wasn't going to be around to care. He released the vacuum on the grips and shoved them back in the duffel next to the Duck tape. Finally, he pulled the sensor off the window. He carried the sensor as he made his way back across the street to the sedan parked in the apartment complex lot. He popped the trunk, put the duffel, shotgun, shoulder holster with the PPK, and sensor inside, and then got behind the wheel.

He left his lights off as he pulled out of the parking lot and clicked them on as he merged onto Illinois Route 120. He pulled his phone out of the center console and brought up the encrypted communications app. He pressed his thumb to the screen and pulled up his boss's contact.

Suddenly, red and blue lights flashed in his rearview mirror.

'*Shit*,' he thought. He pulled over and clicked the dome light on in the sedan. He pulled his wallet out of the center console and shoved the phone back in. He set his wallet on the dash, pulled on a mask, and kept both hands on the wheel.

The officer approached the vehicle, keeping the customary distance between Javier and himself.

"License and registration."

Javier pulled his license out of his wallet and found the registration for the rental under the visor. He handed both to the officer and returned his hands to the wheel.

"Do you know why I pulled you over this morning?"

Javier quickly ran through what he had done after leaving the bank. There was a small chance the officer had seen him come out of the bank or make his way back to his car with the duffel over his shoulder. If the cop saw either of those things ...

He decided to play dumb and see what the cop wanted, but mentally, he calculated how long it would take for him to get the micro-compact SIG Sauer P365 he had stashed under the seat.

"No, sir," he said, turning his head to face the officer.

"You were using your cell phone while driving."

"Ah, yes, yes I was," Javier said, breathing a mental sigh of relief. He wasn't going to have to add this officer to his body count.

"Using your phone while driving is illegal in Illinois. I'll have to write you a ticket for it. Wait here. I'll be right back."

Javier acknowledged the officer's request. He felt himself relax in the seat. The license he gave the officer was clean—he wouldn't find anything in his record that would cause alarm. All he was going to get was a moving violation, and the officer should let him be on his way.

After a few moments, the cop came back and handed his license, registration, and ticket through the window.

"Alright, Javier, here's your ticket. If you'd like to plead guilty, there's the amount. If you plead not guilty, your court date is listed at the bottom of this ticket. My name and badge number are listed at the top. Stay off your phone, and drive safe."

"Thank you, sir," Javier said, feeling another wave of relief as the officer rattled through the typical post-traffic citation rhetoric. "I'll be sure to do that."

The officer tapped his hand on the roof of the car—his wedding ring making a hollow, metallic sound on the aluminum car body—and moved away, heading back to the patrol car parked behind Javier's sedan. Javier tossed the ticket on the passenger seat—he'd just make his boss expense it; it's not like $75 was anything to his employer—shoved the registration back into the visor, and put his ID back in his wallet. He waited another moment for the officer to turn off his flashers, and then he signaled and pulled away.

As he pulled into the hotel parking lot, he sighed and pushed the shifter into park. He took a moment to center himself, and then he opened the driver's side door. He popped the trunk and, after making his way around the back of the car, unzipped the duffel bag. He double-checked to make sure the box was still inside—he didn't know why he felt the need to check but did anyway—re-zipped the bag, and tossed it over his shoulder. He wasn't going to chance leaving the box in the car—for all he knew, some junkie douchebag would come through and steal the rental.

He trudged down the hallway and opened the door to his room. He clicked on the lights and swept the room like he always did. Finding it clear, he took the duffel bag and safe deposit box over to the bed. He had half a mind to open it but really didn't feel like starting in on the next mystery tonight. He knelt down by the bed, pulled the box out of the duffel bag, and shoved the box and the bag under it, blousing the generic gray skirt to hide the items.

After hiding both, he peeled off his night gear and shoved it in his personal duffel in the closet. He crawled under the covers and was asleep in moments.

CHAPTER 52

We left Alex's and drove back to the house. I wanted to try something—anything—with the machine to try and get a reaction. I was getting tired of being split between two times; I had a headache and felt completely exhausted.

My latest episode gave me hope that there was some way to contact the future and figure this situation out. I wasn't sure how exactly, but I wanted to try.

The drive back to the house was uneventful. The three of us sat in silence; the only sounds in the car were the soft tones of the radio and the tires on the pavement echoing up into the vehicle. The air in the car was heavy. We all had our own thoughts brewing, and very few of them were positive.

I didn't say it out loud, but I didn't want to keep Joseph and Leigh involved in this. They had their own lives—normal ones, in fact, up until today. They didn't deserve to have me introducing some bizarre, sci-fi shit, making their lives not make sense. If poking around the machine didn't work, I was going to insist that they go about their lives and forget about trying to help me. Hell, it would be a lonely existence, but I couldn't keep asking them to put their lives on hold. They were teenagers—for real, unlike me—and needed to figure out their own paths.

Joseph pulled into the driveway of the house and shifted the car into park. He sat behind the wheel for a moment and then turned to face me.

"I'm not sure what we'll find in this machine," he said, "but I'm going to do my best to get behind the security that's built in. We've got to get you back home to Mazer." He paused and shook his head. He knit his brow and took a deep breath.

All of a sudden, he pitched forward and grabbed his head. A gasp escaped his mouth, and his forehead broke out in droplets of sweat. He squeezed his eyes shut and covered them with the palms of his hands, groaning.

"It hurts!" he cried, bent almost in half by the pain.

"Joseph?" I said, grabbing his shoulder, "What's going on?"

"My head!" he howled, "It feels like it's splitting open!"

Leigh and I just looked at each other. He had been fine a minute ago, and as soon as he mentioned my dog, he began to writhe in pain.

"Wait a minute," I said, squeezing his shoulder. He looked up at me, his eyes already bloodshot and his pupils were constricted to pinpoints. "Did you say 'Mazer'?"

He nodded weakly and then slumped in the seat. His breathing was labored, but the sweat on his brow had begun to disappear. He closed his eyes and took a deep breath. He waited another moment with his eyes closed, continuing to take deep breaths. When he opened them, his sclera was white again and his pupils were back to their normal size.

"What was that?" Leigh asked, her face pale as a sheet.

I ignored her and stared at my brother. "How did you know Mazer's name? He's my dog, but he won't even be born until, like, 2013. How could you possibly know his name?"

Joseph shrugged, his breathing finally starting to return to normal. "I don't know. It just flashed into my mind. Then there was this searing pain, like my brain was being torn in half. It's like ..." he trailed off.

I sat, anxious to hear what he had to say. I forced myself to wait, even though I wanted to yell at him to spit it out.

"It's like I remembered something. I remembered when you got him and what he looked like. I remembered him running around during game night. It's like this flood of memories just rushed into my head, kind of like when Neo learned his skills from the training programs in *The Matrix*."

"Shit," I said, leaning back in the seat, "how is that possible? It's like ... it's like you're remembering things that haven't happened yet."

"It sounds insane, but could it be because he's spent so much time with you?" Leigh asked, her brow furrowing. "I wonder what effect this is having on him in the future, and if Leona is having to take care of him—"

Leigh's sentence ended in a hoarse croak. Just like Joseph, she pitched forward, grasping her head. Her already pale complexion nearly turned transparent as the rest of the blood drained out of her face. She pressed her thumb into her left temple, pushing against the vein that had started pulsing through her skin. She cried out, squeezing her eyes closed.

"Shit, not you, too, Leigh!"

I didn't know what to do. Now, not only was I screwing up their lives, but I was causing them physical pain.

Leigh slumped in her seat and let her hand drop from her temple. She took a deep breath and raised her head.

"That was like no other headache I've ever had," she said, wiping tears from her left eye. "But, just like Joseph, I remember things now. Things that haven't happened yet. This is weird."

"You guys should stay here. I don't think you should come in the house with me," I said, looking back and forth between the two of them. "I don't want this to continue."

"You don't know how to work the computer. I have a better shot of helping you figure it out. Honestly, even though this is some sci-fi stuff, I have a feeling that the headaches will keep happening while you're in this time, whether we're near you or not," Joseph said, opening the car door. He got out and started to walk around the side of the house, heading to the back door.

"I agree," Leigh said, reaching out and taking my hand. "You know I'm always going to be there for you. It might take another thirteen years in my time, but I remember how much I care about you from that last migraine. I'm not leaving, so deal with it!"

She squeezed my hand and then opened the car door, following Joseph around the side of the house.

I sat for a moment, allowing myself to feel comforted. I hadn't wanted to admit just how much this was wearing on me, and hearing Leigh and Joseph both tell me they'd support me until the end really helped. I may be the one being torn between two times and two different bodies, but I wasn't alone.

In my normal time, I knew that. I had realized just how many people helped lift me up to the position I was in, just like I knew how many people *I* had helped lift. Back in 2006, though, my 18-year-old brain couldn't comprehend just how many people would end up caring enough to be there through thick and thin.

'*Now that's interesting,*' I thought, '*Leigh and Joseph have been starting to take on characteristics of their future selves. Does that mean that I'll start reverting back to my teenage self? Is my adult mind destined to get pulled apart and broken back down to that of a teenager?*'

I furrowed my brow. No, I decided, that's not how it was going to go. I wasn't having headaches. Whiteouts and blackouts, yes, but no headaches. I figured the headache had to be the key to Leigh and Joseph's newfound future memories. By that same logic, if I were going to revert to my former self, I'd be getting headaches, too.

I shook my head, realizing I was thinking far too much

about it. I needed to focus on the here and now and figure out what the link between the machine and I was. I needed to find some way to turn the machine off and end this "journey."

I got out of the car and walked around the side of the house. The back door was standing open, and I ducked through the portal. The house looked the same as it did the last time I was inside, but with all the clutter, it was hard to tell if anything had been moved. There was no noise from the bedroom, which concerned me. I decided I'd better check on the captive, so I walked through the dimly lit hallway to the bedroom door.

I eased the door open, not wanting to draw too much attention to the fact that I was back in the house. The man was where I'd left him, and his bindings were still intact, from what I could tell. The knots looked a little different, but I figured that must have been from him moving around. There was no way he could have gotten himself loose.

A soft snore came from the figure tied up on the floor.

He was sleeping.

Christ.

'Well, it's better than him thrashing around and making a bunch of noise.'

I eased the door closed again and went to the basement. Leigh and Joseph weren't there, so I figured they must have already climbed down the ladder to the control room. I moved through the mess of boxes and to the pit in the back corner. I made my way through the hole in the concrete and down the ladder.

Joseph was already seated at the machine. He looked at me as I made my way around the corner.

"I'm going to try and get through this fake OS," he said. "I shouldn't be anywhere near anything that will mess the machine up, but I just want to make sure you want me to start digging around."

I nodded. At this point, I didn't give a shit if he broke the machine. He was a good enough software engineer, even at his current age, that I had a feeling he would be fine.

I let him work and went over to the wall near the machine. The concrete wall was smooth and didn't catch my shirt as I slid down the wall to a sitting position on the ground. I took a moment to look at the machine—to *really* look at it.

I saw the cylinder-shaped section, what appeared to be the primary mechanism, that strongly resembled a partially-disassembled airplane engine. There were sections that resembled a turbine, and countless little opaque tubes connected sections of the machine. The metallic casing was a dark, gunmetal gray, although there were bright points of color speckled throughout the tubing and connections. There was an alphanumeric keypad, along with a display screen facing Joseph and a snarl of wires that led to the control console. Another snarl of wires attached the primary mechanism to the secondary units. As I followed the wires with my eyes, I honed in on one of the smaller machines: the one that looked like it had an old-school satellite TV antenna attached to it.

I tilted my head to the side slightly. Something about the antenna was interesting. I pushed myself off the ground and walked toward the device, feeling Leigh's eyes on me as I crossed the room.

I ignored her and stepped up to the module.

The antenna itself was similar to a satellite TV antenna, but rather than the typical, rectangular LNB—Low-Noise Block downconverter—it had a pointed, spike-like piece coming from the center of the dish. I looked over the dish and the antenna. Looking closer, it looked as though the whole thing had been cut from two different pieces. I reached up and brushed a layer of dust away, revealing a darkened logo printed on the side of the dish: a red dot followed by four slivers of red created an I combined with the remaining letters to form the word "dish," even if the D and H were faded. The word underneath "dish" was faded, but "etwor" was still clear.

Impossibly, I figured, it was an old DISH Network satellite module, even if the typical offset LNB had been replaced. I looked closer and found that the wires coming out of the back of the dish had been crudely electrical taped together and strapped into a bundle with zip ties. The zip ties had been clipped cleanly, although the electrical tape wrapping looked like it had been done by a drunk electrician or a five-year-old. The wires ran off toward the main machine and disappeared into a hole in its bulk.

I looked over the remainder of the module, noting that the base of it seemed to be made of badly welded pieces of steel, which formed a roughly pentagon-shaped base. The base had been bolted to the floor, although several of the bolts looked stripped.

'*It looks like some lunatic tried to play both mad scientist and electrical engineer at the same time,*' I thought, shaking my head. '*I thought this thing was well built, but it looks like someone was drunk as hell putting it together. That would fit with the lunatic I met upstairs, though. Speaking of which, we should probably try to talk to him at some point ...*'

I made my way around the back of the machine and saw another mess of wires. These all ran to a hole that had been bored out of the cement ceiling. I figured they had to lead to the tape mainframes in the basement above us.

Coming back to the front of the machine, I looked at the display readout wired to the core of the machine. Recognizable but nonsensical numbers flashed across the dot matrix readout. It looked like a counter was running, but I couldn't be sure. Either way, it didn't matter right now. I looked back toward the modules, seeing the two reaction chambers and the antenna.

Something about it bothered me. I couldn't put my finger on it, but something was off. I walked to the far side of the antenna and sat in the chair in front of the antenna module. I looked down and noticed the simple metal chair had been bolted to the ground with large study bolts.

Weird.

I looked back up and found myself facing the antenna module but not the antenna itself. From this angle, I could see the hinge the satellite sat on.

It was lined up facing the chair, but the satellite dish was facing the ceiling of the sub-basement. I looked closely, and I could see the corrosion marks on the hinge; it looked like the antenna had spent a lot of time facing a different direction.

'*No fucking way*,' I thought, feeling my heart rate pick up.

"Hey, guys," I said, following the line of the antenna with my eyes, "do you know what's above us?"

Leigh and Joseph both turned and faced me, then glanced up at the ceiling. Both looked back at me, puzzled.

"Not offhand. Why?" Leigh asked.

"Something about this dish seems off," I said. "The module is pointed at this chair," I said as I laid my hand on the back of the chair, "but the dish and antenna are pointed at the ceiling. You'd think that if the module was pointed at the chair, the dish would be pointed at the chair, right?"

"I guess?" Joseph said. "But it could just be oriented that way by chance."

"What if ... what if it *isn't* by chance? What if it was, I don't know, moved somehow? What if it's *supposed to* point at the chair, but someone made it point to the ceiling?"

"Why would anyone do that?" Leigh asked.

"Because," I said, pointing toward the ceiling of the sub-basement, "the master bedroom is right above this part of the sub-basement. What if this machine is somehow connected to its future version beneath *my* bedroom in 2020?"

"How would anyone be able to communicate across time like that?" Joseph asked.

"How the hell did I get transported here?" I fired back. "Maybe it's like quantum physics: different rules than the normal world. I'm not a quantum physicist, but I've seen enough movies that deal with it to know one thing, and that's 'If nothing makes sense, then that means that *everything* has to make sense.' "

It was circular logic and borderline nonsensical, but given the events of the last couple of days, it seemed to make perfect sense.

"So, what, you're saying that someone somehow moved this antenna to shift you back in time? Who would do that? *When* would they do that?" Leigh asked, frustration starting to color her voice.

I didn't blame her; this was maddening. All I knew was that the position of the antenna made the least amount of sense in this whole situation. If someone went through the trouble of changing the orientation of the antenna, then maybe the machine was started intentionally. Maybe this is some kind of sick experiment.

"Joseph," I said, "did you find anything in the system?"

"I was able to get around the fake antique system," he said, turning back toward the monitor. "It looks like there's an entry right before what they call the 'inception' of the latest test. It was logged with gibberish as the timecode, which doesn't make sense."

"It would if it was somehow coming from the future," I said, peering over his shoulder at a modern-looking user interface. "Here's the thing, though. The entry looks like it doesn't change anything about the test. It looks like it just changes this line right here."

Joseph tapped a phrase on the monitor: COORDINATES.

"Can you pull up the history of tests and see what they labeled the coordinates as?"

Joseph nodded and started typing commands into the machine. Although the interface was more modern, it appeared that it still wasn't a point-and-click setup. In a moment, a list of tests appeared on the screen. Joseph selected the one right before the running test.

As the data appeared on the screen, I began to get a feeling of unease. It felt like we were close to some answers, and I started to worry that they may not be the answers I wanted.

'*Really, though,*' I thought, '*some kind of answer would be better than nothing. If we find out something, maybe we'll be one step closer to ending this clusterfuck of a situation.*'

"Here," Joseph said, leaning forward in his chair, "it lists the coordinates as '0,0,0.' That must be—"

"The origin," we said at the same time.

"What's it set to now?" I asked, the pit in my stomach growing more sour by the second. I looked over at the antenna. If it was going to follow some kind of conventional logic, it was going to be on an x, y, z axis. If 0,0,0 was pointing directly at the chair, then the current version would probably read something like ...

"0,1,0."

I felt like I'd been punched in the gut.

"No fucking way," I said, still breathless.

"If this is right ..." Joseph trailed off, staring at the coordinate on the screen.

"What the hell are you two talking about?" Leigh said, leaning forward to look at the display. Her blue eyes looked over the readouts, noticing the discrepancy in the two coordinate readouts.

"If this is right," Joseph started again, "that means the original versions of this test had the antenna pointed straight at the chair."

He gestured toward the metal chair that had been bolted to the ground.

"Now," he continued, "it's oriented to point straight up."

"Which means, the antenna is pointed straight at where I would be sleeping in 2020. If we make the leap that the machines move together, someone either in 2020 or now, in 2006, moved the antenna right before the test started. Moved it to face straight up toward the bedroom."

"So, that would mean someone intentionally involved you in this?" Leigh asked.

"Maybe," I said, "but it could also be that someone was trying to involve someone here in 2006. I don't know how wide the area of influence is, but it could very well have been pointed at someone sleeping in the bed now, not the future."

"So, what do we do? Do we just point the antenna back at the chair? Do you sit in the chair and have the antenna face you? Would that get you back?" Leigh asked, looking between Joseph and me.

"It's worth a shot," I said. '*What's the worst that can happen? I'm stuck here ... still? It kills me?*' I decided not to add that last part out loud.

"Wait, what if it hurts you?" Leigh asked, her eyes widening.

"Honestly, I'm kind of prepared to do whatever I have to in order to get home. Honestly, I'm sick of being here in the past. It's messing with my head, and I'm having trouble thinking straight. And don't forget—I've lived this once already. I don't need to live it again. All things considered, I'd say it's worth the risk."

Joseph and Leigh looked at each other and seemed to make a decision. They didn't look happy about it, but they made a decision, nonetheless.

"Okay," Leigh said, "let's get you strapped in."

CHAPTER 53

Javier sent the text at 8:14 a.m.:

> **I've secured the package. It was in the safe deposit box. The contents are unknown. Contact for rendezvous and transfer of possession of the documents.**

He tossed the phone on his bed and made his way to the bathroom. He pulled the shower on, making sure to turn the dial as hot as it could go. He went back to the bedroom and checked the phone, finding that his boss had sent him a message back:

> **Rendezvous will be tomorrow at 2230 hours in Knox Park. Coordinates for the drop will be sent at 2200 hours. Bring the package and the weapons used. They will be disposed of. Your auxiliary operation has been authorized. McDougall must be neutralized. Another operative is already camped out in**

the woods around Knox Park. Connect and continue the auxiliary operation.

Javier sat on the bed, staring at the display on the phone. He'd finally received the authorization to neutralize McDougall.

It was about damn time.

Javier typed a reply, asking who the other operative was and how he was meant to make contact.

A moment later, the reply came:

The operative is to be known as Number 4. Your new alias will be Number 7. Use this alias only. You will make contact by reaching out to them by using the attached contact information. It can only be opened via your encrypted phone. Confirm that you have received the contact information.

Javier tapped the contact. The phone indicated that the contact had been downloaded and added to the encrypted contact list. Javier opened the contact list and pulled up the new contact. He tapped out a message and then switched back to his boss's message.

He confirmed that he got the contact information and that he had initiated contact. He closed the phone down and tossed it on the bed. He knew he wasn't going to be able to get away with being absent from the site today, and he needed a shower after his excursion last night.

Fifteen minutes later, he was back in the bedroom, dressing in his usual attire. Having dressed, he went to the bed and pulled the safe deposit box out from under the bed skirt.

The box wasn't very large; it was about 24 inches long and 12 inches across. It was maybe six inches tall. The lid on the top was secured by a keyhole, much like the ones he had shredded to get the box out of the vault. Fortunately, this keyhole was clear of any gunk.

Weird for the actual box but not unheard of, especially if the person storing things in the box had reason to want extra security. Extra security, but apparently, this Bureat character had some way to access the box after it had been locked in the vault. Did that matter? Probably not.

Javier sighed. He would need the drill to open the box ...

... unless he could pick it.

He looked at his watch. He still had time before Tweedle Dipshit and Tweedle Dumbass would come knocking. He wasn't the best at picking high-security locks quickly; he was better with the standard deadbolts, but he could do it given enough time. He walked to the duffel bag he had stashed in the closet and got his lockpick set. He brought them back to the bed and flipped the case open.

He pulled out the torsion wrench and a small, half-diamond pick. He knelt by the bed and slid the torsion wrench into the keyhole. He pulled it slightly to the left, putting pressure on the tumbler. He slid the pick in and began to feel for the pins.

One, two ... five pins total. Maybe it wasn't as high security as he initially thought.

He found the furthest pin back and began to jiggle the pin up and down. He felt a slight *click* as the pin slipped into place.

'*One down, four to go,*' Javier thought.

He continued to work on the lock for another minute and a half. One of the pins was a spool pin, and it was giving him trouble.

'*I guess I was wrong about the lock being a low-security one. This is a pain in the ass.*'

Finally, the lock gave way, and he was able to turn the tumbler fully to the left, opening the box.

He wasn't sure what he expected, but the contents of the

box were underwhelming. The box was full of folders, all bearing the Project Outrigger logo. Under the folders were a mishmash of papers, some printed on old dot matrix pages, others from a more modern laserjet, and some were even handwritten. As Javier pulled the papers out, he caught a glimpse of some of the titles on them. Most of them were just generic reports, lines of text with the odd diagram thrown in. A few mentioned power levels, beam frequencies, and other status-like things.

Javier set the papers on the bed next to the folders and returned his attention to the box. The bottom of the box had ancient-looking, gigantic floppy disks, along with CDs in clear jewel cases. He had half a mind to grab his laptop and see what was on the disks, but he didn't think he'd have enough time.

He started to put the papers back inside when he caught the title of one in particular: `ORIGINAL PROJECT PERSONNEL`. Interested, he pulled the sheet out and glanced over it.

He only got to read a few unfamiliar names when he heard the knock on his door. He shoved the personnel list under the mattress and finished putting the rest of the papers and folders back in the safe deposit box. He shoved the box under the bed, grabbed his gear, and made his way out to the cars waiting to take them back to the site.

CHAPTER 54

It took a few minutes to figure out how to move the antenna. Joseph had finally figured out how to get around the facade of the OS and input commands in a common language. When he finally hit `RETURN`, the antenna slid into place, facing the chair.

According to the monitors, the system was still active, but there was no beam being produced from the antenna. After a few minutes of discussion, we decided that we should try turning on the emitter and firing the beam toward the chair.

The chair I was currently strapped into.

"Are you sure about this?" Joseph asked. "We don't know what'll happen if I fire this beam at you."

I took a moment to think about what might happen if an unknown beam of energy shot through my body. There was a good chance nothing would happen. On the other hand, though, I wasn't even sure what kind of "beam" was going to be produced. For all I knew, it could be some kind of high-powered radiation that would give me lymphoma or something. I was banking on it doing nothing—or sending me home, of course—so I figured I might as well give it a shot.

I nodded to Joseph and set my jaw.

He looked at me one more time, nodded, and turned back to the control panel. I heard the tap of a few keys and then a pause.

"Here we go," he said and punched the `RETURN` key.

For a moment, nothing happened. Then, a low-frequency buzz—more of a vibration than a buzz, really—filled the room. The pitch began to rise and soon became an audible tone. From the two side chambers, a light started to glow brighter, seeming to follow the pitch of the buzz. As the buzz reached near-inaudible levels, the light from the reaction chambers became hard to look at. I squinted, trying to keep my eyes open. On the far side of the room, next to the control panel, Joseph and Leigh were both shielding their eyes from the blue and purple lights coming from the reaction chambers.

From my seat, I could see directly down the point of the antenna. It started glowing a blue-violet, pulsing slightly. I braced myself for whatever was about to happen.

My vision started to flicker. The overhead lights began to look as if they were shaking, almost as if my entire body was vibrating. The flicker became more intense, and the lights almost seemed to strobe.

From across the room, I heard Joseph yell, "It's counting down! Five, four, three, two, one!" On the screen in front of him, I saw the words `CRITICAL MASS` flash in red.

Just then, the buzz stopped. The lights from the reaction chambers seemed to fade, and my vision cleared.

"What the hell—" I started.

As soon as the words left my mouth, a terrifying sound filled the basement lab. A garbled, sub-bass boom seemed to emanate from nowhere. It reminded me of the sounds you hear in an alien movie when the character sees the alien for the first time, the terrifying *BRAAAM* that permeates every part of your being and sends a primordial chill through your entire body.

But no aliens appeared, cast down by a beam of light.

There was no robotic monster waiting under a secret hatch in the floor.

Instead, the blue-violet glow on the tip of the antenna shot toward me, the beam widening as it was produced. A moment later, I was enveloped in the mysterious glow.

I waited for the jolt of pain, telling me my mind had once again been ripped from my body. I waited to stare wide-eyed at my now-lifeless body, slumped in the chair, just like Bruce Banner when the Ancient One punched his soul out of his body.

But I felt ... nothing.

There was no pain.

I wasn't floating away.

Nothing was happening at all.

The *BRAAAM* stopped as suddenly as it started, and the blue-violet light disappeared.

Joseph and Leigh both lowered their hands from their ears and stared at me.

"What in the fuck was that?" Leigh cried, looking back and forth between Joseph and me.

Joseph, with too-wide eyes and a bewildered look on his face, could only shrug and turn back to the computer. He tapped a few keys, and a new readout appeared on the central terminal.

"It ... it didn't do anything," he said quietly. He tapped a few more keys, ensuring that the machine had powered down and had returned to low-power standby. He rotated in the swivel chair to look at me. "Did you see anything? Feel anything?"

I shook my head.

"No," I said, "I didn't feel anything. The only thing I saw was a bright light, and then my vision got kind of," I struggled to find the best way to describe it. "Shaky."

Leigh crossed the room and undid the straps on my arms,

legs, and across my chest. She turned and walked away, moving past the control panel into the southern end of the sub-basement.

Normally, I would have gotten up and gone after her. Instead, I slumped forward in the chair, resting my elbows on my knees. I closed my eyes and took a deep breath. Something felt funny behind my eyes, so I brought my hands up to rub them, trying to soothe the strange pressure I was feeling.

I opened my eyes. Everything was blurry, like I was looking through a piece of dirty, weathered glass. Joseph was still sitting in the swivel chair in front of the panel, and Leigh was still pacing at the southern end of the sub-basement, but I saw something else.

Two men were sitting right next to Joseph at the control panel, and a third was leaning against the wall, right next to Leigh.

But the men didn't seem ... *here*.

They looked blurry; their bodies seemed to shimmer, just like the lights did when I was being hit by the beam from the machine. Their voices, too, sounded muffled, and were hard to understand, like they were talking in an adjacent room rather than being, apparently, right in front of us.

From what I could hear, it sounded like they were arguing about something, even if it sounded like they were talking through a mouthful of cotton:

"We should just pull the plug."

"We can't do that yet; we don't know how this experiment ends. If we don't know how it ends, we can't replicate it!"

"If we start over, we can replicate it."

"Do you even know how to start the fucking thing? I don't. Look at this," the man gestured toward one of the screens. "From the readings, this is the first successful attempt. This thing has been running on auto since Bureat first constructed it! See, right here, in the log. 'JBAUT.' That means Jonathan Bureat Automation. It's a throwaway line in one of the files, but it looks like he set this thing to run an automation. The time scale is left as a variable, though, which is either ridiculous or genius, I can't tell which. But that isn't the point! If it's been running on and off for the past twenty years, and this is the first time it's successfully sent someone back, we *can't just turn it off!*"

The man who was talking all but shouted the last five words.

The older man seemed to scowl and turned his head toward where I was sitting. His eyes stayed narrowed, as if he couldn't see me.

"Hey, can you hear me?" I said, waving my arms at the man looking in my direction. From the panel, I heard a muffled *beep.*

Rather than acknowledging me, he looked back at the control panel.

"What the hell does that mean?"

The other man shouldered him out of the way, pushing him directly into Joseph. Rather than bumping into him, though, he passed *through* my brother.

'*So, wait,*' I thought, '*am I seeing something like I did before when I blacked out?*' Out loud, I said, "Joseph, Leigh, can you both still hear me? Can you see me?"

Joseph and Leigh both looked over and then looked at each other. I knew I was talking crazy again—well, crazy for them, anyway—but I needed to know. Fortunately, both of them nodded. Weirdly, the third man leaning against the wall looked in my direction, too.

'*Okay, so I didn't black out this time, but it seems like I'm able to interact with the future? At least, I think it's the future. Looks like that guy has an iPad, and those aren't even around yet. Now, how do I make contact with these people?*'

I studied the men and tried to figure out what they were doing. It looked like they had pulled up nearly the same graphs that Joseph had, but they looked delayed. I turned my head and looked at the man leaning against the wall.

For the first time, I noticed he had a gun on his right hip.

The hell? What did they need a guy with a gun for?

He seemed to feel uneasy with me watching him. He pushed off the wall and walked over toward the other two men, glancing at the screen as he made his way over.

I turned back to the monitors and noticed that a new spike had appeared on my brother's readout. A small spike, but a spike, nonetheless. A moment later, the same spike appeared on the one the two men were looking at. A small spike identical to the one I saw on my brother's screen.

I raised my eyebrows.

I saw a spike appear.

A moment later, I saw another one.

'*No shit*,' I thought, '*the spikes on the readout are responding to my movements. How in the hell is that happening both here and in the future? Dammit, I wish I understood more about this fucking thing. It's maddening to see something happen and have no idea how in the hell it works! I'm this close to being able to reach the future, but it's like swimming lessons as a kid: They toss your crying ass off the diving board and tell you to swim to the pole, all the while pulling the pole further and further from your outstretched hands. It's like a sick game. I guess that means I just have to play the game, then. Maybe if I make enough spikes appear, one of those two guys will notice and try to do something. Hopefully, the scrawny guy who wants to let this run. The bigger guy sounds like he wants to just shut everything down, which would probably be bad news for me.*'

I started to wave my arms over my head. Instead of multiple spikes, though, a line rose sharply and then hit a plateau. When I stopped moving my arms, the line began to descend back toward the base.

I had an idea.

I waved my arms, counting to three, then paused a moment. Then, I waved my arms and counted to one.

I saw the spikes react just the way I hoped they would.

Joseph was staring at me like I had three heads. I ignored him and watched the monitor. I sat perfectly still, letting the small, weak spikes add space between the larger ones I'd just made.

When I felt like there was enough space, I waved my arms, counting to two. I stopped, counted to one, and then waved my arms again. I waited one more time and waved my arms the same way.

Three short spikes flashed on the monitor.

I counted again, this time waving my arms for a count of three each time.

Three long plateaus appeared on the monitor.

'Hell yes, it's working!'

I waved my arms for the short spikes again.

. ↑ . ↑ .   - - -   . ↑ . ↑ .

S→ O→ S

I didn't know Morse Code worth a shit, but I knew that three dots, three dashes, and three more dots was the universal call for help. I'd seen plenty of movies and read plenty of books where they'd used that particular code.

I watched, hoping that the two men at the console would see the readout changing.

"What the hell is that?"

The third man seemed to take the other two by surprise. They both looked back at him, and he was pointing toward the monitor with the spikes appearing.

"What are you talking about, Javier?" the older man asked, putting his hands on his hips. "Aren't you supposed to be guarding the ladder?"

The man named Javier seemed to ignore him: "Look at the monitor. Why is it spiking and plateauing like that?"

"Who knows ... or cares?" the smaller man asked, glancing over his shoulder. "McDougall is right; go watch the ladder."

"I'm serious. That pattern looks ... familiar," Javier said, leaning forward to peer at the monitor. "Make it go back, and let me see the whole pattern again."

"What the hell for?" McDougall, the older man, asked forcefully.

"God dammit. Jeffrey, just do it!" Javier growled, glaring at the man sitting in the chair.

The man named Jeffrey sighed, "Fine, but you've got to stop talking to me like this. I'm your boss, not some piece of shit lab tech you can just treat like a trained monkey."

Jeffrey keyed in a few commands, and the readout reappeared on the upper-center screen. Javier watched as it began to scroll, and he saw my test spikes and plateaus. A moment later, my SOS signal appeared.

"Pause it," he said.

Jeffrey tapped a key, and the readout froze.

Javier stared at it for a moment, as if he didn't believe what he was seeing. "Do you know what that is?" he asked, looking back and forth between Jeffrey and McDougall.

Both men shook their heads.

"It's probably just readings from the machine. Fluctuating power levels or something. It's just noise." McDougall said. Jeffrey nodded but looked somewhat hesitant.

"No," Javier said, pulling out his phone and tapping a phrase into it. "It's Morse Code. That's the universal signal for SOS." He flipped his phone around and showed the two men the image on the screen.

"How the hell is it Morse Code? That means it isn't just fluctuations but an intelligent response. Wouldn't someone have to be influencing the machine?"

All three men looked up, as if they could see through the layers of concrete, steel and lumber.

"You don't think ..." the man named Jeffrey said and trailed off.

Javier nodded.

"I think it's the guy in the bed upstairs."

I felt my heart skip a beat.

'*No way*,' I thought, '*this guy put it together!*'

I stood up and started to move toward them, hoping I could continue the contact—

—but the shadowy figures faded, slowly and completely disappearing, as if they had never been there at all. I looked over at Joseph and the monitor behind him, but the readout had flatlined.

"Shit!" I said and started to wave my hands, but nothing happened. The line stayed flat.

Panicking, I sat back down in the chair and closed my eyes. I opened them, hoping that the shadowy figures would be back again.

But they weren't.

I knew I looked like a jackass, but I waved my arms again, willing the line to start jumping like it had a moment ago.

Nothing.

"Fuck!" I shouted. Leigh whipped around from where she'd been pacing and stared at me, mouth agape. Joseph flinched backward in the chair, as if he'd been slapped.

Joseph looked at me, his eyes wide, "What happened?"

"Bring up the graph you just had on the screen," I said, moving quickly across the space between the two of us.

Joseph looked bewildered but turned back to the keyboard. He tapped out a few commands, and the readout appeared on the upper-center screen.

The graph appeared, just like it had when that guy Jeffrey entered the commands. This whole thing was giving me a hell of a feeling of *déjà vu*.

Regardless, Leigh, Joseph, and I stared up at the graph as it slowly played from the beginning. After a few seconds, at the right-hand side of the screen, we saw the first spike.

"That's where I moved, and that's when I saw the shadows of three men."

We kept watching the waveform. We saw the plateau and the short spike.

Leigh and Joseph looked at me, a question playing behind their eyes. "Morse Code," I said.

"How the hell do you know Morse Code?" Leigh asked, shaking her head.

"Does it matter?" I asked, "If I'm right, they saw the spikes and plateaus."

"Okay," Leigh said, "so you think this message got transmitted via Morse Code. Now what?"

I thought for a moment. I was really just hoping that one of the three people milling about the sub-basement understood Morse Code and could do something about it.

From what it looked like, the third man—the one who was closest to Leigh—looked like he understood Morse Code and tried to bring it to the attention of the other two. The man named Javier. The other two men hadn't looked like they wanted to listen to him, but I was almost certain that Javier understood Morse Code and had connected it to my almost lifeless body in the bed above them.

"I want to try engaging the machine again."

Joseph and Leigh looked at each other and then back at me.

"Are you sure you want to go through that again? We don't even know what kind of energy is passing through your body. What if it's harmful?" Leigh said.

"She's right," Joseph said. "What if this isn't actually letting you see the future? What if it's just causing some kind of overload in your brain and making you hallucinate these things?"

There was a very real possibility that they were right. For all I knew, the machine was just causing me to slump over in the chair and drool like a moron, the radiation making me think I was seeing three imaginary men from the future.

The fact that Joseph and Leigh were still relatively calm and not rushing to make sure I wasn't dead led me to believe I wasn't turning into a drooling mess.

The visions I'd had of the future weren't hallucinations. Even though it doesn't logically make sense, it made sense to me that they were actually small glimpses into my own timeline.

"I get why you're concerned," I said, looking back and forth between Joseph and Leigh, "but I really think that I've had glimpses of the future. I don't think it's been some kind of radiation hallucination or something. Wouldn't you two have seen me, I don't know, slump over or pass out or something? The only way to know is to try it again. I doubt it will happen, but even if I end up braindead in the chair, it's a risk I'm willing to take."

I looked at both Joseph and Leigh, putting as much sincerity into my gaze as possible. They looked more than just skeptical; they looked worried.

"I don't know about this," Joseph said. "I know you want this to work, but what if it doesn't?"

"That's a risk I'm willing to take," I repeated. "I can't stay stuck here forever; something has to be done to try and get me home. Just cue up the program again. Please."

Joseph closed his eyes for a moment, shaking his head. He set his jaw and turned back toward the computer. He wasn't happy, but he was going to start the program again.

"Thank you," I said.

He didn't respond. He just kept tapping commands into the terminal.

I turned to face Leigh. I knew she was just as mad at me as Joseph was. She was quiet and refused to look at me. I could see the tears starting to well up in her eyes and her bottom lip starting to quiver. She crossed her arms and stared in the direction of the computer, her eyes working their way over the monitors and commands Joseph was typing.

"Here it goes," Joseph said. "Three, two, one, Enter."

I heard the click of the Enter key and braced myself for the hum. For the blinding light. For the ear-shattering *BRAAAM* to fill the sub-basement.

But nothing happened.

The screen in front of Joseph popped up a message. Before, it had warned that the machine had reached Critical Mass and was about to fire the beam that had been produced in the two reaction chambers. This time, it showed a message blinking in red: ENERGY RESERVES DEPLETED.

Joseph tapped a key, and a text document appeared. I couldn't read the whole thing around his head, but I was able to see a few words.

> RESERVE POWER ONLY.
>
> REACTION CHAMBERS RECHARGING. ESTIMATED TIME TO FULL CHARGE IS 36 HOURS.
>
> BEAM UNABLE TO FIRE UNTIL ENERGY IS REPLENISHED.
>
> CURRENT EXPERIMENT WILL BE MAINTAINED ON RESERVE POWER.

Joseph turned around in the chair, the look on his face was like a doctor about to give you some bad news. He opened his mouth to speak but saw me shaking my head. The look on my face must have told him that I already knew.

I wasn't going to get another chance to try and make contact with the future. With the energy depleted, I was still stuck here.

Still.

Shit.

CHAPTER 55

A woman's voice cut into Baumann's thoughts, "Sir, there's been a development."

Baumann looked up from the book he had been reading at the young woman standing in the doorway to his study. He marked the page and pushed himself out of the overstuffed leather armchair.

He followed the young woman through the house, making their way to the lab in the basement. She pressed her thumb to the security plate and then leaned in for a retinal scan. After a moment, the door popped open, and they both made their way into the lab.

She sat down at a terminal and pulled up what looked like a graph of energy readings.

"We detected the surge about twenty-five minutes ago. Something caused the machine to initiate another cycle. What's strange is that it happened while the experiment was still running. We haven't seen that happen before."

Baumann stared at the readings and saw the spike of a massive output of energy. He had seen that same spike before: Every time a new automated test started, the energy level spiked just like it did on the current graph. But it wasn't supposed to happen during a test. *That* was new.

"The energy spike itself is weird, but what happens next is even weirder," the young woman—Baumann thought her name was Annie—said. She tapped a few keys to move the graph forward. "Here, we start seeing smaller spikes appear. They're more than just baseline readings and more than the occasional power fluctuations we see during experiments. They look almost ... *intelligent*."

Baumann and Annie watched as the graph continued to scroll. At first, there were just short spikes. After a moment, there were longer plateaus, suggesting some kind of sustained input. They watched in amazement as the graph returned to baseline, followed by three short spikes, three long plateaus, and three more short spikes.

"What the fuck?" Baumann said, breathless.

"SOS," Annie said, looking over her shoulder at her boss, "but you probably already knew that."

Baumann didn't respond. He glared at the readout, wondering how another cycle could have started. He knew the control panel for the machine was still active, but it should have given an error message.

"Pull the logs for the machine. I want to see what's been accessed and when."

Annie set to work inputting the commands. Baumann ran his hands through his hair and exhaled sharply. He pulled a file folder off the corner of the desk and flipped it open. Inside, there were three printouts: one for Javier, one for Jeffrey, and one for McDougall. The three primary people working on the site. Baumann set Javier's to the side. His operative was certain to be able to get around any errors, but he hadn't authorized him to work the computer. As insolent as Javier could be, he still knew how to follow orders. Mostly.

He looked back and forth between the faces of the other two men. All reports suggested that neither of them was adept enough to work around the computer system running the machine. They could likely access portions of it but would not be able to work around the errors they would encounter if they tried to initiate a new test.

"Sir, I've got the logs," Annie said, turning slightly in her chair.

Baumann flipped the folder shut and set it back on the corner of the desk. He peered over Annie's shoulder and looked at the timestamps for the logs. The last entry was a garbled mix of gibberish.

"That," Baumann said, "why is it garbled like that?"

Annie pulled up the last log and expanded the details. Unlike the usual reports that Baumann was able to access, this one was woefully thin on information. As he looked through the log, he was surprised to note that the laser actually fired during the sequence. As far as he knew, that wasn't supposed to happen; it would risk putting the subject into another transport state.

He looked at the keylog from the test and found that several of the steps normally taken to initiate it had been skipped. Really, it was impressive how the workarounds had bypassed the system. Whoever ran the commands must have been a high-level programmer with a vast knowledge of coding languages.

Baumann wasn't impressed very often, but whomever this was ... they were good.

"I get it now," Annie said, her eyes darting back and forth across the characters on the screen, "the person who initiated the test didn't engage the drive. See here? It looks just like it's supposed to, but the actual temporal displacement drive never received the command to activate, so the subject wasn't placed into a transport state. The only thing that happened was the laser was fired, just like it's supposed to at the genesis of the test. So, rather than firing the main engine, only the reaction chambers fired. It looks like that was enough to anchor the subject in the past but gave them the ability to communicate to both versions of the machine. It's really quite amazing. I'm surprised no one ever thought of just using the reaction chambers on someone who's already in a test state."

Suddenly, an alert popped up on Annie's screen.

`ALERT: BREACH DETECTED`

"What the hell?" Annie muttered, closing the log and switching the screen to her network diagnostics. "No way. This isn't supposed to be able to happen."

"What kind of breach? We're supposed to have military-grade encryption. How can we have a breach?"

"Fuck, it's coming through one of the ports used for the lab equipment. That stuff isn't secured, and someone found a way in through" —she paused as she tapped a command— "a fucking printer, of all things. Dammit. They're past the firewall and working on breaking through the port that the printer is connected to."

"Shut it down before they get in!" Baumann shouted.

"I can't," Annie said through gritted teeth. "Once they're past the firewall, it's just a few commands to get through the port to the computer. The damn printer was connected to the network, but it was outside the firewall. I guess IT didn't think they needed to secure an in-house laserjet."

"They're all fucking fired," Baumann growled. "Take the mainframe offline. There's got to be an Internet kill switch."

"I can try ..." Annie trailed off, furrowing her brow and typing ferociously. The force she was putting into each keystroke sounded like she was about to punch a hole in her keyboard. The monitors in front of her flashed as she whipped from one open window to another, trying to kill the Internet connection to the server as fast as possible.

Finally, after what seemed like an eternity of typing, she declared: "There!"

"Did you get it offline?" Baumann asked, his brow still furrowed.

"Yes," Annie answered, "but I'm not sure if I got it fast enough. Whoever was getting into the system knew how to cover almost all their tracks. While I was trying to get the mainframe offline, I was running a tool to see what information the intruder was accessing. The tool didn't find much, but it was able to find that they were going after the test logs. Unfortunately, the tool wasn't able to figure out which ones they were going for since they're named to be deceiving, just in case something like this happens."

"Well," Baumann said, running his thumb along the knuckles of his right hand, "if it was just the logs, there isn't much valuable information there. Plus, they're named to look like something else, right? It shouldn't be a big deal. Run a full system scan and see what else they might have gotten their fingers into. After that, get that goddamn printer removed from the network, or at least behind the firewall!"

Baumann stormed out of the lab, leaving Annie sitting in front of her computer.

She pulled out a Post-it and scratched his instructions on it. With that done, she turned her attention to the trace program she'd used to try and trace the intrusion into the system. She tapped a few commands into the trace program's UI and watched as a list of all compromised files appeared.

The majority of the files compromised were log files for the machine. Annie called up one of the files and ran through the information listed. Realistically, there was nothing in the file that was terribly confidential. The log files listed things like power levels and the date and time of tests that had been run. All the log files were from dates well in the past; the intruder hadn't even tried to get to the files from the current situation over at the test site. Those were stored in a different subdirectory and hadn't been moved to long-term storage yet.

Annie closed down the log file and continued to sift through the rest of the compromised files. She found what she expected to find, until she noticed that the shipping and receiving server had been breached.

'*What the hell?*' she thought, cueing up the files accessed through that server.

By all rights, there was nothing that some hacker should want in shipping and receiving. The files she pulled up were manifests from shipments of lab parts and building materials dating back to the initial stages of turning the mansion into Baumann's personal lab.

Each of the manifests showed a different array of materials. Most were shipping orders received through distribution centers. A few showed lumber; others showed computer components. Annie looked through the billing information listed on the manifests and found nothing that would be useful.

'*What could they be going after with the shipping manifests?*' she wondered. She was about to write it off as a failed attempt to find financial information when her eyes went wide.

"Shit," she muttered, "they weren't looking for what was ordered or for billing information. They were looking for *where* the materials were going."

She pulled the manifest back up and found the shipping information. It was right in front of her the whole time:

The mansion's location had been compromised.

CHAPTER 56

Javier was convinced that the readouts he had seen were because of the guy in the bed upstairs. Somehow, he was able to link the two versions of the machine and send an SOS. McDougall still wasn't convinced. He insisted that the readouts couldn't possibly be intelligent communication from someone under the influence of the machine.

"There just isn't any way for that to happen," he had said.

Javier disagreed. The readings up until that time had all been similar: small spikes in energy, yes, but nothing as profound and varied as the readouts they had just seen. Plus, how the hell did McDougall know what could and could not happen? He was just as blind in this as the rest of them.

Jeffrey, looking for any excuse to keep the experiment running, had agreed with Javier.

"This just proves that we have to keep this experiment running!" he all but shouted in McDougall's face.

McDougall had stormed out of the sub-basement, leaving Jeffrey and Javier alone with the machine. Javier shook his head, thankful that McDougall's temper tantrums would be over that night. He glanced at his watch. It was getting toward evening. He told Jeffrey he was heading back up into the main house. Jeffrey just waved a hand over his shoulder and continued to sort through graphs and text files.

As Javier pulled himself up the ladder into the sump well, he considered the all-but-comatose man in the bed upstairs. By all rights, he was still actively alive, but his brainwave readings were at the level you'd expect of someone in either a deep, profound sleep or a coma. At least, they had been the last time anyone had checked on them. Javier made a note to go take a peek at the readings.

What did it mean, though?

Javier still couldn't figure out if the man's brain was actually powering two separate bodies or if he was just being projected into some kind of dream world.

Hell, maybe not even a dream world. Maybe he was literally in a different time or space. From the reports and the information he'd gotten from his employer, it seemed the machine was meant to transport someone through time. What if it just didn't transport the body? What if it only transported the mind? It was pure science fiction, but it was the only thing that made any amount of sense.

Those questions were more than Javier wanted to deal with. Right now, he had an objective to accomplish.

Although he was in a hurry to leave, he turned right at the top of the basement stairs and went into the man's bedroom, fully intent on taking a look at the EEG readout before he left the site.

The man was right where he'd always been, and he didn't look any different. Even the monitors hooked up to him looked and sounded normal. His pulse was steady, and there didn't seem to be any indication of the SOS they'd received.

Javier crossed the threshold and went to the bed. The dog was right where he'd been since Javier let him out of his kennel. He looked up at Javier with sad, bloodshot eyes and whimpered slightly.

"I know, buddy," Javier said, reaching down and scratching the pup behind his ears. "I'm sure you're wondering what's going on with your master and why all these big, clumsy idiots are milling about your house. You're being a really good boy, though; I don't think I'd be as chill with all these random assclowns wandering through every inch of my space."

The dog cocked his head, almost as if he really understood what Javier was saying. Javier scratched his ears one more time and then considered the man in the bed. He glanced at the readings on the monitors and checked the fluids that were being intravenously fed into his arm. The EEG looked a little odd, but Javier wasn't exactly qualified to read it with any accuracy. It looked to him like the machine was malfunctioning and creating a very faint shadow under the waveform. He tapped the machine on the side, trying to fix the readout. With a shrug, he turned back toward the man lying before him.

"Can you actually hear what's happening to you?" Javier asked the seemingly unconscious man.

The readings on the monitors didn't change.

Javier shook his head, wondering for what felt like the millionth time just what the hell was going on. Sure, he'd been assigned to work with the Project, but that didn't mean he actively understood everything that could happen when the machine was turned on. His handlers only gave him enough information to assimilate into the project culture; they didn't give him enough to know the intricacies of the machine and its potential to send a subject through time.

He looked at his watch and found that it was getting even later in the day. He had to go and meet the other operative soon, and he needed to make sure he was on time.

He gave the dog one final pat and left the bedroom, working his way to the front door.

Fortunately, no one tried to stop him as he left the house and made his way back to the hotel.

CHAPTER 57

Javier arrived back at the hotel about an hour later. He'd stopped on the way to get something to eat and spent some time taking notes on the current state of affairs while he ate.

His notes, though, were basically worthless.

He was documenting the situation and adding his own theories, but he didn't really have anything concrete. His notes looked like a frustrated man trying to find a way to keep himself from losing his mind.

As he let himself into his hotel room, his mind was still on the SOS signal that had seemed to come through the machine earlier that day. The output signal had looked too uniform to be some kind of random or natural occurrence. Granted, he hadn't seen a full readout of the machine's power levels, but what little he had already seen didn't seem to suggest that it was possible to create three short peaks, three longer plateaus, followed by three more short peaks. It *had* to be some kind of intelligent response. There was no other option.

Wearily, he threw the lock on the door, made his way to the bed, and sat down, reveling in the momentary comfort the soft seat offered. He wasn't going to be comfortable later tonight, but he had a mission to accomplish.

A mission he was actively looking forward to.

First, he had to rendezvous with the Collector and hand off the materials he'd procured from the bank. Then, he and the other operative would execute their "auxiliary mission."

Javier checked the time. It was already past 2000 hours. He had about two and a half hours to kill before he had to meet his contact to hand off the materials from the safe deposit box and hook up with the other operative to complete their mission.

He went to the side of the bed and pulled the safe deposit box out from under the bed skirt. He opened the box and considered the contents.

His cursory look earlier hadn't revealed any documents of interest except the one he had hidden under his mattress. Before he looked at that document, Javier decided to take a closer look at the remaining contents of the box. As he started pulling folders out, he began to make piles on the bedspread. Most of the file folders were battered and well-worn, having been passed among scientists and bureaucrats many times over.

Javier flipped one of the files open and glanced through the contents. Most of the papers inside the folder were technical readouts and other reports on various experiments the machine had run. As he flipped toward the back, he found several memos intermixed into the readouts. The memos were mostly interoffice communications, reminding workers about various policies and advising them of the experiments being run.

One memo caught Javier's eye, though.

The memo had been folded hastily and appeared to have been shoved toward the bottom of the file. He pulled the yellowing paper out and undid the cockeyed fold.

The memo was addressed to J. Bureat, and it was sent from H. S. Baumann. Those were the only two names on the memo;

the other memos were addressed to different subgroups of workers, with Bureat cc'd on each one. This one, however, looked to be a private communication between the two men.

The typed content of the memo outlined Bureat's professional dismissal from the project. Phrases like "unprofessional behavior," "increasingly erratic," and "borderline insanity" stood out as Javier read through the memo. At the bottom, there was a handwritten postscript:

> *You rat bastard. I know you're just fucking with me to steal this research. I hope this dismissal fucks up all your plans. Rot in hell, you son of a bitch!*

Javier stared at the handwritten portion of the message. He knew both of the players and had heard that there had been bad blood between the top two men at the project, but this ...

He stood up and grabbed his laptop. Propping himself against the wall, he logged into the encrypted drive and pulled up the personnel files for the various people associated with the Project. He knew his boss had kept detailed files on everyone, the only exception being the head honcho himself: Herman Samuel Baumann. For whatever reason, his boss never found much information on the murdered research genius.

Driven more by curiosity than anything else, Javier pulled up the file for Jonathan Bureat, looking for anything that might be relevant and interesting. In the file, he found the typical biographical information: age, date of birth, degrees and honors, employment history. He even found sections detailing finances, investments, and debts.

All of the information was written in a clinical, detached manner, just like all the rest of the files. Oddly, though, much of the narrative elements held a distinctly negative aura—almost as if the writer was actively opposed to writing down the information ...

... which didn't make any sense. Why would anyone give a shit what this guy accomplished or how much he was worth? It was just facts, right? Why, then, would the narrative about his life and employment seem so standoffish? As far as Javier knew, his boss was the one who wrote and compiled the files. He could be wrong, of course; it could be some random employee whose only task was to research and compile personnel files.

But that didn't square with how controlling Javier knew his boss was. From everything he'd read and heard, his boss liked to be intimately involved in nearly every operation. That *had* to include researching the people he was interested in.

Javier closed down the laptop and furrowed his brow. Something wasn't adding up, and he was starting to get the idea that it had to do with his employer. The more he thought about it, the less he liked how the information had been written.

During his years of employment, Javier had read a number of files just like Bureat's. The difference was that they were written in an almost overtly negative way.

His phone chirped, interrupting his train of thought. He grabbed it off the bed and opened the message.

> [Restricted]: ***En route. Rendezvous behind Alpha 1. Eta 3 minutes.***

Javier replied with a simple "**Acknowledged**" and wiped the messages. It was finally time to get some answers and be rid of a particularly massive pain in his ass.

As he made his way out of his room and toward the side door, Javier ripped a piece of duct tape off the roll in his closet. Fortunately, even though the door claimed to be armed with an alarm, it didn't work. That would come in handy. As he passed through, he smoothed the strip of duct tape over the strike plate, stopping the door from locking him out and allowing the two operatives to gain an unnoticed entry to the building.

He walked casually around the side of the building and toward the back. A line of trees bordered the hotel, throwing the gravel walkway into complete darkness; there were no lights on the backside of the hotel. As he walked, Javier felt the crunch of glass under his boots.

The security light mounted on the eaves looked to have been broken out. He reached into the small of his back and withdrew his ultra-compact SIG P365. Keeping his finger off the trigger, he moved slowly into the shadows.

Although he was anticipating the other operative, he still wasn't taking any chances. Working for the Project—especially in his double-agent role—had caused him to think a little more carefully about wandering unarmed into the shadows behind a building, especially one with a seemingly recently broken security light.

Taking slow, deliberate steps, he moved along the back of the building, glancing toward the woods every couple of steps. Halfway across the back of the hotel, he heard a muffled *thump* from behind him.

Something—or someone—had slid off the roof.

As he spun around, bringing the muzzle of the pistol up, a black-gloved hand shoved the weapon off the centerline with enough force to send it flying toward the woods. Javier pulled himself back two steps, sinking into a crouch, bringing his hands up, ready for a fight. The figure dropped into a crouch, mimicking Javier's pose.

Both Javier and the mysterious figure stood stock still, staring each other down.

Suddenly, a lightning-fast sidekick was hurtling toward Javier's torso. Reacting, he trapped the leg against his body and took a step back, pulling the figure off balance. Gritting his teeth, he pulled the figure forward and off balance. He spun, sending the figure flying. Pressing his advantage, Javier rushed in. As Javier's left knee hurtled toward its face, it brought its hands up and blocked the blow. Without stopping, Javier shifted his weight, bringing his right arm around in a devastating haymaker.

The blow connected with the side of the figure's head, and the figure dropped like a stone. Breathing heavily, Javier stood over the collapsed body. He knelt down and pulled the ski mask off the figure's head, revealing a lean, hard-jawed face and a rat's nest of black hair.

The man's hand flew up and swatted Javier's hand away.

"That is enough," he said, a thick Russian accent making the words sound hard and angular.

"Who the fuck are you, and why in the fuck did you jump off the roof and attack me?" Javier growled, still standing over the man on the ground.

"I am Operative Number Four. You can call me Volkov," he said, holding out his hand. When Javier looked him over dubiously, he continued: "In *Bratva*, I am referred to as Wolf. I ambushed you because I needed to know that you were who the director said you were. You cannot be too careful when it comes to this business. Now, would you mind helping me up?"

Javier grabbed the man's forearm and hauled him to his feet. As Volkov dusted himself off, Javier walked to the tree line and, after a moment of searching, found his SIG and slid it back in the holster in the small of his back. He turned toward Volkov.

"Okay," he said, crossing his arms, "so you're here to help with this operation. Let's get going. We're going to interrogate a man named McDougall, and once we find out all he knows, we're going to execute him."

"Interrogation and execution is messy," Volkov said. "Police will be called. This is not a good thing."

"I've got a way around that," Javier said. "I'm not going to enjoy it very much, but it'll keep the cops off our trail. The Collective will be clear."

"How will you do this?"

Javier just smiled.

CHAPTER 58

I hauled myself up the ladder, feeling more exhausted than I'd ever felt in my entire life. The last handful of hours had been thrilling but draining, especially given my disappointment at the latest attempt to reinitiate contact with my original timeline.

I walked slowly through the maze of boxes and piles of random objects, making my way to the creaking staircase. As I walked up the stairs, I thought of the man lying tied up in the master bedroom. Although he was crazed, maybe his mind somehow held the key to the machine that was running two floors below him.

If, of course, I could somehow get him to be lucid enough to answer my questions. I figured it was worth a try, although, given how insane he was on our first meeting, I didn't hold out much hope that he could actually help. If I thought he could, I would have asked him first thing. I'd just assumed he'd give me nothing but nonsense.

At the top of the stairs, I turned right and walked toward the bedroom door. I opened it and cautiously went inside. The man was basically where he'd been the entire time—hands bound behind his back, lying face down on the carpeted floor. I looked at the knots in the rope; they looked to be intact, although they seemed to have, again, shifted slightly. I chalked that up to his struggling. His breathing was regular but not nearly slow enough to indicate sleep. When the door creaked open, he turned his head to face me, looking up at me with eyes that looked significantly less crazed than they had been during our fight.

"I was wondering when you were going to come see me," he said, his voice gravelly but calm.

I stood in the doorway, looking down at the man, my mouth slightly agape. I hadn't expected him to talk to me, let alone to be calm while doing it.

"Would you mind sitting me up?" he said. "I'm starting to get stiff from laying here on my face."

Before I knew what was happening, I was moving toward him and hauling him into a sitting position. A moment later, he was sitting cross-legged in the middle of the floor in front of the bathroom door, and I was leaning against the wall in front of him.

"Why did you think I was going to come talk to you?" I asked.

"Well, it makes sense, doesn't it? You're here, in my house, poking around my basement. I assume you found the lab in the sump well? Surely you must have."

"How the hell—"

"Don't tell me you haven't figured it out yet," he said, his eyes dancing mischievously. "You seem like a smart man; you must know."

"Seriously, old man, I don't know what the hell you're talking about. Why don't you enlighten me?"

He dropped his chin to his chest, heaving a sigh. For a moment, he sat still.

Then, he began to shake.

He snorted.

Laughed.

His laughs grew in intensity until he was hysterical.

I sat dumbfounded. I was wrong. He wasn't lucid. He was just as fucking crazy as he was when he attacked me, only this time he wasn't violent. He was just batshit crazy.

"You dumb motherfucker," he said, still cackling, "you still don't get it? Who the fuck do you think brought you here?"

I felt my eyes widen.

Felt the left side of my mouth twitch, like it always did when I was on the verge of becoming irrationally angry.

"What did you say?" I said, my voice low, rage barely controlled below the surface. I could hear the shake in my voice and hated it.

"You heard me."

In a flash, I hurtled myself forward, grabbing him by the collar. My face inches from his. I could smell the stale cigarettes on his breath and the subtle rot of his teeth.

"You did this to me?" I said, the muscles in my arms and cheek twitching with anger. "You fucking did this to me?"

"That's right. Who else could operate the machine? Some dipshit from your time?" He snorted a laugh. "Not a chance. They don't even know that the machine is able to be used to view the past and future. They think it's just for projection—for time travel, although it's really more akin to consciousness travel—but it's so much more! I've been watching, waiting to find a suitable test subject. Someone whose mind is stable enough to handle the transportation but open enough to be receptive to the travel beam. It can't just be anyone; it has to be someone who *believes in the madness of the universe*! Someone whose mind won't break when they wake up in their new body. I've tried so many people, and all of their minds turned to jelly! But not you. No, not you. You're different. You made it work! You were able to receive the gift of consciousness travel!"

"The gift?" I said, my voice shaking. "The *gift*? You think this is a fucking gift? To be trapped here, in my eighteen-year-old body? To be a grown-ass man, living as a teenager? You can *keep your fucking gift*!"

The rage bubbling under the surface was starting to bleed through, threatening to completely overtake my rational mind. I had only gone truly berserk a few times in my life, and it felt like I was about to add another notch to that belt. I felt the red mist start to cloud my eyes, but I tried to hold it back.

I forced my hands to release his collar and pushed myself off the ground. I turned my back on him and took a deep, steadying breath, willing the rage back down.

"How do I get back?" I said, still facing away from him.

"You can't. Not from here. This machine can only sustain the experiment. It has to come from the target date. Someone in the future has to figure out how to stop the experiment," he replied, his voice carrying a note of manic excitement.

"*What?*"

I whipped around, staring at the man sitting on the floor. He was laughing again, his eyes taking on the glassy, crazed look they had held earlier.

"That's right!" He cackled. "You need someone from the future to save you! Get used to life as a teenager! You're stuck here!"

"Maybe I ought to drag your ass down to the lab and beat you until you decide to fix this. How does that sound, you piece of shit?"

"Oh, beating me won't do any good," he laughed. "Even if you drag me down there and stuff me down the sump well, I can't do anything from this side. I told you: It has to be someone from the time the consciousness is drawn from."

As I stared at him, something seemed to detach in my mind. Before I could stop myself, I had crossed the distance to him. Next thing I knew, my foot was cocked back and swinging toward his stomach. As it connected, I heard his breath escape in a pained *whoosh*. He doubled over, wheezing and trying desperately to refill his now-empty lungs.

I knelt down, grabbing him again by his collar, steadying him. My right hand shot forward in a brutal straight, collapsing his nose with a stomach-churning crunch. In the space of five seconds, I had closed his left eye, split his lip, and dislodged his right canine. He continued trying to draw a breath, but now his wheezes were mixed with gurgling half-breaths.

I yanked the man to his feet. He was able to support his own weight, but only barely. I pulled my right hand back and let loose a vicious cross, connecting with the left side of his jaw. I followed with a backhanded fist, knocking his head back in the opposite direction. Grabbing his collar with both hands, I brought my knee up into his stomach once, twice, three times, until he was painfully gasping for breath.

As I let go of his collar with my right hand, he began to slump forward. I brought one final fist to the back of his skull, forcing him to his knees.

I let his collar slip through my fingers and watched him slump face-first back into the carpet. Blood pooled on the carpet under his broken lips and nose.

After what seemed like forever, his breathing began to even out.

"Does that make you feel better?" He groaned, struggling to raise his head and look at me through his good eye.

"A little, yeah," I said as my right hand continued to shake. "I'll keep going if you don't tell me how to make the machine send me back."

He took a deep, rattling breath that sounded painful. On some level, I registered that I'd probably broken something on the inside. On a deeper level, I didn't give a rat's ass. The manic fuck deserved it.

Hell, he deserved more.

"It won't do any good. You can beat me to death, but it won't change the fact that you've got to tell the future to bring you back."

Tell the future.

I turned back toward him and glared down at his prone form. "What did you just say?"

"The same thing ... I've been saying. It can't be done ... from here."

"No, you said something else. You said, 'Tell the future.' What the hell did you mean by that? *How do I tell the future?*"

I stared down at him, but he didn't respond. I knelt down and pulled him into an upright position. His good eye had rolled back in his head, and his breathing was shallow.

The son of a bitch had passed out.

"Fuck!" I shouted, letting go of his shoulder and letting him fall face-first back to the floor. "You crazy, fucking piece of shit! God dammit!"

My foot swung forward, catching the man in the ribs. I lashed out again and again, finally hearing a sickening *crack* deep in the man's abdomen as one of his ribs broke. My foot flew twice more, forcing another audible *crack* as another rib shattered. Breathing heavily, I stood over the man.

Suddenly, I felt the walls closing in on me. The feeling of claustrophobia was overwhelming. I needed out.

I spun on my heel and stormed out of the bedroom, shoving the basement door shut on my way past. I threw the sliding door open and stormed out toward the center of the backyard, through the snow dotted with tall grass, weeds, and the last pitiful remnants of wildflowers.

The March air was cold enough to start cooling my anger off, although my face still felt hot. I was sure it was red and somewhat blotchy from my outburst. As I gulped in breaths of the cold air, I looked down at my hands and, seeing that they were both shaking, clenched them back into fists. The knuckles of my right hand were red and raw. The middle finger knuckle was already starting to swell and showed a deep, dark red split in the skin.

The rest of the knuckles were covered in abrasions.

Abrasions and blood.

His blood.

"Shit," I muttered, dropping to my knees, and wiping my hands on the weeds, trying to get his blood off me.

As I was frantically trying to wipe off my knuckles, I heard a *whooshing* noise in the snow behind me. Somehow, he had woken up, gotten free, and was trying to blindside me. I whirled around, my right arm cocked back, ready to throw a punch.

Leigh flinched and threw up her hands. Joseph stopped a few feet behind her, his eyes going wide and his mouth dropping open.

"Whoa, dude!" she cried, taking a step back.

"Don't, it's just us!" Joseph yelled, holding up his hands.

I dropped my fist and opened both hands, palms out toward them.

"I'm so sorry," I said. I felt my eyes go wide as I realized what I had almost done: I'd almost attacked my brother and my future girlfriend. Holy shit. "I'm sorry." I dropped my eyes, unable to look at either of them.

"What the fuck is going on? You went upstairs, and then we heard a bunch of noise. It was faint, but I was already heading up the ladder after you. Joseph"—she gestured over her shoulder—"was only a few rungs behind me. We heard the basement door slam and then the back door open. What happened?"

"I ..." I trailed off, searching for the words. "I ... snapped. That guy we found in the house ... he told me something. He told me ..."

Both Leigh and Joseph were staring at me; both had a mixture of concern, fear, and curiosity on their faces.

"He told me," I started again, "that the only way I can get out of this is to contact the future. The only problem with that is I beat him into unconsciousness before he could tell me how to do that. Guys, I beat him bad. I think I broke something inside him."

I moved past them and back into the house, taking slow but deliberate steps through the kitchen, down the hall, and into the master bedroom. Inside, it was worse than my anger-clouded mind remembered. The man was crumpled, face down, a dark stain spreading from his mouth and nose. On the wall near him, oblong droplets of blood speckled the once-white surface. Circular, gravitational drops marked the carpet near the man, clearly the result of the blood dripping off my shaking fist.

They both took an involuntary step back at the scene of violence. Back in my time, they both knew how angry I had been in my teens and twenties, but this was the first time either of them had actually witnessed the aftermath.

It was the first time I'd lashed out at another person in that way.

Looking at the bloodied and broken man, I began to feel something let go behind my eyes again.

A feeling of becoming unmoored.

My knees gave out, and I collapsed. I felt my head pitch forward, my chin coming to rest on my chest. My dark hair hung over my face, obscuring my features, just like the beating I'd given this man obscured his.

"Guys," I muttered, "how am I going to get home?"

Leigh and Joseph looked at each other.

No one said a word.

CHAPTER 59

Javier and Volkov slipped back into the hotel and made their way down the hall to Javier's room. Volkov had retrieved his pack from the roof shortly after their initial confrontation and had slung it over his shoulder before they entered the hotel.

Back in Javier's room, Volkov opened the duffel bag and began pulling out gear. Inside, there were two sets of black 5.11 TACLITE tactical pants, MultiCam tactical shirts, and Under Armour face masks and gloves. On top of the clothes, he set two tactical pouches containing a variety of tools and gear, along with a pair of shoulder holsters.

The two men began to dress, neither having much to say to the other. Javier had filled Volkov in on the plan, and although he had initially disagreed, Javier pulled rank and told him it was an order. While Volkov wasn't happy about it, he would follow Javier's lead.

Once they were dressed and had their gear pouches fastened around their waists, Volkov pulled out a pair of handgun cases and popped the clasps. Inside were two Glock G22 pistols with threaded barrels. From a second, smaller case,

Volkov pulled two suppressors. Both appeared to have been hand-milled for the modified Glocks. Javier picked up the first Glock and the matching suppressor. Using gloved hands, he fit the suppressor onto the threaded barrel and tightened it until it was snug.

Volkov followed suit and looked at Javier when he was done.

"Preparations are complete, Operative Four."

Javier rolled his eyes but followed the script: "Acknowledged, Number Seven. We proceed."

The men moved to the door, Volkov in the lead. He cracked the door open and peered out into the hallway. Javier once again rolled his eyes, making sure to keep his snort of amusement silent. It was just a goddamn hotel in suburban Illinois, for Chrissakes, not some burnt-out hotel in Chechnya.

'But then, he is Russian, after all. All doom and gloom and secrecy. Whatever. He can be paranoid if he wants to. McDougall isn't gonna do shit; he's a coward.'

Volkov turned back and, bringing up his right hand, fingers pressed together, gestured to move forward. Javier nodded and walked out into the hallway. Volkov, bringing up the rear, moved forward, stepping lightly in an infiltration crouch. Again, Javier snorted lightly. He walked down the hall to McDougall's room and pressed himself against the wall outside the door. Volkov took a similar position on the other side of the door.

Javier reached across the door and gently grabbed the doorknob. He turned it slightly, wondering if McDougall was actually dumb enough to leave his door unlocked.

The handle turned with a soft *click.*

'Are you fucking kidding me? This idiot is just asking for it,' Javier thought, thankful his low opinion of his boss wouldn't last past tonight.

He pushed the door open, letting it swing on its surprisingly well-oiled hinges—the door didn't make a sound as it opened into the room.

The room itself was dark, leaving much of it in shadow. The only light came from the TV perched on the dresser, accompanied by the low volume of some mindless show. Javier and Volkov lightly stepped in; there would be enough commotion to come, and they didn't need the festivities starting before they were ready. As Javier moved forward, Volkov closed the door. The click of the latch bolt in the strike plate was almost inaudible over the soft sounds of the TV.

In the bed, McDougall was snoring lightly, his head resting on the pillows. He had no idea what was coming.

Just as Javier intended.

He moved forward, footfalls barely making sound on the industrial carpeting. In a moment, he was standing over McDougall, staring down at the man. Volkov stood near the door, presumably keeping guard and letting Javier take the lead.

As Javier stood over McDougall, the man began to stir, almost as if he could sense someone else in the room with him. His eyes opened and seemed to take a moment to focus. When they did, his eyes shot wide, the light of the TV reflecting in his terrified gaze.

"What the fuck?" he said, trying to sit up in bed.

Javier didn't say anything. In a flash, his fist shot forward and caught McDougall across the left temple, stunning the man for a brief moment. Javier pulled the punch at the last moment. He didn't want to knock McDougall out, just stun him long enough to get him zip-cuffed to a chair.

As McDougall rolled on the bed, clutching his face, Javier grabbed him by his shirt collar and hauled him out of the bed. One-handed, he grabbed one of the chairs by the table and spun it around to face the center of the room. He pushed the man into the chair and, pulling the set of FlexiCuffs from his pouch, zip-tied McDougall's hands to the stiles on the back of the chair. Again, from the pouch, he pulled a roll of duct tape, tore a piece off, and, a little too roughly, slapped it over McDougall's mouth.

McDougall's head hung, his chin resting on his chest. A small trickle of blood had begun to trail from where Javier had hit him. His breathing began to quicken as he picked his head up and saw the two masked figures in front of him. He pulled the other chair out and set it in front of McDougall. Sitting down, he leaned forward, resting his elbows on his knees.

"McDougall," he said, putting some gravel in his voice to mask his identity, "we have some questions. You have the answers. Answer our questions, and I can promise your end will be as painless as we can make it. Resist, and, well, let's just say it'll take a lot longer and be a lot more painful for you."

McDougall glared at Javier. A sudden fire in his eyes surprised Javier; he figured McDougall would roll over and spill any information, just to try and save his pitiful life. It looked like McDougall had a spine. Who would have guessed?

Javier smiled inwardly. All the better. Maybe he would get to use some "advanced interrogation techniques" on him after all.

Javier reached forward and pulled the tape from McDougall's mouth.

"Fuck you, you'll get nothing from me!" he said, his voice wavering and completely undermining his tough-guy bravado. He struggled for a moment against the restraints, rocking the chair back and forth, his face becoming redder with each passing moment.

Javier stood, gazing down at the man. His arm tightened, and he was sure McDougall saw the motion. McDougall's abdomen tightened as Javier brought his fist to bear. Even though he braced for it, Javier's fist slammed into his stomach just below his ribs, causing McDougall's diaphragm to spasm. McDougall's breath shot out of his mouth with a pained "gah!" He pitched forward, his head crumpling into his chest.

"Ready to talk yet?"

McDougall wheezed, unable to pick his head back up. Javier pushed his head off his chest with two fingers, watching as it lolled around, leaving McDougall staring at the ceiling. From the doorway, Volkov grunted. Javier looked over at him, and Volkov gestured for Javier to come closer. Javier narrowed his eyes but made his way toward the door.

"What is it we are hoping to learn from this man?" Volkov asked, bending his head closer to Javier and lowering his voice.

"Don't worry about it," Javier said, keeping his voice low. "I'll handle it. You just make sure Jeffrey doesn't crash the party."

"Who is this 'Jeffrey' you speak of?"

"McDougall's lackey and, technically, my boss," Javier said.

"Will this man come to the room tonight?"

"Who knows. He's probably still fucking around with the equipment over at the site. If he comes, handle it. If he doesn't, then it's irrelevant."

Javier turned and walked back to McDougall.

He sat back in the chair and leaned forward again.

"Alright," he said, "let me explain how this is going to work."

McDougall's head lolled forward again, coming to rest on his chest.

"Hey!" Javier said, slapping McDougall across the face, bringing his attention back to the man sitting in front of him. "Do I have your attention now?"

"What the fuck do you want from me?"

Javier smiled, staring at McDougall. He brought his hand around and hit him with a backhand, snapping McDougall's head to the side. "If you would pay attention, I'm trying to tell you, you idiot."

McDougall glowered, clearly not used to people having the audacity to speak to him like that. Wisely, though, he kept his mouth shut.

"It appears I've got your attention. Thank you. Now, as I

was saying, allow me to explain how this is going to work. I'm going to ask you some questions, and you're going to answer them. If you do, your end is quick. If you don't, I'm going to take my time, making you wish for death. But, as much as you wish for it, you won't get it. Not until *I'm* ready for you to die. Even then, though, it won't be quick or painless. You're going to take a long time to die. If you want to help out, things will be much smoother. I'll let you think about that for just a moment."

Javier fell silent, letting his words hang in the air. Although he hadn't told McDougall just what he would do, the threat of violence made the air in the room thick and oppressive.

"I'll take your silence to mean you're ready to cooperate."

McDougall glared at Javier but didn't say anything.

"First question: What does the Project plan to do with the machine after it removes it from the site?"

"How do you know about tha—oof!" Javier's fist slammed into McDougall's stomach again, cutting off the questions before he could complete it.

"You really don't get how this works, do you? And to think you consider yourself to be intelligent. I ask"—he jammed two fingers into McDougall's chest—"you answer."

"They plan to study it, you prick," McDougall finally answered.

"What's their objective?"

"Time travel, plain and simple. We contracted with DARPA, trying to recreate the original machine that Baumann and Bureat built. We failed. When our lackey detected a time-space anomaly, we had a feeling it might be something we could use. Turns out, it was a working version of the machine we'd been trying to recreate. We came here to investigate, assuming we would be able to figure out why our version of the machine didn't work. Turns out, we weren't even close to making our version work.

"My bosses figured out that if we couldn't recreate the different aspects of the machine, we might as well dismantle it and bring the entire thing back to the lab. We found that we couldn't dismantle the machine to appropriate or recreate parts because an experiment is already running. It's a simple fix: end the experiment. Unfortunately for us, there's a problem."

Apparently, once McDougall got talking, it was hard to shut him up.

All the better for Javier, though. Let the dipshit talk and spill all the secrets.

"And that problem is?" Javier asked, prompting McDougall to keep talking.

"The problem," he said, pausing for dramatic effect, "is that someone is connected to the machine."

He said this as if it was some massive cliffhanger revelation. Unfortunately, Javier was already aware of this. He knew what McDougall wanted to do about it, too. Javier wasn't interested in any of that; he just wanted to know what DARPA wanted with time travel.

"Fine, there's someone connected. I don't give a shit about that. What does DARPA want with the machine?"

The question seemed to take McDougall off guard.

"Why ..." he trailed off, eyeing Javier's right hand.

He caught himself before he could ask a question, obviously hoping it would stop Javier from dealing another blow to his diaphragm.

He was wrong.

Javier's left hand came to rest on McDougall's shoulder, and his right fist flew forward again and connected with the already tender spot on the man's abdomen, causing another cry of pain to come from the man. Tears began to form in his eyes as he doubled over, as much as the zip cuffs on his wrists would allow.

"Well?" Javier said, patting the man on the shoulder and pushing his back against the chairback.

"DARPA ..." McDougall wheezed, "has interests in advanced technology. That's what they do. Can you imagine what time travel would mean? What the military would do if they could send someone's consciousness back into a younger version of themselves? Think about it! High-value assassinations. No more military casualties from surprise attacks. Whoever they hooked up to that machine would go to whatever time period they wanted with *all the knowledge they currently possess.* The United States wouldn't just be *a* superpower; it would be *the* superpower. The possibilities of what they would do are nearly endless. That"—he again paused dramatically—"is what DARPA wants. That's why they sought this project out and why they brought me on board."

Javier sat quietly for a moment, letting the implications sink in. From what he knew about his own organization, DARPA sounded like they wanted to use the machine for a very similar purpose. The only difference was that DARPA would use it in a military fashion. Truthfully, Javier had no idea what the Collective would use the machine for, outside of sending operatives around time-space. McDougall was right about one thing: the possibilities were nearly endless.

McDougall's voice broke into Javier's thoughts: "There, now I've told you everything. Please, let me go. I won't say a word about this. You'll both be safe, I promise!" The man's voice held a pleading quality that Javier relished.

Javier stood up and moved around the back of McDougall's chair. From his pouch, he pulled a knife and flipped the blade open, allowing McDougall to hear the spring-loaded *snap* as the blade clicked into the locked position.

"Thank you," McDougall said, relief washing over his voice and causing his tense shoulders to relax. Javier quietly set the knife on the table.

"You're welcome. We'll set you free ..." he trailed off momentarily, letting McDougall think that he was being sincere. "Until the end, anyway."

"What?" McDougall cried, unsuccessfully trying to turn

around to face Javier. He thrashed against his restraints, lobbing curses over his shoulder. Javier just smiled. He pulled the Glock from its shoulder holster and racked a round into the chamber. Even though McDougall wasn't a gun guy, he knew that sound; he stopped thrashing and swearing and sat bolt upright.

"No, please," he whimpered, "I'll give you anything you want!"

"I've been looking forward to this for a long time, *boss.*"

McDougall's head slowly turned, craning his neck to see behind him. Javier pulled the face mask off, letting McDougall see his face.

"What is this?" Volkov said from the doorway, shocked that Javier had revealed his face to their captive. Javier just smiled at him.

He brought the Glock up and, in one swift movement, pressed the suppressor to the back of McDougall's head. Before he could even cry out, Javier squeezed the trigger. It only took five and a half pounds of pressure to discharge the .40 S&W slug into the back of McDougall's head. The point-blank shot rocketed through his brain, punching a half-dollar-sized hole through his forehead, splattering blood, bone, and brain matter on the chair Javier had been sitting in moments earlier. McDougall's now lifeless body slumped forward, straining against the zip cuffs. Javier let the pistol drop back to his side as he looked down at the carnage he had just created.

'*Sucks for whoever gets to clean this shit up,*' he thought, '*but, really, his brain is more useful congealing on the carpet than it ever was in his head. Good riddance, you useless fuck.*'

Volkov had moved forward but had stopped before he stepped through the gore splattered across the room.

"The objective is accomplished," he said, pulling the face mask over his head. "I will take this information back to our group. You are sure you want to do this next part, yes?"

Javier flipped the Glock around and held it by the barrel, extending the firearm toward the other operative. Volkov reached a gloved hand forward and took the weapon from Javier.

"I suppose this is your answer," he said, pulling the slide back, checking that a round had entered the chamber.

"You know what to do," Javier said, nodding at Volkov.

Without a word, Volkov aimed the pistol at Javier and fired.

The last things he felt were a blinding, searing pain, collapsing to the floor, and darkness washing over him, enveloping his being in nothingness.

ABOUT ATMOSPHERE PRESS

Founded in 2015, Atmosphere Press was built on the principles of Honesty, Transparency, Professionalism, Kindness, and Making Your Book Awesome. As an ethical and author-friendly hybrid press, we stay true to that founding mission today.

If you're a reader, enter our giveaway for a free book here:

SCAN TO ENTER
BOOK GIVEAWAY

If you're a writer, submit your manuscript for consideration here:

SCAN TO SUBMIT
MANUSCRIPT

And always feel free to visit Atmosphere Press and our authors online at atmospherepress.com. See you there soon!

ABOUT THE AUTHOR

Kevin Rowlett is an American author, teacher and musician. He holds a Bachelors of Music from Northern Illinois University, but has always loved the written word. Prior to publishing his first book, Kevin wrote stand-alone short stories centered around science fiction for a small audience. His first major novel, *Travel*, is the result of many years of hard work, imagination, and research into the northern Illinois area. He lives in Wonder Lake, IL with his wife, two dogs and two cats. Kevin would like to thank his wife, Nikki, for pushing him to follow his dreams.

www.ingramcontent.com/pod-product-compliance
Ingram Content Group UK Ltd.
Pitfield, Milton Keynes, MK11 3LW, UK
UKHW032043030225
454636UK00013B/152/J

9 798891 325883